Fish Out of Water

Fish Out of Water

An Ozarks Lake Mystery (#1)

Marc Jedel

BGM Press
San Jose, CA

Published in the United States by BGM Press.

ISBN 978-1-7327164-4-5 (Paperback edition)

Cover designed by Molly at CozyCoverDesigns.com

Other Books by Marc Jedel

SILICON VALLEY MYSTERY SERIES

Book 1. Uncle and Ants
Book 2. Chutes and Ladder
Book 3. Serf and Turf
Book 4. Hit and Mist

Sign up for Marc's mailing list to receive free content, learn of new releases, and receive special offers:

http://www.marcjedel.com

1

Monday Morning

Elizabeth

"You have the right to remain silent," said Trent.

I stood there in confusion as my ex-boyfriend accosted me outside Harps grocery store. His sheriff's squad car had come screeching to a stop when he caught sight of me chatting with the old codgers out front. He now stood stiffly in front of me spouting off this nonsense.

"Boy, where were you when my wife was alive? I could have used a deputy to tell her she could remain silent once in a while," said Colton Buck, perched on the bench near the entrance.

Cackling from his seat next to Colton, Billy Ray watched my bewildered reaction to Trent's statement and elbowed his buddy in the ribs as he tried to one-up his lifelong friend. "Son, you need to work on your pickup lines. This one doesn't seem to be succeeding very well."

Was the old fool right? Was Trent trying to rekindle our relationship? His demeanor did seem odd. Maybe he just felt as awkward as I did, standing in front of each other after ten years apart. He must have been surprised to find me here, and now he was putting on a show for these old-timers, making the situation even weirder. Mom had told me he'd become a sheriff's deputy but had neglected to mention how good he looked in his uniform, even with the nervous look on his face.

Feeling uncertain about the right etiquette for greeting an ex-boyfriend you hadn't seen since high school, I took a step toward him and reached out to give him a hug.

But Trent stepped back. "Lizzie!" His right arm was tense as it moved to his hip. Tight-lipped, he asked, "Do you understand your rights as I have explained them to you?"

When he paused, I figured he'd finished with his little soliloquy. "Okay, okay, very funny. It's cool to see that you became a sheriff like you always wanted. But hush now and let me finish telling my story to the boys."

Trent's jaw clenched. "Lizzie, you need to come with me. Now."

I waved my hands at him. "Stop fooling around. Hey!" I objected as he grabbed my wrists and cuffed my hands together.

Colton and Billy Ray laughed as my sputtering protests were ignored.

"I know plenty who would frown on that technique for catching yourself a woman," said Billy Ray.

"Yup. And I'm not sure he'll be able to reel in that one," added Colton, returning his neighbor's nudge as Trent pulled me to his squad car.

"Hey! Don't mess with the hair," I complained as he pushed my head down so I fit into the back seat without smacking into the roof of the car.

"Guess we'll have to catch the rest of your story later," called Billy Ray as Trent slammed the door.

"Yeah, later, like in ten years to life," shouted Colton, cackling at his own stupidity as he turned to Billy Ray for reinforcement.

Old men were far less funny than they thought they were.

When I first saw them, fond memories of growing up here in Jenkins, Arkansas, had flooded back. Even the air still smelled the same: pine trees mixed with the musty, almost grassy odor from the lake. Colton's twang evoked images of visiting with my Pawpaw and his friends at this very meeting spot. Remembering the good things about Jenkins helped balance the memories of the more challenging aspects of growing up here, which were brought back all too vividly after spending the past day with my mother.

Recalling the Colton from my younger days, I started to shout back that he would never have made that remark when his wife was alive. Then, realizing that would sound just like my mother, I held my tongue.

Trent closed the driver's door as he got in, buckled up, and started the engine.

"You know, Trent, if you wanted to see me, you could have just said hello like a normal person. You didn't have to grab me off Main Street and throw me into the back seat."

The back of his neck turned red as he pulled away from the curb. "I didn't throw you—"

Oddly pleased that I could still mess with his head after all this time, I interrupted him. "I don't remember you being into this sort of thing back in high school." I waved my cuffed hands so he'd be sure to see them in his rearview mirror. As the blush extended up to his ears, I tried to flip my hair over my shoulder but only managed to clunk myself on the forehead.

Trent cleared his throat. "Careful not to hurt yourself, Lizzie," he said softly.

Many years had passed since anyone called me by that nickname. To the best of my memory, he was the only one I'd ever allowed to use it. Continuing to stare at his reflection in the rear mirror didn't feel right, so I looked out the window.

The buildings on Main Street, built separately but jammed together, looked the same as always, although some needed a touch-up of paint here or there. I smiled at the eclectic array of different colors, materials, and shapes that constituted the haphazard collection of downtown Jenkins.

As if to break the uncomfortable silence, Trent said, "Sheriff Tucker is still pretty new in these parts. He's been positive about my work so far and I wouldn't want him to write me up for hurting someone while in custody."

I frowned. He was keeping up this act for far too long. "Wouldn't be an issue if you hadn't put these on me." This time I used my head to gesture toward the cuffs. "You sure you're not just showing off and acting all macho in front of me?" Lowering my voice to make it sound sultry, I added, "I used to like it when you did that." I paused and shook my head slightly, trying to regain control of my emotions. I kept my tone light so Trent wouldn't figure out that his gag arrest had started to make me nervous.

The blush deepened in Trent's pale cheeks. Teasing Trent was an easy habit to fall back into. That was how most of our interactions had gone during senior year in high school—well, those that involved talking.

Teasing him also helped to distract me from the embarrassment of his little scene in front of men I hadn't seen in ten years. They'd been friends with my grandfather before he died. As much as I missed Pawpaw, I counted it as a small blessing that he wasn't around to see my latest public incident.

Blinking back the unexpected tears, I turned my head away again. The familiar blocks we passed on the way to the sheriff's station had a lot of open space for the buildings to breathe. I had forgotten what it was like to be able to see the hills from anywhere in town, where nothing was taller than two stories except for a few churches. Jenkins was so different from Portland and the other bigger cities where I'd lived since leaving.

I wouldn't have returned if my grandmother hadn't passed a few months ago. The trip back for Mimi's funeral had been a blur, and I don't think I even left Mom's house. Learning later that Mimi had left her ranch to me—both the house and land—had been a shock. I loved that ranch. In my childhood, I felt more at home there than at my mother's place. But I had my life with Jonas in Portland to look forward to. Someplace far away from Mom. I had only returned to help Mom clean out Mimi's house and prepare it for sale.

Bumping over a pothole that had probably been there since I was a kid brought me back to the present. "I don't even know why you insisted I wear these. You know I'm not dangerous. Why couldn't I sit in front with you?" I half-heartedly waved my hands again, but the cuffs were heavy and tight on my wrists. This prank was getting old, fast.

"Standard operating procedure." Trent still spoke in a breezy tone that didn't match the tension in his shoulders and neck. He didn't sound like the Trent I remembered, as if he was forcing himself to act this way. "It's policy and it keeps everyone from getting hurt."

As he pulled up the uneven driveway into the sheriff's parking lot, I slid around a little on the hard, plastic-molded seat. With these unpadded seats, sheet metal covering the backs of the front seats, and wire mesh covering the windows and separating me from the driver, police cars were certainly not designed for pleasure rides. Besides, riding in the back seat always made me car sick. Even though Trent had driven only a few blocks from the grocery store to the sheriff's station, my stomach was starting to feel queasy and I was already claustrophobic. No wonder they called these cages. Only here for a few minutes and already I felt like a rat.

"Well, you didn't have to be so mean about it. You know I wouldn't hurt you." I cringed, remembering a time when I had hurt him.

Trent parked and twisted around in his seat, his fake smile fading. "Lizzie, this is serious. That argument that you and Mr.—"

"I know, I know. I shouldn't have gotten into it with him yesterday. I was tired from the long drive and just wanted to pick up some food for dinner." My contrite tone automatically turned annoyed. "Suddenly Duncan Fowler . . . ugh . . ." After what he'd done to Mimi's land, just thinking of him left a bitter taste in my mouth.

Duncan was a teacher at the local high school and always seemed to take on odd jobs, like as the property manager for her ranch. My anger at Duncan had animated my words in my conversation with him a bit more than I had intended.

Trent opened my door and held himself rigidly as he helped me out, his face stern. I knew I shouldn't have interrupted him, but when I made up my mind about what I wanted to do, I did it right away. I didn't have the patience to wait around for some magical "right" time or politely ask permission. Mom always said I took after Mimi. She meant it as a criticism, but to me, it was high praise.

I took a deep breath to calm down as I faced Trent. "He was just . . . right there. In my face. I couldn't stop myself."

Trent looked taken aback. "So, you . . . you admit to it?" he stammered, eyes wide.

"I could hardly do otherwise. Those old-timers were sitting right there. Half the block must have heard or seen it. I ran into him as he was leaving Harps and just let him have it. Maybe I should have let him walk away. But you know me, I get worked up easily and then—"

Trent raised a large, rough hand to stop me. "Enough."

I let out a sigh. "Okay. You made your point. I won't get into a yelling match with Duncan Fowler outside Harps again." I was careful to be specific in my promise because Duncan was surely going to get another talkin' to, as Mimi used to say. If he thought he could just get away with how he'd devastated Mimi's land, he was going to get another piece of my mind. I wasn't about to commit to never yelling at him again.

As Trent pulled me toward the building, I objected, "Hey! I promised. We can just stop this already. You don't need to put me in prison."

"It's jail, not prison," Trent corrected in a blunt tone.

Spending this quality time with Trent was helping me remember some of the reasons why he was an ex-boyfriend. Starting with him still being right here—in the same podunk town where we'd grown up, still with the big chest and strong muscles. Same ole Trent, all brawn and no brains.

"Prison is where you go after you're convicted." Trent held the station door open and jerked his head sideways for me to go inside first.

"Convicted?" I paused. I'd thought he was teasing me. Although he did look fine in that tight deputy sheriff uniform, he was starting to annoy me. I stood my ground, ignoring his direction, and narrowed my eyes at him with my best ex-girlfriend glare. "What are you talking about? It's time to stop this nonsense."

The glare must have lost its sizzle, as Trent merely frowned. "Lizzie, Mr. Fowler's body was found floating in the river at Roundtop Bend this morning. He was murdered."

"What?" The air suddenly disappeared and my head felt light. My knees buckled but Trent quickly stepped near and caught me before I fell.

"Whoa. You okay?" Trent supported me for a moment, but his arms around my back didn't feel like they used to.

Once the blood started flowing to my brain again, I shook him off. During all of this, my mouth had opened and closed a few times without forming actual words. Finally I said, "But, when I last saw him—"

Trent interrupted again. "You probably shouldn't say anything more. I read you your rights. Do you understand them?" His tone was friendlier. Although his expression hadn't changed, he was less tense after seeing my reaction to his news.

I nodded meekly, still shocked.

Trent led me into the station. "Come on, I need to get you processed. Do you want me to call your mother once we're through to let her know?"

"No," I said in a more subdued voice. "Call my husband, Jonas."

2

Monday Mid-Morning

Jonas

My phone rang. Although I didn't recognize the number, it was an Arkansas area code, so I answered in case Elizabeth had run into some car trouble.

"Is this Jonas Trout? Elizabeth's husband?" The unfamiliar male voice faltered a bit on the second question.

Concerned why a stranger knew my name, number, and relationship to Elizabeth, I halted in the doorway after returning from loading a box of frames into the car. "Yes, that's me."

"This is Deputy Trent Walker. I'm calling from the sheriff's office here in Jenkins." He spoke slower than I would prefer, but it allowed me to stop pacing and take a grounding breath. I told myself there was no sense in getting worried prematurely. Speculation would solve nothing.

"How can I help you, Deputy?" I spoke a bit faster than normal, as I was eager to learn why he was calling regardless of what the rational side of my brain might tell me.

"We arrested . . . " Again a hesitation. "Your wife. She's been charged with murder."

I blurted out, "Murder?" causing Mary, my mother-in-law, to

jerk to a stop a few steps away in the kitchen of Elizabeth's grandmother's house.

"Yes, for the murder of Duncan Fowler."

"Duncan?" I felt stupid repeating the deputy's words but couldn't seem to stop. Having difficulty processing conversations wasn't like me.

Mary grabbed the phone. "What sort of nonsense are you up to now, Trent Walker?" she demanded.

She listened for a moment. "What does that have to do with Ella Mae?" She stepped past me onto the porch, searching for a better signal.

Elizabeth had warned me that reception inside her grandmother's house was poor. Combined with the lack of Wi-Fi, the whole experience was like living in a time warp. Even hearing Mary use Elizabeth's childhood nickname felt strange. Elizabeth had told me she didn't care for it but her family still used it. I adored Elizabeth—both the name and my wife.

But Mary—pacing back and forth at the far end of the porch—wasn't about to change just because her daughter wished her to. She was a force of nature. That personality was well-suited for a woman who worked as a doctor in small-town Arkansas while raising an equally headstrong daughter mostly on her own, not to mention being elected recently as a county commissioner too. It must have taken a lot of drive for her to succeed as she did. Elizabeth might not like to admit it, but that was one personality trait where she resembled her mother—even if her time away had softened her edges some.

The two of them didn't seem to have much else in common, aside from their DNA. Mary was always the practical, disciplined, get-it-done-my-way-now type while Elizabeth carved her own meandering yet distinctive path.

Nearing me, Mary suddenly burst out, "Oh, poppycock," and

then hung up without waiting for a response. She glared at the phone for a moment before handing it back to me. "Let's go."

"What happened?" I asked.

"Duncan's dead. Floating down by the river. Probably drowned. And some nonsense about proof." She spat all this out as she was on the move, collecting her jacket and purse from the dining table as I trailed behind her.

Turning as she pulled on her jacket, she noticed the third person in the house waiting patiently by the table. "Sorry, Sebastian, but we'll have to continue later. Looks like we've got to go down to the sheriff's office to get Ella Mae."

As Sebastian Edwards, the estate assessor, stared at Mary, they formed quite the contrasting image. She was petite and slightly heavy, in khaki pants and a simple, light blue button-up collared shirt. Sebastian stood reed-thin and tall, in light gray suit pants and a white dress shirt with a bright blue bow tie. He also wore thin leather gloves to protect any valuables he touched.

Sebastian frowned and tilted his head. "But, ma'am, we have a lot to do to get the house sorted and categorized before Sunday."

"Don't be a nervous Nellie. Sunday's a long ways off. We'll just have to work harder when I get back." Mary snatched his suit jacket off the back of a kitchen chair, where I had neatly folded it in half lengthways and had been careful to drape it so the matching blue pocket square faced up and wouldn't get creased.

As Mary thrust his jacket at him, Sebastian caught the pocket square in mid-air as it fluttered to the ground. "I could stay here and—"

"Nope. Not gonna leave you alone here. Go get some coffee somewhere. Isn't that what all you big-city types do?" In one fell swoop, Mary managed to imply Sebastian was dishonest and insult my preference for coffee not made from a Folgers can.

But I let her comment roll off my back as I waited by the front door, more concerned about Elizabeth. I couldn't imagine why she'd been arrested. It made no sense.

"I expect we can start again in an hour or so. We'll reconvene here after I pick up Ella Mae from the sheriff's office." As she shooed us out the door ahead of her so she could lock up, she muttered, "Certainly won't be the first time."

We hurried the thirty yards from the house to where her car was parked under an outdoor shelter. The carport consisted of a heavy-duty fabric stretched across the top and attached to metal poles, which were cemented into the ground adjacent to a stand-alone garage.

As Mary raced us down the narrow dirt road that served as a driveway for this house and another farther up the road, I looked out the window to avoid considering possible outcomes from her driving. I'd rather be surprised than watch an accident develop in front of me.

Much of the cleared land across the dirt road also belonged to Elizabeth's grandparents. Elizabeth had taken it quite hard when her grandmother—or Mimi, as she had told me to refer to her—passed away a few months ago. The two had been close when she was growing up, with Elizabeth spending a lot of time here at their small ranch. Their land was too hilly and rocky for farming, so like many of their neighbors in western Arkansas, they raised cattle and even had a mid-sized chicken house before it burned down from a lightning strike. Now the land looked more like an overgrown meadow, with young trees starting to hit full height and tall grass everywhere.

The car fishtailed as Mary gunned it onto the county highway running down the ridge to town.

I closed my eyes and began counting to one thousand by thirteens.

"We'll be fine. I've been driving here my whole life," she snapped.

"Mmhmm." I didn't point out that her statement would remain true even if she killed us today.

Fortunately Elizabeth didn't share her mother's driving style. Otherwise, our cross-country trip from Portland would not have been enjoyable. On the drive, she'd confided that Mimi's passing made her feel like she had lost her last connection to her childhood. When I mentioned that her mother was still very much alive, Elizabeth reminded me that her grandfather had died before she'd started high school. I decided to let this go as she explained that driving to her hometown was part of her "healing process." We had made the trip into a vacation of hiking and sightseeing across the beautiful countryside of Idaho, Wyoming, and Colorado.

We traveled well together. Elizabeth didn't want to spend any time planning and relished surprises, so she did most of the driving while I plotted out the next day's adventures. I enjoyed double-checking maps, figuring out the perfect day's plan, and comparing several review sites to find the best hiking trails, scenic overlooks, and vegan restaurants along the way. We were both happy.

"Have you decided what you're going to do next?" asked Mary.

I cracked one eye open only to catch her zooming around a slow-moving pickup and narrowly avoiding an oncoming big rig. I closed my eye again and took a deep breath.

She must have noticed. "What? You never played chicken when you were younger? We had plenty of room."

I practiced my yoga breathing and answered her earlier question. "No, not yet."

Before we left Portland, I lost my job. With a lot of unexpected spare time on my hands and the prospect of a whole lot more ahead of me, I had begun systematically experimenting with a wide range of possible hobbies. My goal was to find one I might get passionate about.

Elizabeth had done this, turning her innate artistic talents into a career as an independent graphic designer. She could be dreamy and unfocused at times, but the whole starving-artist lifestyle never appealed to her. As an independent contractor, she kept busy designing websites, ads, and other marketing materials for her clients. I appreciated how she'd turned her passion for drawing into a paying job. I needed to find something to do or I'd go stir-crazy.

I liked dogs, so perhaps dog training or animal rescue work could be worth exploring. Running was more of a hobby than a profession. I enjoyed the tired euphoria I felt after running, but too much of that during a week could lead to knee problems. Plus, it wasn't terribly fun to run during rain, which fell quite often in Portland. Only a single attempt each was sufficient to eliminate birdwatching and rock collecting. While stamp collecting was still an unexplored possibility, I struggled to see the point to it. Boredom will inevitably interfere with a hobby's sustainability.

During our trip here, a side excursion to Dinosaur Ridge, just outside Denver, led Elizabeth to suggest dinosaur bone collecting to me, but that wasn't a realistic proposal. We'd need a much larger place if I actually found anything. She thought I was being funny, but even a small skeleton wouldn't fit in our garage.

Our week had been enjoyable until we hit Kansas. Apparently Elizabeth could only take so many miles of endless flat cornfields and wind turbines with no hills or mountains in sight. Fortunately, I had noticed her "I'm going berserk" expression before she took her plan to test how long our car would stay on the ruler-straight highway under cruise control without her hands on the wheel past the conceptual stage.

Perhaps she wasn't as different from Mary as I thought. Nonetheless, I had driven through the rest of Kansas while Elizabeth flipped through the radio stations, fiddled with her phone, and listened to podcasts she had downloaded. Quiet contemplation was more my style than hers, but nature liked balance and opposites attract.

I opened my eyes as the car sped around a corner, wondering

if the driver's side tires had actually lifted off the road. Mary had turned off the county road onto Main Street, finally slowing down. "Did he tell you anything else about what happened?"

"Nothing that made any sense," she answered. "We'll be there in a minute."

We drove past an interesting collection of both new and old houses—some with well-kept lawns and others junked-out and full of refrigerators, broken-down cars, and spare parts. Well-designed buildings with bricks and neat paint jobs neighbored those with cheap vinyl siding and peeling paint. Despite being so close to the small downtown portion of Jenkins, even the modest homes we passed stood on quarter-acre lots or larger.

The sheriff's station was a modern building with a neatly-maintained grass lawn alongside the parking lot. After Mary screeched to a halt, we scrambled out of the car as if saving a few seconds could rescue Elizabeth from some terrible fate.

I'd never been inside a sheriff's station before, but the lobby's red plastic seats, gray concrete floor, and thick glass separating the front desk from the waiting area matched my image of any modern police station.

Mary didn't slow down to take it in, barreling through the door I held open for her and marching up to an older officer who was sitting in front of a computer and eating potato chips. Leaning forward to tap the glass, she demanded, "I'm here to pick up Ella Mae."

"Dr. Banks, good to see you," said the officer as he finished chewing. "Sure been a while since you've had to come here and say that, hasn't it, ma'am?"

He leaned back in his chair, but his wink must have taken the sting out of his words as Mary didn't explode. Instead, she leaned back and took a breath. "Lucas. How's Sally doing? Haven't seen her in ages. Y'all doing well?"

"No complaints. She's still working at that dress shop down yonder. You know, the one over in—"

"Excuse me," I interrupted. I needed to get to Elizabeth, not learn about this man's family history.

As the officer scrunched his thick gray eyebrows and looked at me, Mary explained, "He's from out of state. Lucas, please meet Jonas, my son-in-law, from Portland, Oregon."

Lucas stood, brushing crumbs off his shirt. His belly extended out past his belt by a good few inches. He leaned over the desk and slid the glass divider out of the way, then stretched his hand out to shake mine as he nodded at me pleasantly. To Mary, he raised one of those bushy eyebrows and queried, "Ella Mae married a Yankee?"

"Oregon's on the West Coast. We're not Yankees, we're Ducks or Beavers." It was a matter of critical importance for Oregonians to choose whether to be a fan of the Oregon State Beavers or the University of Oregon Ducks. I'd known families that had stopped speaking over divided loyalties.

"Huh?" asked Lucas.

I started to explain, but Mary jumped in. "Ella Mae, Lucas?"

"Oh yeah." He picked up his desk phone, pressed a button, and said something quietly into the receiver. Then he nodded and buzzed us through the door to join him in the station's back area.

We stood there awkwardly staring at each other in silence for a few minutes before a nearby office door swung open and a tall, lanky man with gray streaks at his temples stepped out. A slight frown shadowed his face as he caught sight of us before he quickly made it disappear.

In three strides he stood before us. "Mary," he said with a slight incline of his head. The shiny badge attached to his uniform read "Sheriff Tucker."

"Owen," she answered with an equal lack of warmth. "What's this nonsense about my daughter?"

He bristled. "There's no nonsense here. This is a serious matter. She's been arrested for the murder of Duncan Fowler."

"Pshaw." Mary dismissed this with a wave of her hand. "Ella Mae's no killer. Maybe she had a loud argument with him yesterday—"

I wondered how Mary knew that, as Elizabeth hadn't mentioned anything to me, but she continued, "That just proves she's excitable, not a murderer. Besides, why would she kill him?"

The sheriff answered, "I'd hate to speculate too early, but she did go to high school here, right?"

"Along with most of the town. What does that matter?" Mary asked.

"Well, you know he teaches there. Maybe she held some grudge against him—"

"He's a foreigner here," Mary interrupted. "Like you." She practically spat the last sentence at the sheriff.

Lucas spoke up. "Sheriff, Duncan Fowler's only lived here for seven years. Ella Mae was long gone by then."

The sheriff shrugged. "She was the last person seen with him—"

Mary burst out, "Seen on Main Street, in front of Harps. A dozen other people must have seen them hollerin' at each other outside that grocery. Half them codgers probably egged her on, as it was the most entertaining thing they'd seen all day."

The sheriff puffed out his chest. "Be that as it may, we also have physical evidence against her."

"What evidence?" Mary's voice dripped with disbelief.

"We found a woman's T-shirt with bloodstains hidden on the side of your house on a clothes rack."

Mary's eyes glittered with anger. "You've been to my house?"

"Yes. A little while ago, we found a bloody woman's shirt stashed—"

"You can't just break into someone's house and rummage through their stuff." Mary wasn't quite yelling, but her voice had risen.

"Actually, yes, we can." The sheriff waved a dismissive hand at her complaint. "That's exactly what a warrant grants us permission to do."

"I've got medical records at my house. You're not allowed to look through patient records without—"

"We didn't look at any records," he interrupted. "We were looking for clothing or possible murder weapons and found something."

"How would you even know it's her shirt?" Mary demanded.

"It's a woman's long-sleeve T-shirt in her size with 'Mt. Hood Portland' printed on it. We also found an impression of one of her fingerprints in the blood on the shirt. Pretty conclusive evidence."

Shocked by his accusation, I said, "That's too obvious. Elizabeth is not stupid. If she killed someone, she wouldn't leave the evidence in plain sight."

The sheriff turned a haughty gaze to me. "And you are?"

"I'm Jonas Trout, Elizabeth's husband."

"How much experience does your wife have in planning murders?"

"What? None. Of course none." I was starting to get annoyed. He sounded like he'd already determined she was guilty when I knew Elizabeth couldn't have done this.

"I understand you've only known her for a couple of years and been married for just one. Do I have that right?"

"What?" I was taken aback. How had he learned our dating and marriage history? Had he investigated us already?

"It's a small town, son." Noticing my surprise, Lucas gripped my elbow in a friendly fashion. "Everyone gets all up in each other's knickers."

Ignoring Lucas, the sheriff challenged me. "What can you tell us about where your wife was late yesterday afternoon and evening?"

I opened my mouth to respond, then paused. He didn't know it, but he was right—I hadn't seen much of her yesterday in the late afternoon and early evening. I had fallen asleep on the couch in Mary's living room, still worn from the long drive and being put to work immediately at Mimi's place. Elizabeth had left me to nap while she went to the grocery store to pick up food for dinner. When I woke after dark, hours later, she was in a different shirt with her hair freshly washed. She said she'd wound up going for a hike down by the lake and up the river trail. At the time, the important aspect to me was she hadn't picked up any groceries and I was starved. We wound up eating a late dinner of spaghetti with a jar of sauce from Mary's cupboard.

Seemingly satisfied with my non-answer, the sheriff nodded. "And I'll bet you don't know her past very well either, do you?" He paused to observe my reaction. "Do you know why we have her fingerprints on file?"

I started to object that the past didn't matter, but arguing wouldn't help matters. Besides, I didn't like to lie, and he was right that I had only known Elizabeth for two years. We had met during her ill-fated attempt to take up running and bonded over some volunteer stints at rescue dog adoption events and hiking outings. But two years was long enough to know that I loved her and she was no murderer.

Was it really her bloody shirt that the sheriff found? But who else around here would have a Mt. Hood Portland shirt? She hadn't mentioned anything to me about an injury. How did you get a shirt bloody walking along the lake? Why were her fingerprints on file at the sheriff's office? I frowned.

"Is it Duncan's blood?" Mary's piercing eyes focused on the sheriff as she calmed just enough to re-engage with him.

"We don't have DNA results back yet—"

Mary interrupted, "We don't even know it's murder for sure until I get my hands on the body in the morgue."

During our trip, Elizabeth had told me about Mary's as-needed gig serving as the local medical examiner. She didn't want me to be grossed out if Mary started talking about it over a meal, but she'd forgotten I had plenty of experience with dissections during my biology training. Mary acting in this role was logical. After all, a small town had little need for a full-time medical examiner, so they outsourced the job to a local doctor willing to undergo the necessary training.

The sheriff looked startled. "You can't go there."

"Have you forgotten I'm the town M.E.?" Mary rolled her eyes in disgust.

"No, of course I remember." The sheriff's voice was no friendlier than Mary's. "But you can't touch his body. Your daughter is accused of the murder. That's a huge conflict of interest. I called in an M.E. from Little Rock. He'll be here tomorrow to do the exam."

With Mary now looking ready to explode, I interjected, "Can we get Elizabeth out on bail, or see her at least?"

The sheriff's face puckered as if he had something sour in his mouth. "Apparently the answer to that is yes. When Deputy Walker called to arrange the bond hearing, Judge Hardy told him that bond was approved without a hearing since it will be more than forty-eight hours before she can get here. The judge is covering for some vacationing judge in the next county with a full docket this week. Elizabeth's hearing will be next Monday."

Then the sheriff produced a thin, unfriendly smile. "But since it's a capital case, bond's set at one hundred thousand dollars."

Lucas and Mary gasped.

I gulped but reached into my pocket. "Who do I make the check out to?"

3

Monday Noon

Elizabeth

"Lizzie, looks like you're going home after all." Trent stopped in front of my cell and flipped through a set of keys.

"About time you came to your senses," I snapped as I got up from the bench against the wall and waited for Trent to let me out. I was worn out from the stress of the whole arrest. Trent had questioned me in an interrogation room, asking me where I'd been yesterday evening, who could confirm it, why I had been so upset with Duncan, and on and on. Someone must have been watching from behind the one-way mirror because Trent never called me Lizzie and stopped when I finally insisted on talking to a lawyer before answering any more questions.

"Lizzie." Trent shook his head, as if he were the one who'd had to endure sitting in the gross jail cell for what felt like the last few decades. "You're getting out on bail but you're still accused of murder."

"You know I wouldn't kill anyone, although you're rising on my list of possibilities," I snapped, though still in control enough to avoid touching anything in the cell.

"Stop saying things like that. If the sheriff heard you, he'd get your bail revoked."

I gulped and clamped my lips together. I wasn't diplomatic like Jonas; keeping quiet was my best option to avoid more trouble.

Trent instructed me to walk in front of him out of the lockup area, but this time I didn't think it was so he could look at my rear. I was past the point of caring anyway.

I felt desperate to put this whole mistaken accusation behind me. Ignoring my own resolution not to speak, I blurted out an idea I had been chewing over in the cell. "Did you find Duncan's cell-phone? You know you could use that to track where he was on Sunday? Maybe he called whoever really killed him?"

"Lizzie, we're not stupid. We know how to do our jobs."

I let out a frustrated sigh. It was the only idea I had come up with. How great would it be if they could have used his cellphone records to solve this murder without involving me?

Trent must have thought I was upset at his response because he explained, "We didn't find his phone. We think he had one of those pay-by-the-minute ones because the phone companies don't have any account for him. There wasn't anything electronic at his place at all, not even a TV."

"Oh," I mustered. So much for the easy solution.

"Who can live without a TV?" Trent wondered aloud.

Apparently Duncan had tried, bless his heart. I wondered why he had worked so hard at different jobs if he lived so simply.

A few steps further, Trent asked, "You rich now or something?"

I half-turned and threw him a puzzled look.

"Your husband wrote a personal check for one hundred thou-sand dollars to bail you out. Who has that kind of money?"

I didn't respond as I suddenly remembered the truth. The idea that Jonas and I were those kinds of rich people was shocking. When we'd met, Jonas was the same as me, making an average salary with his college degree. He was employed as a biologist for a small biotech startup where he'd been the fifth employee, hired right out of college and granted outsized stock options typical for risky startups. Jonas had even talked about quitting his job but hadn't decided what to do next when the company was acquired out of the blue by some big pharmaceutical firm. We hardly blinked and Jonas's shares had been cashed out for a huge sum of money right before he was informed his services as a junior biologist were no longer needed by the acquiring company.

That had only been two months ago. We hadn't decided what to do with all the money and had just started interviewing financial advisors to help us manage it. Mom had made a good point that we should clear Mimi's house soon so it could go on sale around the end of the school year when more people shopped for homes. I thought this trip back to Jenkins would be a good break for us and give Jonas time to figure out what to do next.

I halted in front of the heavy steel door separating the cells from the rest of the sheriff's office to wait for Trent to unlock it.

He reached around me and handed me a business card. A phone number had been scrawled on it. "It's my cell—"

"Trent, I'm married," I turned and said firmly. Had I led him on too much with my earlier teasing?

"I know." He cleared his throat. "It's not that. It's just . . . I don't think you killed Duncan."

Without thinking, I lunged forward and hugged him. "Thank you," I said, stifling a sob as I released him quickly and stepped back.

He stepped back too as he glanced around. Being seen hugging inmates couldn't be good for his career. Looking at me, he said, "Last week, the sheriff made me the acting lead for the town of Jenkins. It's a big opportunity and I want to show him I can solve an important case like this murder." He rubbed the back of his neck, not meeting my eyes. "The sheriff made me go arrest you. He's convinced you're guilty." Then he pointed at his card. "If you think of anything useful or hear anything to move the investigation along, let me know."

I swallowed and gave a quick nod. "Thank you. I will." I put the card in my pocket, trying to hold back my tears.

Trent then entered a code in the number pad near the door and it buzzed open.

We stepped through and I took a deep breath, feeling instantly better. Leaving the cellblock and seeing desks, windows, and sunlight, blessed sunlight, lifted a weight off my chest. I also felt a huge sense of relief that Trent believed I hadn't killed Duncan.

Jonas and Mom stood with two older officers not far away. The distance evaporated as I hurried over to hug them both at once. Jonas's lean runner's body felt warm and reassuring. Despite the comfortable air temperature in the office, I trembled. I didn't even flinch when my mother kneaded my back with her fingers in that annoying habit of hers.

We stood there for a moment until one of the older officers cleared his throat. "Mrs. Trout, I'm Sheriff Tucker."

Our little circle broke apart, but I kept a tight grip on Jonas's hand. I took a closer look at the man Mom, as county commissioner, had voted against hiring to fill the remaining three years of the previous sheriff's term. Sheriff Owen Tucker was in his mid-forties, mustached, and strong, looking like he came by his muscles naturally. He stood erect with that indescribable aura of command around him. Other than him falsely arresting me, I had no beef with the man. As usual, Mom and I had something to disagree about.

"Sheriff, can we go now?" asked Jonas.

He looked from Jonas to me, giving me a slow, appraising stare, as if looking for an excuse to say no, before reluctantly nodding at the heavyset officer standing near the front desk. "Lucas can help Mrs. Trout sign the last of the paperwork."

Mom broke in, waggling her finger at Trent. "Young man, you

better not have left my house a mess like the last time you were in there without my permission."

Trent blushed and glanced away.

At another time I might have found it funny that he remembered the house party we'd thrown when Mom was supposed to spend the night at some medical conference in Little Rock during our senior year of high school. Some nosy neighbor must have called her cell to tattle on me. Next thing I knew, she was swooping in the front door well after midnight like an avenging angel, breaking up our party, grounding me for the next twenty years of my life, and threatening to call all my friends' parents.

As the sheriff gave him a confused look, Trent replied without mentioning any ten-year-old infractions. "No, ma'am. It's as neat as we found it. Not like Duncan's—"

"Deputy," interrupted the sheriff sharply.

Trent shoved his hands into his pockets. "Sorry, sir."

After a stern gaze at Trent, the sheriff turned to me. "You are not to leave the state without permission. Also, we'll need to keep your driver's license."

My mother and I both exclaimed, "What?" at the same time.

"Do you have a passport?" the sheriff asked, ignoring us.

"Yes," I answered indignantly. How dare he treat me like a criminal. But then I realized that technically I was one until they dropped the charges. I squirmed, not liking the feeling.

"We'll need that too," he said.

My mother was fuming and let loose one of her patented glares in the sheriff's direction. "By what right—"

I interrupted. "It's at home in Portland."

The sheriff, somehow not melting, ignored my mother's glare. "Okay, then your driver's license will do for now. We can't have you jumping on an airplane to flee the country and avoid prosecution."

"I'm not fleeing anywhere. I'm here to settle my grandmother's estate." It was my turn to glare at the sheriff. It was none of his business that I hadn't been ready to deal with her things right after the funeral. Of course, if I had, none of this would be happening now because I'd be home in Portland.

"I reckon I've heard about as much nonsense as I care to put up with for one day. I'll meet you two back at the car." My mother stormed out the door.

The sheriff looked at Jonas. "I think you should take your wife home now, and remember, don't leave the area."

I started fuming at the sheriff's blatant sexism. Here he was, right in front of me, telling the man to control his woman. Why if he thought—

Just then Jonas squeezed my hand, interrupting my thoughts before I could jump down the sheriff's throat. I took a breath and squeezed back, grateful for his steadying presence by my side. He always helped me stay on a more level keel, or at least return to one.

I pressed my lips together again to keep the yelling inside my head, then signed the necessary documents and handed my driver's license to the overweight officer at the front desk before leaving without another word.

Jonas stuck to my side the whole time. He was brave to go home with two angry women—one accused of murder and the other who sounded like she could commit murder and had the medical knowledge to dispose of the body.

*****

The ten minutes we spent in Mom's car were excruciatingly endless. She grilled me on what happened, what Trent said after he arrested me, what the sheriff said, and what my plans were to fight this. I finally got her to back off by agreeing to talk to a lawyer she recommended in Ft. Smith. That aspect of her nagging was helpful, but I wasn't in the mood to thank her.

Mom drove back to Mimi's place after dropping Jonas and me off to collect our car and pick up something for a late lunch.

We were in the car heading back up to Mimi's house when Jonas asked, "Where did you go yesterday when I was napping?"

Tears welled up in my eyes. "You too?"

Jonas said softly, "No. Of course I know you didn't kill him." He glanced over from the driver's seat. "But perhaps we should retrace where you were and maybe find someone who remembers seeing you."

I swallowed. "I told you. I went for a walk to the lake and then along the river. After the argument with Duncan, I just rushed off. I don't think I saw anyone." Scratching my head didn't help me remember seeing anyone. "It was late and got dark while I was out. That's why I slipped and scraped my elbow." I rolled up my sleeve and held out the bandaged elbow to show him where the blood on my shirt had come from. "I took off my shirt on the side of Mom's house and slipped in the back because I didn't want another of her lectures on not hiking along the river at night. I didn't realize how much my arm had bled."

"Okay," he said in a pensive tone. "I guess going back to the river won't help much." He paused a beat, then turned and smiled wryly at me. "At least this fall didn't lead to a cast."

Despite the morning I'd had, I giggled. Jonas and I had met soon after I moved to Portland. During a moment of misguided loneliness, I'd allowed my apartment neighbor to talk me into joining her running club. I showed up at the state park running trail in new shoes and cute workout clothes, specially purchased for this opportunity to meet new people.

It had only taken a few hundred yards up the sloping path before my neighbor left me in the dust. Jonas noticed me trailing far behind and slowed to join me. I thought he was cute, and he gained mega points when he didn't say a word about how far I lagged behind the rest of the pack. The whole join-a-club, meet-a-new-friend experience seemed to be working out until we paused after half a mile so I could catch my breath.

Without any warning, I threw up. All over him. Mortified I hadn't realized what was about to happen, I spun away from him and then tripped over a tree root on the side of the path. I tried to grab a branch to stop my fall but unfortunately missed the tree and fell off the trail, tumbling down the embankment.

I was a total mess. My cute workout clothes were spattered with vomit, my hair was tangled with branches and leaves, and my arm was bent the wrong way and hurt like the dickens. Jonas took me to the hospital and conveniently had a camping blanket in his trunk that I wrapped around myself to protect his seats.

In tune with my thoughts, Jonas grinned and said, "I sure got my money's worth out of that blanket."

I looked over my shoulder to where that blanket lay on the back seat—Daisy's preferred perch for our car rides.

When I called Jonas later to apologize profusely and thank him, he'd asked me out. With all the chemicals swirling around in my brain from the painkillers, the pain in my arm, and my humiliation, I may have said yes out of a sense of guilt for smelling up his car and ruining his day. But when he took me the next weekend to volunteer at a rescue dog adoption event, he scored some major brownie points. I mean—puppies!

Jonas won my heart on our next date. When he showed up for our hike with Daisy, a sweetheart we met at the rescue event that he must have gone back to adopt, I was head-over-heels gone. Poor Daisy had thrown up all over "my" blanket in the back seat of his car on the winding drive up to the trailhead.

I reached over and squeezed his hand. Joining that running club was the best decision I'd ever made.

When we reached Mimi's house, Mom was still stomping

around, slamming cabinet doors in the kitchen, and generally letting off steam. I dropped the bag with our lunches on the table and went to freshen up.

When I returned, Jonas had set the table and lined everything up the way he liked.

After a minute of quiet while the three of us ate, Jonas ventured to ask my mother, "Why doesn't the sheriff like you?"

She set down her sandwich. "He found out that I wasn't in favor of hiring him as the acting sheriff. He's held it against me ever since."

"Why?" asked Jonas around a bite of salad.

"Isn't it obvious? Would you like someone who spoke out in a public meeting against hiring you?"

"No. I meant why didn't you want to hire him?"

"Oh." She picked up her sandwich. "I didn't have a good feeling about him. He's moved around a bunch over the last ten years. Never ran a whole police department before and never really seemed successful in any of his positions. Guess I just felt we could do better."

I had some questions of my own. "Why was Duncan working here?"

"There's a lot of land. Someone's got to keep up with the basic maintenance."

"No, I get that. But why him? I thought he was a teacher at the high school. What did he know about ranching or taking care of land properly?"

Mom paused and scratched her neck. "His mother had cancer. Duncan was trying to line up all the extra small projects he could to help pay for her treatments. You know people around here—they'll do their best to help someone in need, even if he is a womanizing jerk." She looked away. "Or was, I guess."

As we were rising to clean up, a pickup stopped in front of Mimi's house. I followed Mom to the door and saw a man maybe ten years older than me, in his late thirties, with dark brown hair, a trim beard, and sunglasses, climb out of his truck.

"Oh, it's him," Mom said with that tone of distaste she used to describe people she didn't care for. At my questioning glance, she added, "Mimi's new neighbor," and jerked her head up the dirt driveway farther from the county highway.

When the man got close to the porch, Mom met him outside with her arms crossed. "Robert," she said with a curt nod.

"Good afternoon, Dr. Banks." Robert removed his sunglasses, revealing a black eye that hadn't yet started to fade. He tilted his head as he looked at me. I had joined Mom on the porch but stood casually compared to her combat-ready pose. "This must be your daughter. Ella Mae, right?"

"Elizabeth," I corrected him. That was my name, regardless of what people called me growing up. No reason to be rude, so I shook his proffered hand. "Nice to meet you."

"What happened to your eye?" asked Mom.

"Ah, this was just me being stupid. Stumbled getting out of a boat and ran into a pole."

"If you came over for me to look at it, you should know I only handle emergencies outside of my office. Make an appointment—"

"No, ma'am, that's not why I came."

"Then why—"

"Would you like to come in?" I interrupted Mom to play the polite host, even if I wasn't in the mood. Mimi wouldn't have stood for Mom acting this rude in her home.

"Thanks," answered Robert.

Mom jumped in. "Just briefly, though; we've got a lot to do before Sunday."

Robert stepped onto the porch. "Ah yes, the estate sale." He paused for a moment, twirling his glasses as he looked at me. "I, uh, heard you had some problems earlier today. With the law."

I frowned, suddenly tense and ready to join Mom's combat unit.

She let out a disgusted snort. "Who's gossiping about my Ella Mae so quickly?" She squinted at Robert. "And why were they calling you?"

"Well, I guess word just gets around." He looked directly at me. "I'm sorry to hear of your troubles."

I muttered some thanks as he continued speaking rapidly without looking away from me. "I imagine you'll be needing money. I hear lawyers can be quite expensive for a murder trial. So I stopped by to offer to buy this place from you."

Mom's face darkened, but he finished, "I'll pay you a fair price and mostly in cash."

When he told us how much he was offering, Mom said, "How dare you!"

"I'm only trying to be neighborly and do what I can to help."

Jonas, standing behind my elbow, spoke up. "How'd you know the property was left to Elizabeth?"

"Like I said, word just gets around," Robert answered.

Mom's face was reddening as her frown turned into a full-on glower. "Why do you want it? And why have all those trucks been going up to your place? What are you doing up there?"

"Just getting some work done to modernize the place," he said, shifting his eyes back and forth between me and Mom. "I would like to have more land. That's why I'm interested in buying. And I didn't like how Duncan was messing with the stream." He pointed behind the house to where a small creek—or "crick," as I'd always heard it called—ran through Mimi's ranch and fizzled out in the corner of his land. "I had words with him. I don't want anyone who moves in here to cause more drainage problems or muck with the landscaping near my land."

Although I was also angry at his presumptiveness, I nodded warily in agreement. Duncan's near-destruction of that corner of Mimi's land was why I had yelled at him outside the grocery store in the first place.

Jonas and I had taken a stroll out there yesterday as soon as we arrived so I could show him my favorite part of Mimi's land before we started sorting through her stuff. I'd been shocked to see what Duncan had done. Mom had hired him to manage the property, not destroy one of my favorite parts. I loved playing among all the trees and bushes along that stream when I was young. "We're not ready to sell it yet," I said cautiously.

Swiveling his sunglasses back and forth, Robert said, "Look, if that's not enough, I'll go higher."

"Thanks, but not interested right now," I said, mentally lacing up my combat boots.

"Like I said, I'm only trying to help. You going to ranch? Chickens?"

When I shook my head to each, Robert flung his hands out in frustration. "What's with this family? If you're not doing anything with the land and not even living here, why do you need it all?" He slid his glasses back on. "Call me when you change your mind. Good day." He swiveled and strode back to his truck, not quite stomping but looking like he wanted to.

As his pickup spun in the gravel before he sped off down the dirt road to his place, Jonas asked, "What was all that about?"

"I don't know." I watched the dust rise behind his truck. "But he sure struck me as a short-tempered man who was mad at Duncan Fowler."

4

Monday Early Afternoon

Jonas

"Jonas, just throw those photos in all catawampus."

"All cat and what?" My question caused Mary to pause mid-stride.

"Catawampus," Mary repeated with a grin. At my confused look, she squatted next to me and tossed a few more frames from the pile on the floor into the box without first lining them up by size and ensuring they all faced forward. I winced as her few seconds of demonstration created disarray in the box, undoing the neat stacks I had created.

"Cockeyed, topsy-turvy." Pointing to her work as she stood, she said, "They don't need to be lined up perfectly to travel the few miles to my house. Just get them in the box and out to the car." She clapped her hands twice. "Get a move on. We've got to make some headway since we lost the morning." Instructions delivered, she bustled off with the estate assessor, Sebastian Edwards, duly in tow.

"I get arrested for murder, but to Mom, it's just a lost morning." Elizabeth poked her head out from the guest bathroom where she was looking through yet another pile of Mimi's costume jewelry.

I smiled sympathetically and then showed Elizabeth a picture of herself as a muddy child, grimacing and squirming to escape the bathtub while her mother looked on with resolve.

"Yeah, maybe I wasn't the easiest kid in the world to raise," she admitted. "But she wasn't the easiest mother to get along with either." She stuck her tongue out at the picture before returning to her sorting.

The struggle between her mother's determination and Elizabeth's willfulness had not changed all that much over the years. It was no wonder Elizabeth had left this small town for college and rarely returned. A high-school-aged Elizabeth, stubborn and opinionated, wouldn't have felt there was enough room in this town for her and her mother—let alone in the same house.

I pulled out another misaligned frame from the box to rearrange the stacks. The picture showed a middle-aged version of Mimi. I had only met her twice—once soon after we got engaged and again during our wedding last year. She made a vivid impression on me both times, a sweet woman with a stubborn streak.

Grabbing the next batch of frames off the wall, I knelt and set them on the ground by an empty box. Before I put them inside, I straightened the remaining ones that Mary had messed up, but I picked up my pace. I did have my orders, after all.

Elizabeth's grandparents had certainly covered their walls with memories. I'd filled a few more boxes and lugged them out to Mary's car before she met me on the front porch.

"Argh, that girl is so ornery," she complained. "Walk with me, Jonas." She launched off the porch without waiting to see if I'd follow.

And follow I did. Mary had that effect on people.

She stopped on the front yard, spinning toward me. "That girl is too pigheaded. Can't you talk some sense into Ella Mae?"

"About what?" I asked.

"She needs to do something about this outrageous arrest."

"She left a message with the lawyer you recommended," I reminded her.

"Well, that's a start," she said. "But she needs to show more gumption." Impatient with the whole situation, she took off again.

Sensing she expected me to follow again, I trailed after her. If I knew of something Elizabeth could do to help her situation, I'd certainly suggest it. But telling each other what to do wasn't our style. Normally Elizabeth did her thing, I did mine. She didn't mess with my ways and I didn't object to her chaos, as long as she kept it mostly contained to her stuff. I avoided the room she used as her office as much as possible. We worked well together under those ground rules. It kept us from rubbing each other the wrong way. It wasn't that we were incompatible. In fact, I thought as I smiled, we were anything but.

Looking from side to side, Mary changed topics. "Have you seen Lucy since we got back here? Help me look for that dang cat."

I followed her glance, but only leaves moved in the light breeze. No cats were wandering around looking for their dead owner. "I'm sorry if Daisy scared her away." I gestured toward our border collie, now sleeping on the couch she had chosen as her own in the master bedroom. She'd exhausted herself discovering all the new smells around the old house and exploring all the rooms.

Mary scoffed. "Dogs can't scare that cat. But I'd like to make sure she's still ticking." She gestured with an imperious finger. "Keep your eyes peeled. Maybe with both of us looking, we'll find her."

She led me toward the barn, located down the dirt road in the direction of the county highway. About thirty yards from the house, we reached the carport, and I stooped to pick up a stray paper flyer stuck in some overgrown bushes by the garage to throw away later. "What about in here?" I asked, gesturing to the detached garage.

"Nah. That workshop of Paw's is locked down. He kept it in good shape for his woodworking, always puttering around with his tools on some project in there. There aren't any holes for a cat to squeeze through." She didn't spare more than a quick glance at the building.

Catching up to Mary, I commented, "Lucy's an odd name for a cat."

"Ella Mae had a dog she named Snoopy when she was a wee little one. She was a big *Peanuts* fan back then."

"Why not name the cat Charlie Brown?" It was the most logical solution to go with Snoopy.

"That cat wasn't a Charlie Brown type. It acted like it was in charge of the place. Besides, she was female."

We passed an old tractor and entered a dilapidated building with wood so old and faded it appeared to remain standing mostly out of habit. The barn creaked even in the light breeze and I flinched, half expecting the roof to fall in at any point.

With a dismissive wave, Mary said, "Oh, this place is fine. It'll last another hundred years." She crouched to look under a wagon that still had dried-out hay pieces stuck in the sides.

"Lucy must be really old by now," I said, trying to remember if I knew how cat years translated into human years.

Mary laughed. "Oh no. That cat died years ago. This is the second, or maybe the third, Lucy that Mimi owned. Calling them the same name was just easier than remembering a new one. It's not like they know any different."

I chuckled. The more stories I heard about Mimi, the more I thought I'd have liked her. "Did Lucy escape out here after Mimi passed away?"

Mary grunted as she stood. "Nah, she's a barn cat. This was her home. She kept it clear of rats and mice so they wouldn't contaminate all the hay and leather out here." Mary worked her way further into the barn, past tools, wood frames, art supplies, and miscellaneous junk.

"Huh," I said, intrigued by the concept of a partially wild domesticated animal. As I focused on avoiding tetanus from the rusty metal items scattered throughout the building and kept my eyes open for movement, I added, "I've never met a barn cat."

"Well, if we find her, she can be your first." She knelt again to look under a workbench.

I frowned, still working through the concept. "Wouldn't they catch diseases from the rats?"

"Most farmers get theirs vaccinated and spayed or neutered. They've got a job like everyone else who works the land." Mary spoke in a matter-of-fact voice with her back to me as she circled around to check the last portion of the barn.

"Guess it saves money on buying cat food," I concluded. Barn cats sounded practical and inexpensive.

"Yup, rats and mice, the original cat food." Mary laughed. "Most farms and ranches are worked in Arkansas. And by regular folks who need to save money where they can. Not like those fancified McMansions out in that big city where you and Ella Mae live. Buying organic cat food while they use exterminators to keep the rats away." She snorted again and left the barn.

I followed her out, grateful to escape that deathtrap, and bent to grab another piece of paper from the weeds.

We returned to the house. As we stood on the porch, Mary asked, "You'll talk to Ella Mae, won't you?" She had her hands on her hips and was looking intently at me.

"Yes," I answered. I fully intended to talk to my wife again, but this didn't seem like the right time to admit that I didn't know what else we should do to clear Elizabeth's name. To avoid her glare, I kneeled to grab the corner of a small paper card from a crack in the porch. Standing, I gestured at the scrap papers in my hand. "Do you have recycling here?"

Mary opened the front door and scoffed. "Does Arkansas have recycling? Where do you think we are, some third-world country?

Of course we have recycling." Catching sight of Sebastian waiting for her in the kitchen with Elizabeth, both holding glasses of water, she added, "Isn't that right, Sebastian?"

He tilted his head, pondering for just a moment. His matchy-matchy style reminded me of my eight-year-old nephew, who had recently visited Elizabeth and me for a long weekend in Portland. The kid had insisted on color-coordinating his underwear with his T-shirt and shorts each day. It was silly, but I understood the comfort derived from having your things exactly the way you expected. Sebastian answered, "I wouldn't know, ma'am. I live in Missouri."

"Well, it's a fact. Recycling's in the kitchen." Mary waved her hand vaguely in that direction, muttering under her breath as she walked past.

Sebastian took another sip of water. He looked tired and was sweating despite the comfortable March weather.

Thanking Elizabeth, I took the water glass she extended to me.

Mary tapped her foot impatiently as the rest of us took a short break. To give Sebastian a chance to finish his drink, I made a comment about his jacket, hanging again over a kitchen chair. "That blue really pops against the light gray, doesn't it?"

Now all three of us admired the contrast and how it shone in the bright sun streaming through the south-facing windows.

Leaning against the wall, Mary placed a fist on her waist and wobbled her head from side to side. "Okay, okay, enough with the fashion highlights. You wore yellow yesterday, blue today, and let me guess, red tomorrow? Your wardrobe selection has been completely analyzed. Now can we get back to work?" She rolled her eyes in case we hadn't noticed her mocking tone.

"Mom!" Elizabeth banged her cup down on the counter and scowled at her mother for a moment before storming out of the kitchen.

Sebastian blinked a few times. When we met him yesterday

afternoon, he'd seemed confident, but Mary had him under her thumb today.

I understood how he felt. Living with Mary, even temporarily, required the ability to maintain a certain level of equanimity. Or else to emulate Elizabeth and argue constantly.

Showing a flash of yesterday's energy, he smiled and framed his bow tie with his hands. "Yes, ma'am, I'm on a primary colors kick."

"Wonderful," said Mary in a clipped voice, closing the discussion. "Well, if we're going to have everything ready for the estate sale on Sunday, this is enough lollygagging. We've all got work to do." She clapped her hands twice again. "Sebastian, you and I need to go check out the basement." Without waiting for a response, she spun and marched off to the basement door, with Sebastian grabbing his gloves and gamely trailing behind.

5

Monday Afternoon

Elizabeth

Despite my best efforts to ignore the elephant in the room, my arrest loomed in the background. The tension finally boiled over when we took our next break a few hours later.

"I'm just saying you should do something about this." My mother paced in a highly agitated state in the kitchen where we had gathered.

"What is there to do? I told you I'd go meet with the lawyer you recommended. I called him and left a message. So there's nothing to do but wait. Going through Mimi's stuff is helping me forget about all the nonsense from today. Trent said he didn't believe I did it, and once that sheriff calms down, I'm sure he'll see that too."

Mom scoffed. "He's an idiot, and you shouldn't be pinning all your hopes on Trent Walker. Goodness, you think you'd have learned that by now."

Despite my annoyance, I focused on Jonas's careful tracking of her jerky movements as he made several attempts to give her a glass of water without spilling.

"You should be more proactive, Ella Mae!" She nodded thanks at Jonas as he successfully executed the hand-off on his third attempt without her breaking stride.

"Mom!" I said even though Jonas's efforts were too funny. I was more irritated at her nagging than truly upset. Yelling was just how we normally communicated. Right now I needed a lot of normal back in my life. "Thanks." I flashed a grateful smile at Jonas as he handed me a glass of water too.

"Well, I'm just saying you need to get out there and beat the bushes to get this thing cleared up. Since when have you allowed someone else to tell you what's what?"

I took a sip rather than pointing out the illogic in my mother trying to tell me what to do by telling me that I never listened to what people told me to do. "What do you suggest?"

Mom nearly tripped as she stopped pacing in mid-stride.

It might have been a while since I'd asked for her opinion.

She recovered quickly enough. "Start by digging up dirt on the victim. Find out who all Fowler had done dirty."

"What did he do? And to who?" I asked.

"To whom, dear," corrected Mom.

I rolled my eyes. Was that really necessary now? "Well, did he upset a lot of people?"

"Oh, heavens to Betsy! I don't know. Not me. And certainly not you," Mom answered.

"Great, we're really narrowing the pool now. It's not like I live here and am up-to-speed on all the latest gossip." I started to wave my hands about but stopped in time to avoid splashing water all over the hardwood floors. Setting the glass down on the counter, I added, "We can't just break into his house or something."

Jonas surprised me by speaking during one of my arguments with Mom. Usually he just sat back and watched the fireworks when I started going off about something. We worked well together because I created enough fireworks for the both of us and he pulled me back from the edge before the explosions became too extreme. "Did he have an office? Somewhere he hung out when he wasn't at home?"

Mom was startled as well and paused for a moment to think. "He worked at the high school. He'd have a desk and stuff in his classroom, I'd imagine."

I said, "Well, we can't just meander into the high school, search his classroom, and start questioning people."

Mom stopped and tilted her head in the self-confident manner she had. "You can if you're on the school board."

"Is Principal Stapleton still there?" I held my breath, hopeful.

"Sure enough," answered Mom.

Frowning at her response, I grunted. "Oh."

Without explanation, Mom walked out to the porch and pulled her phone out of her pocket, apparently deciding to make a call and work her magic. Jonas wandered to the living room and stood near the large windows looking out back. I joined him and said, "Pretty view, huh?"

"Yeah. Pretty amazing."

I snuggled in to hug him. His habitual routines might have gotten a little annoying sometimes, but he got all the important things right.

He continued, "I like that you can see some of the lake and parts of the river from up here."

I paused to take in the view again, trying to see it from fresh eyes. "When I was young, I liked playing here but never really appreciated how nice they had it. For me, it was more about my grandparents, the land, their animals, and the food. Mimi was quite the cook. Every day she made a big deal out of their dinner as if she were cooking for the president, even though it was usually just Pawpaw. Of course, he treated her like she was the first lady. They were so sweet together."

Jonas squeezed my shoulder and I leaned against him.

"Did I ever tell you that this is where I learned how to paint?"

He nodded, understanding that I needed to repeat the stories again.

"Grandpa and I would paint right out there on the porch." As I started to tear up, Jonas pulled me into a hug.

Over his shoulder, an old photograph caught my eye. Pulling away, I picked up the photo from the side table beside us. "This was my favorite picture of him, with his best friend, Amos." I smiled as I realized the old photo taken right in this room showed the two of them at about the same age as I was right now. Funny how I'd always thought of him as old, even though in the picture he showed none of the weathered signs of age I remembered so well.

"That's nice. Did he paint that?" Jonas pointed to the landscape painting hanging between the two friends.

"Yes . . . maybe." I looked to the left. The wall was still painted the same color as in the photo, but a different print now hung there. "It used to be right there." I brought the photo to the armchair where Sebastian sat typing notes into his laptop. He must have experienced his share of family disputes during the process of preparing estates for sale. So far, he had ignored all our drama and barely commented on my arrest. "Sebastian, have you seen this painting in the house?"

He took the photo from me and examined it briefly. "I have not. Was this your grandmother's?"

"Yeah. It was originally my grandfather's. I think he painted it when he was young. If you see it, please let me know. I want to make certain it doesn't go into the estate sale. I want to keep it."

"Certainly, no problem." He held the photo for another few moments before handing it back. One of Mom's friends had recommended Sebastian and his company for Mimi's estate sale. I could tell from the way he carefully handled the photo and committed it to memory that Mimi's things were in good hands.

"We're in. Let's go." Mom breezed back into the room.

"Right now?" I returned the photo to its spot because I recognized this my-way-or-the-highway mood of hers.

"What about the upstairs?" asked Sebastian. "We really don't have time for all this starting and stopping if we're going to finish before the rest of my crew shows up on Sunday morning."

"We'll just have to work harder tomorrow morning," Mom asserted. Once her mind was made up, there was no going back. "Besides, didn't you mention you had other clients in the area?" She didn't wait for his confirmation before adding, "So it won't be a wasted afternoon for you."

Mom was already halfway out the door before we could even process her words. She turned around to look at us, clearly displeased with our slow reaction, and clapped twice. "Let's get going. Time's a-wastin'!"

Mom was locking up the house when her phone rang. She grumbled under her breath but answered, as she always did, because patients came first to her. "Hello. Is everything okay?"

I knew a patient was calling because she walked away from us so her conversation would be private. We said goodbye to Sebastian and waited for her to finish her call so we could go. I hadn't wanted to do this today, but now I was anxious to get it underway.

She returned quickly. "That was Crystal," she said as she jiggled the handle to confirm she'd finished locking the door.

"Crystal from high school?" I hadn't been in contact with her in many years.

"How many other Crystals do you know? She's complaining that she's feeling contractions—"

"Crystal's pregnant?"

"Yes. That's usually when one feels contractions."

How had that happened? Well, I understood the mechanics, but still. "How come you didn't tell me? I want to go see her all preggers." I spoke louder as Mom hurried down the porch steps away from us.

Pausing before she stepped into her car, Mom said, "Another time. And don't use that word. Makes you sound like you're twelve."

Heat flushed through my body at her unnecessary correction. I was twenty-eight; I could talk any way I wished.

Mom didn't give me a chance to react. "I'm going to see her at my office. You two go on to the high school." She got into her car. "Anyway, it's probably just Braxton Hicks. These first-time mothers get overexcited about everything, but I need to check her out just in case." Keys already in the ignition, she shouted out her car window, "You young'uns run along and I'll meet you there if I can."

With her orders delivered, she sped away. It was a replay of my childhood. Dozens, probably hundreds, of times, I'd been left at some activity or event while she dashed away to deal with a medical emergency. Most of the time—but not always—she at least remembered to arrange for someone to take me home. Hurtful as it was to be dumped and forgotten on so many occasions, I did learn to become quite self-reliant. It always caused me some cognitive dissonance to hear how positively other people in town felt about her being at their beck and call when they needed help. Quite different from my own experience of getting dropped like a hot potato when someone else needed her.

Jonas turned from watching the dust rise behind her rapidly accelerating car to look at me and grinned. "I always thought you were exaggerating about her doing that."

Using my larger-than-life Southern accent, I said, "Why Mr. Trout, me exaggerate? Oh, heaven forbid!"

Jonas laughed.

"She's always been a patients-first mother." I shrugged. "I guess we young'uns are supposed to run along and play detective now." Then I grinned and added, "But it's not elementary, my dear Watson. Indeed, we must hit the high school."

"Lead on, Sherlock." Jonas bowed at the waist and leaned forward, sweeping his arm around in a flourish. Only a bowler hat would have perfected the scene.

*****

"What do you think we should look for?" I asked, trying to tamp down my nerves as we parked at the school. It was easy for Mom to tell me to prove my innocence, but how exactly would I go about doing that?

Jonas shrugged. "I don't know. Anybody could have killed him, so let's keep an eye out for anything suspicious."

"It's a high school. Half the student body will look suspicious," I said, only partially joking.

The high school looked much the same as it had ten years ago—same blue-and-white exterior paint scheme, same small visitor parking lot, same dusty glass display case with a few dismal trophies, and same type of sun-faded posters on the lobby walls.

Jonas stopped in the hallway before entering the office and looked to both sides, but the building didn't extend very far. "Seems small."

"It's bigger than it looks. It twists and turns in different directions behind this front part. It was built in fits and bursts over the years and the pieces don't all fit together efficiently." I wasn't sure why I felt defensive about a place I'd never liked.

"It wasn't a criticism," Jonas said. "I like the smaller feel. My high school was enormous. We had over three thousand students."

"Whoa. There were fewer than four hundred total students when I went here—probably even fewer now. Not too many folks with school-aged kids live in Jenkins these days. Most of the younger people left for better jobs in the big city when I was growing up."

"Dallas?" he asked as he followed me through the open office doorway.

I shuddered, mostly out of habit. "No, Little Rock." Any proper Arkansan wouldn't demean themselves by moving to Texas. At least that's what my grandparents and their friends always told me. Portland was far enough away for most of the folks living in Jenkins that it was practically the far side of the moon.

A loud voice was talking inside the principal's office. "It's all his fault. I can't believe he didn't—" A short pause. "But the deadline is next Monday!" After another short pause, the door banged open and a thin kid with messy black hair and bad skin stomped out, slamming the door behind him and rattling the glass in the frame.

Apparently still upset by the conversation, he turned back after a few steps and shouted, "How is that fair?" and flung a plastic Coke bottle at the trash can by the door. It rattled off the frosted glass and clattered onto the linoleum floor. He spun, looking like he intended to continue his dramatic exit.

The school secretary standing calmly behind the counter didn't comment, but the door opened and Principal Stapleton's overweight figure filled the doorway. He opened his mouth as if to reprimand the student for his outburst when he noticed me and Jonas in the office lobby.

While I'd been distracted by the kid's performance and Principal Stapleton's appearance, Jonas had taken a few steps to the side and now stood casually with his hands in his pockets a few feet in front of the kid.

The student seemed startled by Jonas's sudden presence. He shifted his weight to go around Jonas, but Jonas shifted slightly in the same direction and leaned forward onto his toes. Jonas wasn't physically intimidating—he was thin, lean, and a touch over six feet tall—but people seemed to listen to him.

Angling his head and raising an eyebrow, Jonas indicated the bottle still spinning slowly on the ground.

The kid froze.

Jonas raised his eyebrows again, shrugged, and repeated his little head motions.

The kid matched his gaze for a moment before letting loose a disgusted sigh. Shaking his head, he reached down, grabbed the bottle, and flicked it into the small trash can without casting a glance at the principal.

Satisfied, Jonas stepped out of the boy's path, giving him a small smile and nod.

The kid grimaced and heaved another disgusted sigh, then threw up his hands and completed his dramatic exit.

Jonas watched him leave, then looked over at me and winked. That was so Jonas. No yelling—just one look and the kid did the right thing. I'd seen him convince others to clean up their litter—a pet peeve of his—but usually he had to speak to them.

In contrast, Principal Stapleton looked primed to holler at the kid. Just for good measure, he probably would have yelled at me for being a witness to the crime. During my high school years, I'd had my fair share of lectures and shouting matches from him and Mom, and they rarely led me to change course. Their yelling tended to reinforce my innate need to keep doing whatever it was that had upset them. I sure showed them.

As the boy disappeared into the hallway, a broad smile broke out onto Stapleton's fat face. "Well done, young man," he said to Jonas. "And who might you be?"

"I'm Jonas Trout." Jonas shook his outstretched hand.

"Nice to meet you. I'm Lester Stapleton."

Since when did Stapleton have a first name?

His smile disappeared into a thin line when he turned in my direction. "Ella Mae," he greeted me, without offering a handshake.

"Principal Stapleton," I mumbled in reply, with even less enthusiasm.

"Where's that force of nature of yours?" he asked as he looked behind us.

"Mom had a patient emergency—"

"Of course she did. Of course." He rolled his eyes as he pulled his office door closed behind him. "Well, I'm not sure why, but I agreed to your mother's request to show you Mr. Fowler's classroom and I don't have all day. I probably shouldn't let you in there until the sheriffs come by in the morning, but you know your mother." Shaking his head, Stapleton put an arm behind Jonas's back and propelled him down the hall, not caring whether I joined them. "Obviously the whole school is in mourning," he said to Jonas. "We'll have a memorial assembly in his honor, of course, but I've got a lot to organize to make that happen."

"Thank you for your assistance. We'll make this short," said Jonas.

I was quite content to follow behind them and avoid small talk. Being polite to someone who had suspended me three times and hollered at me for all sorts of real—and imagined—incidents during high school was easier when I didn't have to converse with him.

"So I hear you're a biologist," said Stapleton.

"I am. How did you know?" asked Jonas.

From behind them, I inserted, "Small town, Jonas. Small town."

Jonas nodded and then continued an animated conversation with Stapleton as we walked down the hall. He managed to keep the principal distracted so he wouldn't bother me. Jonas was so my hero.

Stapleton opened the door to a classroom right as the end-of-school bell rang. Jonas and I stepped into the room and out of the flash flood of students surging down the hallway. Stapleton stood like a boulder in the river, talking to some of the students as the rest flowed around him.

Ignoring him, we turned our attention to the room and its rows of lab tables neatly facing the bigger lab table at the front. Jonas asked, "He taught science?"

"Yeah, I think I heard Duncan taught chemistry or biology or something," I answered, impressed that the equipment in the room no longer looked older than my mother.

Stapleton leaned into the room. "I've got to speak to someone for a minute. I'll be right back. Don't leave before I have a chance to talk with you." Looking pointedly at me, he added, "Or take anything."

Jonas wandered to Duncan's small desk in the corner, not far from the connecting door that led to the next classroom. I'd always wondered what weird building code had made connecting doors between classrooms a good idea. Regardless of whoever had created the rules, most of the classrooms here had them.

Heading in the other direction, I went to check out the small, open storeroom and bookshelves in the back corner of the room. I had just begun examining the narrow shelves alongside the doorway when I noticed Jonas pick up a piece of paper from a tray on Duncan's desk.

"What?" I called out, stepping back out of the storeroom.

Of course, Stapleton chose that moment to step back into the classroom. "What what?" he asked, looking at me with a suspicious frown.

While Stapleton's head was turned, and much to my surprise, Jonas jammed the paper into his pocket without a word.

6

Monday After School

Elizabeth

Not wanting to call attention to whatever Jonas had taken, I merely said, "Sorry, I thought you called my name."

"No," Stapleton responded crisply. "Okay, how about making this quick. This is a crazy busy time for me. We've got some event keeping me at the school late every night this week. And losing Mr. Fowler on top of that won't help." He wiped his forehead with a handkerchief as if the mere thought of the coming week was enough to wear him to a frazzle.

Jonas and I quickly looked around the classroom, but since we didn't know what we were searching for, we succeeded in finding nothing out of the ordinary. Plenty of boring laboratory and school supplies, but nothing that seemed unusual. With Principal Stapleton watching me like a hawk, I couldn't ask Jonas about whatever he'd found on Duncan's desk.

We exited the classroom only a few minutes later, but already the crush of humanity in the hallway had ebbed as the students satisfied their frantic urge to be anywhere but in school. Only a few still idled by lockers as we walked out.

Suddenly someone rushed up and hugged me from the side with an excited, "Eliza?"

I squealed with delight. Only one person had ever called me by that nickname. "Kelsey Wheeler, as I live and breathe." I hugged her back. Kelsey had been my best friend during middle and high school. I'd gradually lost touch with her when I left Arkansas for college—like I had with so many others. Returning as seldom as possible will do that to a relationship.

"Look at you, all teacher-like and everything." I smiled and stepped back to study her.

Kelsey looked much the same as before, only more mature. She was still short and cute with long, straight, light brown hair, but she was dressed decidedly unglamorously for her teaching job in a loose-fitting sweater, thick glasses, and a long skirt. She had started calling me Eliza in junior year after she'd read *Pride and Prejudice* in our English Honors class and decided I reminded her of the main character. After she told me this, I had to actually read the assigned book to figure out if she was making fun of me. Tricking me into doing the homework so she'd have a helpful study-buddy for the test was just one example of how she'd always been my most clever friend.

"I'd heard a rumor you were back in town." Kelsey put her hands on her narrow hips and threw a level-two glare my way. "But I couldn't believe it because my friend Eliza would have told me she was coming."

Embarrassed, I looked down at my feet. "I . . . I should have—"

Stapleton interrupted, "Ladies, as touched as I am by this heart-warming reunion, I don't have time for this." He turned to Jonas with a smile. "It was a real pleasure to meet you, Jonas."

"You too, Lester," he replied.

Stapleton shook Jonas's hand again and then glanced at Kelsey. "Ms. Wheeler, could I impose upon you to escort Mr. Trout and Ella Mae out of the building when you're done visiting?"

Biting her lip, Kelsey looked up at Stapleton and nodded.

We held it together long enough for Stapleton to sail back toward his office before we burst out laughing.

"Oh my goodness gracious, he still doesn't like you, does he?" Kelsey managed as she gasped for air.

"Can't really blame him, can you?" I watched Stapleton waddle up the hallway. "Well, at least the feeling's mutual."

"And when are you going to introduce the hot guy standing next to you?" asked Kelsey.

Jonas answered, "Hi, I'm Jonas, Elizabeth's husband."

I started to explain why I hadn't brought him by to meet her before, but Kelsey just laughed at me, as easy-going and hard to annoy as ever.

She clasped his hand with both of hers. "So good to finally meet you. I'm Kelsey. I always wondered what kind of man would finally tame Eliza."

"Nice to meet you too." Jonas chuckled. "And if you ever find him, please let me know."

She giggled and I joined in, even though I was surprised that he made a joke. He had a good sense of humor but wasn't the joke-telling kind of guy.

I raised an eyebrow at Kelsey. "How did Stapleton agree to hire you after all we did?" Before she could answer, I noticed Jonas's puzzled expression and explained, "He was a new principal when I went here. We didn't exactly make it easy for him. Kelsey and I got into trouble all the time."

Kelsey chuckled. "Maybe you've forgotten that you got in trouble much more than me. I got pretty good at knowing when to stop right before the hammer came down." With a shrug, she added, "Besides, it's not as if he's got lots of candidates dying to move to Jenkins to teach high school English."

Her words reminded me why we'd come here, so I sobered and asked more quietly, "Did you hear about Duncan?" Seeing Kelsey's serious nod, I added, "Did you also hear that the sheriff arrested me for Duncan's murder?"

She laughed, clearly believing I was kidding around with her, but then her mouth dropped open when I didn't join in. "You're kidding!" After I shook my head, she said, "Why would he think that? You wouldn't kill anyone." She clenched a fist and slapped her open palm. "You want me to line up some of the old gang to act as character references for you?"

Despite the situation, I smiled. Years had passed since we'd seen each other and Kelsey's first reaction was still to support me.

I shook my head, not sure that our old gang of friends would be all that helpful. With my luck, they'd wind up putting another nail in my coffin by bringing up all the things I did that no one found out about. After I explained what had happened earlier today, Kelsey shook her head in disbelief. "That's ridiculous. Couldn't . . ." She shot a cautious glance at Jonas. "Couldn't Trent talk sense into the sheriff?"

I shook my head again and lowered my tone to add a gravelly edge. "He's gone over to the dark side."

Cutting to the chase, Jonas asked, "Can you think of anyone who might have wanted to kill Mr. Fowler?"

Kelsey took his question seriously, chewing on her bottom lip for a moment. "No one jumps to mind, but even though he taught next door to my classroom, I didn't know him that well. He was always on the run, busy teaching biology and managing properties for people. Every time I saw him in the teachers' lounge, he seemed to be working on some scheme or another. He was so busy. When the school bell rang, he was out of here so fast he probably beat most of the students out the door."

"What kind of schemes?" I asked.

"I don't know, he just always seemed to be working some angle with someone, always whispering in some corner to one of the male teachers or talking on his phone." She paused. "But busy is how I'd describe him best. Did you know he was even planning to start a new art class in the fall? Stapleton was offering some extra pay if anyone was willing and he signed up right away."

"They're bringing back art classes?" I was surprised.

"Stapleton is," said Kelsey. Then she smirked. "He was quite the ladies' man."

At my horrified expression, she quickly explained, "No, not Stapleton. Duncan. He was always very friendly to all the women—nothing out of line, mind you. All the women teachers would gossip about him being quite the flirt when the men weren't around. I think he dated a number of the older teachers."

Perhaps responding to my frown, she added, "Not that I was into him or anything. We never really talked besides saying hello."

Jonas followed up with a few more detailed questions about Duncan's friends, but we didn't learn anything that would help me convince the sheriff to investigate someone else.

We headed down the hallway. Walking these halls again with Kelsey felt surreal, especially with Stapleton not too far away. I did feel a surge of power when I realized I didn't have a hall pass and there was nothing he could do about it. I giggled a little and then remembered, "Oh! Did you hear Crystal is pregnant?"

Kelsey chuckled. "Eliza, it's Jenkins. Of course I know." She jiggled on her tiptoes in excitement but still didn't reach my eye level. "Oh, I almost forgot. Her baby shower is tomorrow night. You should come."

I also jiggled, mimicking her eagerness, but then hesitated. "I don't know if it would be right. I haven't kept in touch with her very well." I blushed. "Either."

"Oh, nonsense. She'd love to see you." Seeing my continued reluctance, she added, "I'll text her to make sure, but plan on coming!"

I clapped in excitement, but then, realizing I was picking up my mother's annoying habit, I dropped my hands. Feeling suddenly awkward, I stepped forward and hugged Kelsey.

We made plans to meet tomorrow evening for the shower, and after one last hug, Jonas and I walked to our car. Although this excursion had been a bust, I was happy to have rediscovered an old friend.

Suddenly remembering what Jonas had done in the classroom, I asked, "What was that paper you found?"

"In the car," he said quietly as we passed a few knots of students talking on the sidewalk.

Wondering what was so juicy he wouldn't tell me in the open, I hurried to the car. After I hopped in, I asked impatiently, "What was it?"

After sliding into the passenger seat, Jonas went through his normal routine—locking the doors, checking the vents, and making sure he had remembered his phone. When he started to fasten his seat belt, I tugged on his arm to get his attention. Normally, his drill didn't bother me, and I hoped my interruption didn't throw him off so he'd start it all over again, but I felt like I had ants in my pants.

Jonas glanced over at me and then shook his head, looking like a dog shaking off stress. Back on track, he pulled the crumpled paper from his pocket and opened it. The handwritten note read, "Elizabeth Trout problem?"

"Problem?" I slapped the wheel. "What kind of problem am I?"

"I don't know. Had Duncan been in touch with you before our trip?" He arched an eyebrow.

"No," I said, perhaps more emphatically than necessary. Then I caught my breath, suddenly worried. Did Jonas seriously think I had something to do with Duncan's death?

Jonas touched my leg. "I took it because I didn't want the sheriff to have another reason to harass you."

"Thanks," I said softly. "Thank goodness Mom got us in the

classroom before they searched it." Then I looked him in the eyes. "You know I didn't—"

"I know," he interrupted, nodding.

I ducked my head as warmth flooded through me. He rarely interrupted. I heard cars pulling out from the nearby student parking lot and waited a moment before I asked more quietly, "So why am I a problem? And why would someone kill Duncan Fowler?"

"That's a good question. He seems to have been working for half the town on different jobs. That's a lot of suspects if he angered one of them. Almost anybody could have killed him."

My frustration grew. "I don't know how Mom thinks we can investigate this. We just don't know who was mad enough at Duncan to kill him."

"At first glance, he doesn't sound like someone people would want to kill. Sounds like the women liked him. Hard to get angry at someone who was helping his mother pay for her cancer treatment." Jonas grew silent.

Seeing him staring into the distance, I asked, "What?"

"Well, Principal Stapleton told me Tyler was quite upset at Duncan."

"Tyler?"

"The angry student in the office," Jonas explained.

"Ah, okay. Why would he want to kill Duncan?"

"Lester said—"

"Stapleton. We are not on a first-name basis with that man."

"Hmm." Jonas's response was noncommittal, but he started over. "I was told that Tyler—"

I interrupted, "By the way, that was super chill—your whole stare-him-into-submission thing. It was like a move out of some Siegfried and Roy book on how to handle a wild beast." I touched Jonas's hand. "It impressed me, too. I just didn't want Stapleton to know I agreed with anything he said."

"Yes, I gathered you don't like the man much," Jonas said dryly, then shrugged. "Tyler was angry because Duncan refused to submit a letter of reference that he needs for college. Apparently Tyler thought Duncan had promised he would. He even wrote out a draft for Duncan to sign, but when he brought it to him, they had a big argument about it and Duncan refused. Now that Duncan's dead, Tyler wants Lester . . . Mr. Stapleton—"

"Just Stapleton," I insisted, giving him one of my glares.

"Elizabeth." He tried his taming-the-beast look on me.

His look worked better than mine, although it didn't manage to smooth the petulance out of my voice or keep my lower lip from jutting out just a little bit. "Fine, you can call him whatever, and even Kelsey may have been lured to the dark side, but he's still Stapleton to me."

Jonas smiled and planted a quick kiss on my lower lip, conceding to the compromise.

I loved that he didn't mind my quick trips to crazy town as long as I didn't insist on him joining me. But then I considered all the details that he'd shared. "How do you know all this?"

"Lester and I were talking on the way to the classroom. I thought you were listening." He quirked an eyebrow.

"No," I said firmly. Compromise or not, listening to Stapleton wasn't on my agenda.

Jonas finished his recap. "Tyler wanted Lester to sign the letter he'd written for Duncan, but Lester won't sign a letter he didn't write. He told Tyler he would write his own and send it in soon. Apparently Tyler felt that wasn't adequate, or he worried it would miss the deadline. Regardless, Tyler was angry enough to throw quite the fit in Lester's office."

I corrected him. "In the South, you don't throw a fit; you pitch one. And besides, that boy was having a conniption."

"What?" Jonas blinked several times and rubbed his forehead.

"We're in the South now so you need to understand the difference. A conniption is when things start to get physical; a fit is just words. That boy was slamming things around. He threw his soda bottle at the door and was stomping around. We didn't even see what he did inside Stapleton's office before he stormed out."

Switching gears as I realized Jonas might be onto something, I snapped my fingers. "You're right. It's possible the kid met with Duncan on Sunday, became thoroughly enraged, had the mother of all conniptions, and killed his no-good, double-crossing teacher."

"Tyler," clarified Jonas before pausing to absorb the rest. "Well, it's a theory."

I pressed my lips together and crossed my arms. "It's a good theory. We should tell the sheriff. I know he's under pressure to solve some of the crime around here and this could help him close this case without me behind bars."

"Hmm. Why don't we bookmark this for now and see what else we can discover. I think it would be irresponsible to point the sheriff after a child if he is not the true culprit."

"What about me?" I said, indignant.

"They've already accused you. Can't undo that. But we can make it worse by making false allegations."

I didn't like it when he was so dang right. Sighing, I asked, "Then who should we look into next?"

Jonas responded, "Well, if it wasn't you, it could have been anybody."

"If?!" I felt steam starting to rise.

"I didn't mean it that way." Jonas touched my leg in apology. "Of course it wasn't you. I just meant that we don't know much more than we did this morning."

Quiet reigned in the car for a minute before Jonas spoke again. "It really could be Tyler. He was very angry at Duncan, and Lester said he'd argued with him too. According to how this sheriff operates, owning a shirt from out of town with some of your own blood on it or having an argument is enough to arrest a person for murder."

For Jonas, that qualified as an attempt at humor. But I wasn't willing to stop being annoyed at him. If even my husband was thinking "if," then maybe I really was in trouble.

7

Monday Evening

Jonas

I crossed Main Street, looking for the grocery store Elizabeth had told me was on the corner. She wasn't up for another attempt at shopping, but the visit to Duncan's classroom made me hungry. It was probably the association with the lab equipment—at work, I had often missed lunch because I got so focused on my experiments. At least losing my job meant I was less likely to miss a meal.

This stretch of Main Street was quite different from other parts of Jenkins. The road widened enough for cars to park nose-in at an angle in front of each shop. Nearly every store had an awning extending out over the sidewalk, but all the store owners seemed to have made their own color choices without consulting their neighbors. Green, red, white, striped, and more all hung at different heights and angles. The buildings themselves were a riot of different construction techniques—different colors of brick, stone, and wood fronts. It was as if whoever built the next store along the line just grabbed whatever material and paint were on sale.

Personally, I would have preferred a more orderly plan, but that was more my style in any situation. At least the buildings didn't have that fake look common to tourist-trap towns, but I wasn't sure

I could describe the area as charming either. "Real" was the adjective I settled on—it looked real.

Crossing the street, I aimed for Harps Grocery and nodded hello to two old men chatting on a bench near the entrance. The tiny size of the storefront and its associated awning concerned me. I feared that eating in Jenkins for a week as a vegan would be quite a challenge if I had to make it with the goods sold here.

The inside was much as I'd expected—a tiny and touristy corner market, with even an old wooden pickle barrel stuck between stacks of apples smack in the middle of the store. I stopped in my tracks just inside the entrance, staring at the limited array of grocery items, snacks, and souvenirs and wondering how I'd manage to find something I could eat. I didn't think I'd enjoy surviving on taffy pulls, bags of baby carrots, and peanuts.

"Can I help you, honey child?" asked an older woman I hadn't noticed sitting on a tall metal stool behind the counter.

"Is this everything?" I asked, my gaze settling on the pickle barrel flanked by stacks of green and red apples.

The woman quirked an eyebrow at me and answered in a strong Southern accent. "Sugar, we got both kinds of apple. Red Delicious for eatin' and them Granny Smiths for making pies. Are you a baker?"

"Well, yes. But no, not today. What about Opal apples? Do you have any of those?" What I really meant to say was, "Where are all the vegetables and other items I need to make dinner?"

She smacked her lips. "Opal doesn't work here no more. How about some of them pickles? Them tart." She pointed, in case I hadn't noticed the pièce de résistance of the place.

I put my hands in my pockets and peered over warily, wondering if they ever changed the brine in the barrel. "No, thank you. I'm not interested in a pickle."

"Fran! Stop teasing the poor man." A woman popped out from behind the next aisle where she must have been restocking. "Sir, if you're looking for regular groceries, the rest of the store wraps around back here." As she waved me over, I could see the manager badge on her apron.

I followed her, still hearing Fran cackling from where she reigned on her rusted stool.

"Sorry about that. Fran gets bored when we're not busy. She's supposed to be greeting customers, not harassing them. She is real good with children."

"I'm sure," I said to be polite, and then pulled up short when we turned the corner. A modern and decent-sized grocery store with aisles full of actual groceries stretched out for what had to be the distance to the end of the block.

The store manager laughed. "Yeah, everyone reacts like that when they see the real store for the first time. We bought out all the shops on the back side of the street years ago and just kept the front part to pull in the tourists and visitors who walk along Main Street."

I laughed too. I'd let my preconceptions about small-town Jenkins fool me. Much the same as that sheriff's assumptions seemed to have blinded him from seeing anyone other than Elizabeth as the murderer. My smile faded. I hadn't wanted to scare Elizabeth, but I was worried. If the sheriff didn't investigate other people, then she'd be facing a full-fledged trial, and those could be unpredictable. We had to do something. I'd research local private investigators tonight.

"Most of our regulars enter from the parking lot back here." The manager pointed to another entrance. "By the way, that pickle barrel holds individually-sealed pickles in plastic. The state health board wouldn't find it very hygienic if we allowed people to reach in and grab one."

I thanked her and was able to collect most of the food on my list. I was especially pleased to find fresh, high-quality coffee beans. Doubting Mary had a home grinder, I ground them with the store's machine and made a mental note to resolve Mary's kitchen deficiency at my next opportunity.

The same manager was staffing the register when I reached the checkout line. When she checked my driver's license to compare it to my credit card, she said, "Oh, are you Dr. Banks's son-in-law?"

When I nodded in surprise, she explained, "I heard you were coming to town with Ella Mae."

There was certainly no need for a local newspaper around here.

She tsked in dismay. "I was so sad to hear about her troubles. I'm sure she's innocent. No daughter of Dr. Banks could kill someone."

Although I agreed Elizabeth was innocent, I couldn't attribute that to any resemblance to her mother.

"Is it true they arrested her because of the big argument she had with that man?"

"I don't . . ." My voice trailed off as I tried to decide how to avoid explaining that the sheriffs had also found Elizabeth's bloody shirt in the side yard.

Without waiting for me to finish, she went on, "Well, it's terribly unfair if you ask me." She continued bagging my groceries while she gossiped. "Why Brent Hollands had his own argument with that Duncan Fowler right here in the store, not three days ago. You don't see the sheriff arresting Brent, now do you?"

I was about to ask who Brent Hollands was and what they argued about when she handed me the groceries and said, "Sorry to hurry off, but I just saw a delivery truck pull up and I've got to take care of that. You have a good evening now."

She dashed off, leaving me with a bag of groceries, my cards, and some unanswered questions. Picking up the bag, I left from the front since that was the fastest way back to Mary's house.

"Y'all come back now, ya hear, honey," said Fran as I passed her, still on her perch.

I looked around for the people she was talking to before realizing that she meant her "y'all" for just the singular me. "Thanks," I said in a tentative voice as I tried to sort this new grammar into a coherent framework I could understand. "Y'all" made sense if you were talking to a group of people, yet around here I'd heard people use "all y'all" and even "y'alls" when speaking to a group.

While I'd slowed down to ponder these new Southern expressions, a teenager hurried past me, hunched over with his hands thrust in his jacket pockets. As we crossed through the sliding door at the same time, I heard crinkling sounds from under his jacket.

I put a hand on the teen's shoulder, causing him to jump, right as I noticed the group of men near the entrance had expanded. The two older men on the bench were still there, along with Lester Stapleton and another I didn't recognize as a fifth man strode up to the group.

Gripping the boy's arm, I leaned in. "You still have time to go back inside and decide if you're going to pay for those things in your jacket or just put them back."

The boy flushed and shot a glance at me.

Just then, a burst of laughter from the gathered men drew our attention. The latest newcomer, smiling along to whatever comment one of the older men had made, was showing off a business card. "Yup, brand-new design. Nice, huh?"

As Lester leaned forward to take one, the boy jerked back in surprise at seeing the principal so close. "You're not going to rat me out, are you?" he whispered urgently.

Based on his reaction, I assumed he went to the local high school and recognized Lester. "There's nothing to tell the principal if you either pay or put them back. And promise not to do it again."

The teenager gulped and then nodded. "Yeah. Okay." Casting another nervous look at the men, he turned and walked back inside the store.

I figured I'd have to settle for only a fifty-percent success rate. Unless I planned to plant myself on the bench next to the men for the foreseeable future, I had no doubt the kid would try to steal something another day. I shrugged. I'd done what I could, and although fifty percent wasn't a passing grade, it would make a great batting average.

"Jonas. Come on over, I'd like to introduce you around." Lester smiled as he noticed me hovering by the door.

I smiled back and raised a finger. "Be there in just a minute." I whipped out my cellphone, pretending I had received an urgent text I needed to handle.

The teen dashed out of the store a moment later, stopping short when he saw me still standing there.

I didn't speak, just rose an eyebrow in query.

He grimaced and flicked open his jacket to show me he had decided to return the item.

I nodded with approval and he hurried off, heading away from the men. Returning the phone to my pocket, I joined them. "Hi again, Lester."

With the sharp eyes of a principal alert to student infractions, he'd noticed my interchange. "Everything all right?"

"Absolutely."

He waited a moment, but when I didn't elaborate, he nodded. "Gentlemen," he said, interrupting one of the old-timers who sat on the bench. "I'd like to introduce you to someone."

Before he could continue, the handsome, hearty man beside him boomed, "You must be Jonas Trout."

At my startled reaction, he laughed. "I'm Dale Cooper, mayor of this here flourishing metropolis."

"How do you know my name?"

"Oh, don't get your knickers in a twist. Lester was just telling us about you," said the fifth man, who was wearing a green John Deere cap with the name "Blake" sewn in script on the side.

"Now Blake, be nice," said Dale. "It ain't every day that one of our promising young women returns to town, married to a smart young man."

Upon hearing Dale's description of Elizabeth, Lester's face twisted as if he had just sucked on a lemon, but he didn't comment.

One of the older men said, "So you mean Ella Mae jumped from the Banks to become a Trout?" He guffawed, and his seated neighbor joined in.

The mayor said, "Now hush, Colton," and extended his hand to me. "Sure as heck, I've heard all about you. How long are you two planning to stick around?" Dale stared at me with piercing, cool blue eyes that weren't as friendly as his words.

"No plans. We're just here for a brief visit and to sort through the things at Elizabeth's grandmother's house."

Dale relaxed and nodded. "Yup, makes sense. Clean it out before putting it on the market. Well, you came to a great place for a vacation. You looking to get out on the water?" He gestured toward the lake at the end of the street. "With a name like yours, I'll bet you're quite the angler, am I right?"

The men all chuckled. I installed my polite smile. It wasn't as if I hadn't already heard every variation of joke about my name. "I do enjoy the outdoors, but I've never been much for fishing. It's just my name."

"Yup, yup." He nodded again, continuing on as if I hadn't spoken, and then raised a finger. "You know, speaking of names, since you're a smart cookie and not from around here, I'm hoping you'd be kind enough to help settle our little dispute." Dale swept his hand to indicate the group.

I set the bag of groceries on the ground. Extracting oneself from conversations around here apparently required a set of skills I had yet to acquire. This was definitely different from the bigger cities I was accustomed to where strangers didn't invite you to join their conversations. "How can I help?"

"I want to change the name of the lake. Lake Capitola doesn't mean anything to anyone since the capital isn't here in Jenkins. The folks way back when hoped that giving it that name would influence the legislature to make this the state capital. Now we're stuck with it and it doesn't have a lot of pizazz." He rolled forward onto his toes and tensed his arms unconsciously as his gaze grew intense. "We need a more exciting name if we're gonna attract more tourists. Am I right?" Although one of the seated men guffawed, Dale looked like his question was serious.

Deciding it was faster to take his bait so I could make my exit sooner, I asked, "What do you want to call it?"

Dale said, "I think it should be—"

Blake interrupted, "Just 'cause you're the honorable mayor and all doesn't mean you can just change the name of the lake all willy-nilly. It borders three counties. All them county boards would have to agree and then the state. Probably the federal government too since there's a federal park over yonder."

Dale responded, "But it's not impossible. Change has to start somewhere. A better name will help us get more visitors."

Colton blurted out, "Should call it 'Findyaown Lake.'"

"Come on, I'm serious," said Dale.

Colton's buddy snorted and threw in his own contribution. "Lake Nunyabizness."

Colton guffawed. "Nunyabizness. That's a good one, Billy Ray."

"Stop it," Dale snapped. "You know the state's going to decide on the location for the final Arkansas casino license soon. If we get it, that could be a game-changer for the whole area. With that and a cool name, more people will vacation here. That means more tax money." Realizing his comment on taxes hadn't yielded the level of enthusiasm he'd expected, Dale added, "More money for the high school's football program."

Lester nodded and Colton grunted in approval. "That's one positive point," Colton said. "But I don't want this town overrun with even more people." He waved broadly around us in complaint.

Instinctively I looked from side to side. Besides our little cluster, only three other people were visible along Main Street.

Colton continued, "If you want lots of tourists, go to Hot Springs or Branson. We like it quiet here."

Billy Ray agreed. "Yeah, you just want more visitors so you'll make more money in your store."

I looked in the direction that Billy Ray had waved—at a store painted bright yellow and situated next to the lake.

The mayor, noticing my glance, puffed out his chest. "Yup. Bait, Boat, and Float is my place," he boasted. "We rent boats and floats for the lake and river. My daddy started it as a bait shop, but I've been expanding."

"Too bad ole Duncan didn't rent a float," interjected Colton. "Floating face down on his own in the river didn't work out too well for him, did it?"

His words landed abruptly, silencing the group. Everyone seemed as shocked as I felt by the old man's comment. Then Billy Ray snorted. "Yeah, Mayor, you lucked out on that. It wouldn't have been good advertising if he had rented one of your floater thingies and then turned up dead."

Dale shook his head. "Nah, not likely. Typically only visitors rent those."

With the old men already on the subject of Duncan, this seemed like a good opening to ask some questions. Mary had admonished me twice before I left for the grocery store to find out whatever I could about the murder. "Did you see Duncan out on the river before . . . before . . ."

"Before someone drowned him?" finished Colton.

Billy Ray added, "Damn shame."

Surprised by his comment after his earlier laughter, I asked, "So you liked Duncan?"

"No. Damn shame Ella Mae's all caught up in this mess."

Before I could agree and thank him, Colton added, "Ain't nobody liked Duncan."

While I took a moment to parse the double negative, Billy Ray responded, his eyebrows waggling, "Excepting women."

Although the two older men laughed, the others didn't, exhibiting a combination of frowning, fidgeting from side to side, and looking away.

Clearly looking to distract us with a change of subject, Dale continued his sales pitch to me. "We've got tours too, you know, if you want to take one." Then he paused. "Well, those pretty much don't start until the summer, on account of that being our busy season and all."

I leaned over and picked up my bag of groceries, deciding I'd learned about as much as I could from the men. Unfortunately none of it was new information. Only the store manager's tidbit about Brent Hollands was worth sharing with Mary and Elizabeth. Who was he and why had he argued with Duncan a few days ago?

Before I could extract myself from the gathering, Billy Ray said, "Now don't be worried, young fisherman. Everything will be just fine. Everyone knows Ella Mae wouldn't hurt nobody."

I replied with a quick, tight smile of thanks, noting that his opinion wasn't universally shared by the other men. A jury trial would be risky.

Dale tried to hook me in with another change of subject, blurting, "You're from Seattle so you know about coffee." Without waiting for me to correct him, he added, "I've been thinking of squeezing in a coffee nook. You like coffee, am I right?"

Involuntarily, I squeezed the bag of fresh ground coffee that I'd just bought. Reassured that we'd finally have a decent cup, I said, "I do."

Dale jabbed a finger toward the older guys. "See there. If I add coffee service, more people would stop in."

Billy Ray teased him, "Yeah, but what would you call your place then?"

Curious despite myself to hear his response, I watched the mayor rub his chin while he thought. Then he grinned. "I'd add *Jolt* to the end." He looked at his store.

I looked too. He'd require a larger sign for Bait, Boat, Float, and Jolt.

Colton turned to me. "While we're waiting for the mayor's plans for world domination to reach fruition, you interested in making a donation to our local high school booster club? Billy Ray here is the president. We're trying to upgrade the lights in our stadium so we can have proper Friday night football games."

"Well—"

"Come on," nudged Billy Ray. "You heard the mayor, this is an up-and-coming town. Ella Mae was a cheerleader once upon a time. You'll be helping those children—"

Colton, perhaps thinking he had a sucker cornered, interrupted. "You can start out small. A thousand would—"

"Dollars?" That was a surprise. I didn't know much about small towns, but this seemed out of order. He'd just met me and here he was hitting me up for a substantial donation.

Billy Ray said, "We heard you was rich."

"No," I replied, still not accustomed to my new status and unlikely to admit it in any case.

Colton didn't back off. "We heard you don't have to work no more."

"That is correct, technically, but—"

Billy Ray nodded. "That means you're rich." Barely pausing for breath, he added, "Even a hundred dollars would really help those poor children. And ole CB here is the play-by-play announcer, so you can come visit and hear him work his magic."

Lester came to my rescue. "Guys, how about backing off the hard sell here. Jonas here just got to town."

I nodded a grateful thanks for his intervention. "I'll talk this over with Elizabeth and get back to you," I promised the men.

Colton brightened as if I'd already handed him a hundred-dollar bill. "Oh, and tell Ella Mae she needs to come down here and visit with us a spell."

Like a lightning strike from out of the blue, Dale suddenly cried, "And pizza!" Still preoccupied with thoughts of future improvements to his store, his face was dreamy as he stared into the distance. As his hands framed his grand vision, he said, "We could sell pizza too. Coffee in the mornings and pizza at lunch and dinner."

Billy Ray elbowed Colton, and asked, with a twinkle in his eye, "So what would you call your place then?"

I waved goodbye to Lester and nodded politely to the others but backed away slowly in order to hear the mayor's response.

"Bait, Boat, Float, Jolt Pizzeria," said Dale in a singsong voice before pausing to scratch his chin as he pondered the name. He smiled brightly. "Now that's a name with pizazz."

8

Tuesday Afternoon

Jonas

On my own again. The quiet felt like a relief after this morning's chaos. Dinner after my successful grocery store run had been a welcome change as I introduced Mary to my excellent African sweet potato stew with spinach, mushrooms, and peanuts. On the other hand, I worried that sitting around with nothing to do was how I'd wind up spending my time from now on.

The clue about Duncan arguing with Brent Hollands that I'd picked up from the grocery store manager hadn't yielded anything yet. Mary knew Brent Hollands. That much didn't amaze me after what I'd already observed in this nosy town. But Brent turning out to be Mimi's neighbor down the hill was quite unexpected.

Mary had called Brent Hollands this morning before we left her house but got no answer. We agreed to try him again tomorrow before Elizabeth called her deputy friend to see if he could check into Brent's alibi for last Sunday.

Then Mary had called a friend of hers in the sheriff's office. He'd quietly informed her that the sheriff was still convinced Elizabeth had fought with Duncan, causing her shirt to get bloody, and then hit him on the head and killed him with a branch. Elizabeth broke into tears after Mary had repeated this.

Mary then left to go to Mimi's house. Elizabeth and I followed about twenty minutes later after she regained her composure. At Mimi's, things had been fast and furious. Mary needed to finish her tasks before lunch because she had patients to see in the afternoon. She'd kept Sebastian hustling so much that his face had turned almost as red as today's pocket square. He'd been pleased with the effort, however, as he was able to finish assessing and tagging the rest of the basement and start on the rooms upstairs.

While Elizabeth flitted from room to room, looking for specific things she remembered from her childhood and calling me in periodically to reminisce about them, I was a little less driven. These weren't my keepsakes, so I'd taken the opportunity to savor my fresh-ground coffee from the thermos I'd brought along. Although the store hadn't displayed the coffee's origins, I wondered if it came from Latin America given the citrusy acidity I detected. Regardless, I had been quite content to indulge my coffee snobbishness once again.

Elizabeth and I left at noon and returned to Mary's house to eat lunch.

"How about stopping by Brent Hollands's house just to see if he's home?" I proposed, figuring we could ask him some questions about where he'd been on Sunday evening.

"I suppose . . ." Elizabeth sounded skeptical, but before she could continue, her phone rang. "It's Trent," she said, and eagerly answered. "Hi, Trent. Did you guys catch the real killer?"

I watched as her excitement dimmed and her side of the conversation became more and more quiet until she hung up.

"He said they haven't found any evidence linking anyone else to the crime. The medical examiner just started looking at Duncan's body. The sheriff still thinks I did it so they're going to continue investigating me." Her voice caught.

I hugged her for a long minute before she pulled away. "I'm

okay," she said. "Nothing changed from yesterday. I just need to distract myself so I don't dwell on this."

Her phone dinged with a text. She glanced at it. "Oh." Her voice became more upbeat. "It's the publishing company. They said it's urgent. I gotta call them back." She shook herself, then twisted back and forth a few times to limber up.

When I smiled at her warm-up routine, she said, "Gotta get my game face on." Then her face fell. "Wait, you don't think they've heard about my arrest, do you?"

When I shook my head, she breathed a sigh of relief. "We've got to clear this up before my clients find out. I don't want them to drop me." With a newly somber expression, she hurried off to her childhood bedroom to call the client, a publisher of children's books. Elizabeth loved working on book covers for kids, probably because she got to draw all sorts of crazy-looking creatures.

While I waited for her to return, I lay down on the couch and petted Daisy while pondering my future.

Of us all, she seemed the most satisfied with the situation.

I swung my feet to the floor. Daisy raised her head, soft black eyes locked on me, concerned her special attention was coming to an end. I scratched the sweet spot behind her ears, and her head flopped back down with contentment.

I wasn't so easy to please. Turning into one of those old codgers sitting outside the grocery store all day did not appeal to me. Maybe in another thirty or forty years, after I'd done enough things with my life to earn the right to be a grumpy old man. But getting behind a lab bench again wasn't particularly appealing. Absent-mindedly, I shifted some of the magazines on the coffee table to even out the stacks.

"Hey, hon." Elizabeth reappeared at the edge of the room. "I'm so sorry but I have to do some work today."

"What about Brent?"

"We'll go tomorrow, I promise." She started jiggling her leg. "It's an urgent crisis and, well, you know."

I nodded, recognizing this mood. Her mother wasn't the only one who tended to put her clients first. "Where does Brent live? Maybe I'll go for a run and stop by."

"It's a ways up the river," answered Elizabeth. "Are you sure it's safe for you to go by yourself?"

Daisy shook herself and did a fine downward dog, getting ready for the exercise she must have sensed was imminent.

I smiled at my smart dog. "Daisy will come with me. I won't go inside his house and I'll be careful."

"It's a long way. If you don't feel like it, we'll go tomorrow. Promise." Elizabeth stood there, still looking uncertain.

"I'll be fine. Promise," I echoed, and she finally nodded. I stood, satisfied that the magazine stacks were now lined up and even.

Elizabeth gave me a sheepish grin. "Okay, have fun." She beat me back to the bedroom and was engrossed in her work before I finished changing clothes.

Daisy waited eagerly outside the bedroom door, looking like she'd have put on her own leash if only she had opposable thumbs. While I ran, I planned to think through what little we knew about Duncan's murder. I often got my best ideas while running, and this would be a good time for one to pop into my head. If nothing came to mind, I would look into private investigators when I got back.

Daisy and I left the house and started jogging toward the lake as I gazed out at the distant hills. These weren't proper mountains like we had around Portland but still quite pretty, covered with green pine trees and the first blossoms of early spring.

I trailed a half block behind an attractive older woman for a while until we crossed the river over the old bridge. I'd seen her out running yesterday morning as well along with only a few other early joggers. Then Daisy and I turned up the hard-packed dirt trail that paralleled the river. The path started to peter out as we went further from town, but a thin yet detectable path still wound around trees near the river.

Daisy and I went out almost four miles but didn't come across Brent's place. I didn't have a good sense of the distance to his ranch along the river since I'd only glimpsed the upper parts of it from Mimi's place high on the ridge. When I reached a bend in the river, I was able to see a long stretch ahead of me, but no house was in sight. I sighed and turned back. Although I might be capable of a longer run, this was about Daisy's limit.

Even though I traveled the same path for the return, it felt different with new vantages of the river and hills to appreciate. Flowers had started to emerge along the banks, poking through the dappled light of the foliage next to the trail. As I ran, I passed through shade-speckled clearings made by the shadows thrown by the hickory, oak, and pine trees growing all around me. Birds sang and called out to greet me, the only sound other than the running water. It was certainly a welcome change after running in downtown Portland, where no matter which direction I went, I had to watch for traffic.

I kept an eye out for any signs of the area where Duncan's body had been found but never noticed anything. I wasn't exactly sure what I would do if I came across the crime scene. The sheriff's people had undoubtedly collected any nearby evidence. It wasn't like I could walk past it now and find a confession note from the actual killer.

Running downstream felt like I was racing the water as it flowed past the lush landscape. Small rapids and eddies appeared whenever the river swirled and twisted around rocks as it snaked down from the higher ridges beyond Mimi's land into the lake below. When we crossed the bridge back into Jenkins, I slowed to a walk, catching my breath while I looked out at the lake. Although a pretty view, it didn't yield me any ideas on how to get Elizabeth out of trouble. At least running came easier than it had a few months ago—one positive side effect of not working was getting into better shape.

For variety, I took a different street back to Mary's house. The center part of town wasn't tiny, but it was no Northwest District of Portland either. The major streets seemed to be Front Street paralleling the lakefront, Main Street running into Front Street at the lake, and a few other streets that ran on both sides of Front Street. That constituted the entire Jenkins downtown business district, while the side streets were filled with small homes with mostly well-kept yards.

The homes varied widely, some small one-story houses with inexpensive siding and others brick or stone facades, and even the occasional two-story building. Every home seemed to have one or more pickup trucks parked out front, and garages that were little more than overhangs made of tent fabric were common.

As Daisy and I walked past a nicer two-story red-brick house with white wood-framed windows and a large porch with white columns that ran the length of the house, she turned her head as she heard something. I looked too, expecting to see a squirrel or cat that caused her to pull on the leash. But instead, Tyler, the kid stomping around the high school yesterday, emerged from the other side of a pickup truck carrying a pile of broken pieces of lumber.

He saw me and froze.

I didn't want Tyler to think I was a stalker following him to make sure he wasn't throwing Coke bottles around. "Hey there." I waved and tried to look friendly rather than strange. "Tyler, right?" Then, realizing we hadn't actually been introduced, I hurried to add, "I'm Jonas. Principal Stapleton told me your name."

"Great." Tyler's surly tone and tense posture made it evident that my efforts to put him at ease weren't working. He continued walking toward us. "Now Stapleton's going around telling everyone about me."

"No, I . . ."

"He tell you all about Fowler screwing me over too?" Tyler asked.

"Yes." Seeing him grit his teeth, I added, "Sounds rough. What happened?"

"I made it simple for him. All he had to do was sign my letter. Except he refused. And then Stapleton did too." A few pieces of wood scraps fell on the ground as he complained, his voice rising with bitterness.

I took a step backward as Tyler continued moving even closer toward me. I didn't think he'd attack me just for asking a few questions, but he seemed quite upset and it didn't hurt to stay on the cautious side.

"Tyler!" an angry voice called from the porch. "Don't put that wood junk in the garbage can. How many times do I have to tell you?" Mayor Dale Cooper was standing just inside the house with one hand on the door.

He glanced my way and, with a politician's panache, stepped outside and flicked on his friendly mode. "Well, if it isn't Jonas Trout. How are you doing this fine day? Stop by to give me more ideas for my coffee nook?"

I gave a small chuckle to be polite. "No. I just went on a run and am on my way back to Mary's house."

"Well good for you. Wish I had more time for exercising." He patted his ample stomach and then held up his index finger. "Hang on a moment." Without skipping a beat, he jabbed the finger toward his son. "Tyler, I just reviewed your video of the river from Sunday. You didn't finish the run. I told you it needs to show the whole way into the lake. What happened?"

I whipped my head around to stare at Tyler. Had he gone running on Sunday and encountered Duncan? Was he guilty of murder?

Tyler's sour expression didn't change, so I flicked my eyes back to Dale.

He glared while waiting for Tyler's response, but when his son only grumbled, Dale said, "When you get done saying your howdies, put that junk in the truck and take it to the dump before they close. You'll need to finish the video tomorrow."

Tyler said, "Can't. I've got a project due and a test later this week."

His father frowned. "Then maybe Sunday." Dale switched his gaze back to me, the gregarious mayor personality resurfacing as he plastered a smile on his lips. "Sorry for all that, Jonas. It's good to see you again." He glanced at his watch. "Oops, I wasn't paying attention to the time. I've got to dash for a call with my accountant." As his phone rang, Dale quickly added, "Stop by my store sometime and I'll show you around."

As I nodded, he waved goodbye briefly, answered the phone, and stabbed his finger at the truck a few times in case Tyler had already forgotten his instructions. Then he shut the door behind him.

In the sudden silence, Tyler let out a long sigh as his shoulders slumped.

Yesterday, I had suspected Tyler might have been angry enough to attack Duncan, and now his own father had basically placed him at the scene of the crime. Could I get him to reveal a little more? "Tough getting a word in edgewise, isn't it?"

"You're telling me." His posture was no longer assertive; instead, he looked like a tired kid who had too many chores. He trudged back to the truck carrying the wood pieces while he complained, "It's always 'Tyler do this,' and 'Tyler do that.'"

Interrogating a minor didn't seem right, but I felt stuck. How else would I learn something that could help Elizabeth? Today had been a bust so far, so I had to try. I eased in with a simple question. "What video are you making for your dad?"

"Oh, it's some stupid marketing thing. He wants me to use a GoPro to film a kayaking trip down the river—from where we drop people in all the way to where the trip ends in the lake. He's going to do some time-lapse video editing to turn it into a two-minute movie to put on his website." He shook his head. "He's always trying to promote something, or has some get-rich scheme."

I couldn't stop thinking that Tyler had been kayaking on the river on Sunday, the same place where Duncan was found. How late had Tyler returned home? Why hadn't he finished the trip?

"Did you see anything unusual on the river?" I probed.

He dropped his load into the back of the truck with a clatter and gave me a perplexed look. "No. Same ole river. It's nice, but I've done that trip like a gazillion times."

"So why didn't you finish the run?" I held my breath, wondering if his answer would include a confrontation with Duncan Fowler and not sure if I'd blown my opportunity with a foolish question.

Tyler slammed the truck's rear gate shut and yelled, "Geez! Why is everyone on me about this? I'm a freaking high school senior, I can stay out late if I want to." He stomped toward his backyard. "And it's none of your business," he said over his shoulder as he banged the fence closed, leaving me alone on the street, speculating over whether I'd just chatted with Duncan Fowler's killer.

As I walked the rest of the way back to Mary's house with Daisy, I considered whether I should notify the sheriff. Last night, however, Elizabeth and I had agreed to wait until we spoke to her lawyer before talking to him again. She and I had read enough legal thrillers to know that the defense sometimes needed to establish reasonable doubt by casting suspicion on another person. As Elizabeth had said before we fell asleep, "Let the lawyer do any dirty work. They chose that profession, after all."

Now I wasn't so sure. Ruining Tyler's life by wrongly accusing him of murder felt terribly irresponsible. But if it meant saving Elizabeth, I would do almost anything.

9

Tuesday Evening

Elizabeth

Jonas and I talked about Tyler as the possible killer when he returned home, then repeated most of our discussion with Mom when she came home for dinner. None of us really believed the kid had killed Duncan, but we disagreed on whether to call the sheriff or Trent yet.

Remarkably, my mother and I were on the same side, although for different reasons. She had known Tyler since he was born and simply didn't believe he had killed Duncan while I preferred to let my lawyer use him in a trial. Jonas had wanted to notify the sheriff but agreed to give it another day while we made a more focused effort to investigate tomorrow.

I was a bit surprised that Mom hadn't disagreed with me—on principle if for no other reason. She must have been argued out, mellowing in her old age, or just plain tired. Going through Mimi's stuff, hosting two guests in her house, and doctoring half the town was a lot to handle in the same week. Not to mention the added bonus of having to collect me from the police station—not for the first time, although a murder charge was much scarier than my previous experience. Maybe I'd hear something useful from the women at tonight's baby shower.

As I stood on the front porch, I took a deep breath and enjoyed the cool, clean evening air. Even if we hadn't been at each other's throats, it still felt great to get away from the house for the night. Painting pottery wasn't a typical baby shower activity, but Crystal wasn't the typical mother-to-be. I didn't even feel guilty about leaving Jonas home alone with Mom. His feathers didn't seem to get ruffled by her the way mine did. Of course, he tended to straighten out his feathers and keep them neat and organized no matter the situation.

I tried to convince myself that I was walking slowly to Crafts n' Creations to stargaze and enjoy the outdoors. Truth be told, I felt nervous. I hadn't exactly been invited to this baby shower—Kelsey told me she'd checked and Crystal was happy for me to come along. Yet I hadn't seen Crystal in forever. I was excited to see her, but what if the feelings weren't mutual? And did Crystal want to associate with an accused murderer? Despite my worries, I snorted. Crystal would probably be annoyed at whoever had actually killed Duncan, causing me to be falsely accused. The real murderer had better watch out. The sheriff might have to protect them.

I slowed further as the store neared but was soon close enough to see a small crowd of women inside, standing around some crafting tables and talking. I finally approached the door, then paused with my hand on the doorknob as I hesitated to enter.

What if the other women gave me the classic cold shoulder all girls perfected in middle school? I had no reason to expect standard Southern hospitality to be extended to people who'd chosen to leave the South. I wasn't a casual visitor, after all; I'd deserted Jenkins as soon as possible after high school and hadn't looked back. Now, this arrest might make me an involuntary resident of Arkansas. I shuddered.

The knob was pulled out of my grasp as Bianca Delgado, the shop's owner, opened the door wide. "Ella Mae Banks!" she greeted me loudly, saying my name partially over her shoulder to announce me to the crowd.

"Trout," I corrected. Feeling off balance as I blinked in the store's bright lights, I straightened and smiled. "I'm married now."

"Well, my goodness. Good for you. That's one brave boy you landed. Well, don't just stand out there, come on in and join the fun." Bianca pulled me into the store.

"You came!" shouted a very pregnant Crystal, looking much the same as the last time I'd seen her, with one notable exception, as she rushed over and flung her arms around my neck.

I laughed as her belly bounced into me, knocking me slightly off balance again, this time in the most delightful way. "Yes. Thanks for letting me crash—"

"Oh, you're not crashing. I'd have invited you if I knew you were going to be in town."

I stepped back to take her in. "You look positively radiant."

"You are so sweet, but I feel bloated and hot. I can't wait for this to pop." She patted her stomach. "Another month unless she decides to make her mama happy and show up early."

"A girl?"

"Yes! We found out early. You know me; I don't like surprises."

I giggled along with her. "Speaking of surprises." I started to hand Crystal her gift. "Here. This is for you."

Bianca swooped past at that moment. "I'll put it with the other gifts," she told Crystal. Then, noticing I was removing my jacket, she pointed at an open seat. "And I'll just put you at this table over here."

She took my jacket and hung it on the back of a chair, one of four tall ones around another large crafting table. "We're not using this table today," she said, pointing to the one next to where Crystal and I were standing. "The drawers are still stuck so the guys have to come back to fix it." Bianca pursed her lips and shook her head, clearly disapproving of her contractor's poor workmanship.

"It's fine. We'll all be able to talk," I said.

"Do you want the good stuff or the fake stuff? We have wine or non-alcoholic drinks for pregnant women and Baptists." Bianca winked, then steered me around the unfinished table to get to the drinks. "The remodel was supposed to be finished already. I thought I'd have plenty of time to move back in and be ready to reopen on Monday. But things kept falling more and more behind. It's been a mad dash getting things ready enough to have the party here tonight."

I'd been so focused on Crystal, Bianca, and the other women that I hadn't even noticed her place looked different. I used to stop by all the time during high school, spending whatever allowance I managed to hang onto on the various art supplies that Bianca sold. "It looks great," I said, appreciating the work tables on the side of the store. Paintings for sale hung on the walls and several rows of shelves with ready-to-purchase pottery, puzzles, and other crafts were close to the entrance.

After pouring me a drink, Bianca paused, put one hand on her hip, and looked around. "It does, doesn't it?" She laughed, then handed me the glass before hurrying off to her next task.

"Thanks," I said to her back, and took a long sip of wine while I surveyed the small group. I'd managed to introduce myself to some women I didn't know when a sweet-smelling pair of hands covered my eyes.

"Uh," I squeaked and flinched, but managed not to spill my wine as I pulled away and turned to see who had crept up on me.

"Don't you know better than to sneak up on a woman with a glass of wine?" I said to Kelsey, then took a long sip to settle my nerves. "I almost spilled some on my dress."

"Guess I'm glad you didn't have a shotgun." Kelsey gave me a wicked grin. It was so good to see her again. "Sorry I'm late. We had a final rehearsal for Friday's show. Can you believe I'm an advisor to the drama club?" She snorted and then eyed my drink. "Aren't you going to offer me any?"

"Sure." I finished off the glass. "Here you go. Please get me a refill when you get your own glass over there." I pointed and grinned when Kelsey stuck her tongue out at me.

Drinks settled, Kelsey sat next to me and we both got busy painting our plates that would get fired in the kiln. While I worked, I listened to the conversations swirling around me. The polite talk of church, jobs, and volunteer activities quickly turned into gossip about husbands, children, and neighbors—some of them I remembered and others I'd never heard of. More of the women had jobs outside their home than I remembered growing up. The familiar lilt of the women's Southern accents as they discussed upcoming church activities, family events, and everyday life was a welcome comfort and served to make me feel less out of sorts.

I spoke a little about Portland, but those people, habits, and activities seemed odd to most of these folks. Going to church in Jenkins was as much social as religious, and hitting the latest trendy restaurants and bars just wasn't a thing. In Jenkins, it was mostly the men who went to drink at the ratty bars, and pretty much the same restaurants were still around from a decade ago.

It was a nice evening, and I'd relaxed, slowed my speaking pace to match the others, and started enjoying myself—and the wine—when the bells of the craft shop's door chimed.

"Okay, ladies, let's get this party started!" exclaimed a familiar, and unwelcome, voice from the doorway. Susie Q had arrived, complete with her hair extensions, highlights, and fake tan. As if she wasn't already too good-looking, she used artificial means to show off.

"You didn't tell me she was invited," I hissed to Kelsey, feeling my blood pressure shoot up.

She grimaced. "Oh yeah, I forgot about you two."

Susie Q was actually Suzanne Quentin, my high school nemesis.

Kelsey and I called her Susie Q after the Creedence Clearwater Revival song that my grandfather used to play all the time for us. I'd heard she was married too, but not to whom. Or what.

Susie approached Crystal and delivered two air kisses with her overly glossy, puffy, bright-red lips, cautiously avoiding smudging any of her carefully applied makeup. All the while, she loudly called Crystal "darling" and told her how amazing she looked. Her loud performance grabbed everyone's attention—just as Susie Q had intended.

I almost barfed. I'd brushed my hair and teeth before coming tonight, while Susie had turned herself into a glamour girl for a simple baby shower, striving to outdo us all, yet again. My only hope was that she hadn't yet heard about my arrest or she'd ruin this evening for sure.

The Drama Queen's entrance had been par for the course. She earned the title Drama Queen—if only in my head—because she had captured all the major roles in the plays during high school while I had to settle for supporting or bit parts. Just because her mother served as the drama club advisor, chaperoned our trips to local theaters, and did all the hair and makeup for the casts seemed to give Susie Q the right to play every leading part.

I finally gave up in our senior year and worked tech crew in the theater. Without competing with Susie over roles, I didn't have to deal with her arrogance and could spend my energy finding places to fool around with Trent backstage, or up in the lighting box, or wherever.

Even when we were kids, Susie and I had never gotten along. She was always tattling on me for something or other. Such a sissy, she couldn't take a joke like finding a frog in her lunch box or having mud pie substituted for her brownies.

It got worse during high school. There might have been a boy named Trent involved . . . who I stole. Well, all's fair in love and high school. Right? I bit my lip and looked down, pressing my mouth to my fist to keep from laughing.

"Why look, it's Ella Mae gracing us with her presence. Oh, bless your heart. Aren't you such a dear to come to Crystal's party despite looking so tired and probably straight from a hard day of traveling?"

Susie Q had demonstrated the perfect Southern use of a polite phrase—"bless your heart"—coupled with a criticism. I hadn't heard this typical expression from back home in years.

Kelsey heard me start growling and jumped in. "Oh, why don't you give your histrionics a rest? Tonight's supposed to be about Crystal. Just go drink some wine and chill out like the rest of us."

"Oh, Kelsey." Susie Q looked down her nose in distaste. "Go drink some more wine." She glanced between the two of us, then sniffed as if she had caught whiff of a bad odor before twirling away to greet the other women with more air kisses and obnoxiously loud chatter. She made her way to the drinks and picked up a glass while fluttering her unnaturally long eyelashes and observing the room's reaction.

I returned my attention to painting my ceramic plate, hoping Susie would ignore me for the rest of the evening. My hopes were dashed as soon as I felt her eyes on me again. I didn't even have time to look up before she commented in an overly loud voice, "Speaking of drama, apparently Ella Mae made quite the lively return to town."

Susie arched an eyebrow in mock dismay in my direction, then turned to Bianca and added in a patronizing tone, "You're allowing criminals into your establishment now?"

I ground my teeth together. An involuntary rumble started in the base of my throat as I squeezed my glass. I might have thrown my drink in her face if Kelsey hadn't laid a steadying hand over mine. I'd seen Susie Q for all of a few minutes and already we'd reverted to our high school behavior. All I needed now was for Principal

Stapleton to walk in right as I took a swing at her and suspend me, or worse, confiscate my wine. Then my trip down memory lane would be complete.

Crystal stepped in front of Susie. "Um," she started as she twisted her wedding ring.

Susie interrupted, "Oh darling, Ella Mae and I didn't mean to upset you."

I gritted my teeth at her attempt to include me in her disruptive behavior.

But Susie kept going. "We don't want your water to break and make a mess of everything here, now do we? We was just teasin'. Besides, I'm fixin' to skedaddle. I only had a teensy bit of time to stop by your little shindig and say howdy—Oh!" Susie stopped herself mid-sentence and raised one hand as if to stop life from moving on until she was ready. She rummaged through her purse with her other hand, finally pulling out an envelope. "Here you go, sweetie." She handed it to Crystal. "It's a gift from my momma and me—a year's free visits to Shear Heaven. Lord knows you'll need some pampering once the baby is born."

Stepping back and taking a critical look at Crystal, she added, "Why don't you stop on by this week. You want to look your best in your baby's first pictures, now don't you?"

Being the definition of sweetness, Crystal said, "Oh, thank you." She hugged Susie Q again and made a funny face at me over Susie's shoulder. "Well, thanks for stopping by, I guess."

Having set down my glass, I focused on my breathing and managed not to say anything. Or throw anything. I decided to forgive Crystal for inviting the devil to her party and chalk it up to her hormones.

"Darling, it was my pleasure," cooed Susie. "And, Ella Mae, looks like you should stop by too. Out of Christian charity, we'll give you a discount so you'll look nice for your trial and all."

I growled dangerously again, but Kelsey kicked me under the

table to distract me as Susie Q flounced out of the craft shop, leaving the place temporarily hushed as though she'd removed the oxygen when she left.

"Well, that sure was memorable," I said, rubbing my shin and gulping my wine.

"Hun, she and her mother think the sun comes up just to hear them crow. Them Quentins are a proud family," said Bianca.

"What does Anita have to be proud of?" I scoffed. "It's been a long time since Susie starred in a play."

"Just be careful." Bianca patted me on the shoulder as she buzzed around the table to refill my glass. "I think you need more of this nectar of the gods."

"Amen to that," I said, and raised my glass in thanks.

Kelsey and I painted in silence for a while, letting the other conversations and background music wash over us while I tried to forget all about Susie Q. Why did she still bear me such ill will? After all, she hadn't seen me in years.

"Oh wow!" Crystal stopped by my chair as she meandered around the room and picked up my plate. "Look at this, everyone! Look at Ella Mae's painting."

I sat quietly as the other women made a fuss over my work. It did feel good to have them recognize my skill as an artist since they'd never seen anything I'd done since I left town. Of course, whose fault was that? I hadn't intended to do anything special tonight, but getting annoyed by Susie Q had made me focus on my work. Painting had always been an escape for me.

"And what is yours supposed to be?" Crystal snickered as she pointed at whatever it was that Kelsey had painted on her plate.

Kelsey stuck her nose in the air, imitating Susie Q. "It's a new form of abstract impressionist work with aspects of pointillism." She pointed to where drops of paint had fallen by accident and dried on her plate.

Crystal laughed and shook her head. "Sorry, I'm not buying

it. Ella Mae, what's that style of painting called when it's really bizarre?"

"Surrealism," I answered. An art degree had to come in useful sometime.

"Yeah. Kelsey's work is surreal for sure." As Kelsey stuck out her tongue at Crystal, she added, "It's a good thing English teachers don't need to do pottery."

"Oh yeah, bet I can recite more Shakespeare than you," said Kelsey.

"Like you'd find that a real challenge." Crystal chuckled and then moved off to the next table.

I was still grinning from their exchange. "You two seem to be pretty close."

"Yeah, we've become good friends. But don't worry, I can have two besties." She raised her glass and we clinked before taking another drink.

I went to refill our glasses. When I returned, Kelsey asked, "Anything new on your arrest?" She didn't look me in the eye as she spoke, perhaps nervous about how I'd react.

I sighed. "Not really."

"I heard the sheriffs found Duncan's place all trashed up," said Kelsey.

"He was a slob," confirmed Bianca as she walked past. Then she halted as she noticed Kelsey and I staring at her. She cleared her throat and added, "Or so I've heard from people."

"What people?" Kelsey's forehead crinkled in confusion.

"I don't know. People. Shop owners hear all sorts of gossip." Bianca waved her hands around in the air. "Someone must have said something." Without pausing, she picked up a bottle from the side table. "More wine, anyone?"

Kelsey and I took refills, but as Bianca moved to the next table,

Kelsey murmured, "Hope *people* aren't talking about how messy my place is."

I snorted and then coughed as the red wine burned my nostrils. Bianca turned back with a frown, but I managed to sputter, "It went down the wrong way. I'm fine."

More quietly, I leaned over to Kelsey. "One of Mom's friends at the sheriff's office told her the sheriff still thinks I did it. He's convinced I fought with Duncan, got my shirt bloody, and then whacked him over the head with a stick. It's crazy."

Kelsey's nostrils flared. "No! Still?" She set her glass down hard enough on the wood table for Bianca to glance at us again.

After she turned away, I nodded glumly. "I don't think he's looked into any other suspects. We've got a meeting with a lawyer on Thursday. Trent said they didn't find any more physical evidence—"

"You're talking to Trent again? Is that smart after how you two—"

"That was the past." I waved an apology for interrupting her. "I'm married now. The sheriff seems dead-set on pinning this whole thing on me. Trent doesn't believe I did it, and at least he'll share a little with me."

Kelsey bit her lip. "Well, be careful."

The back of my neck felt warm at her implication. "Nothing's happening. He just told me they didn't find any clues about Duncan's death at his home or his classroom."

Kelsey's nose crinkled. "Hmm. I didn't notice anyone searching in his art room."

"Art room? Where? Since when is there an art room at the high school?" I asked.

"It's across from my classroom. Just cattycorner from Duncan's room. Well, it's not an art room right now, not since we ran out of funding. But it will be next fall. Duncan would go in it now and again to get some supplies for some of the truly committed students." She shrugged. "If it's not online these days, most kids aren't interested."

We continued chattering like the old friends who hadn't seen each other in a long time that we were. Different women passed by on their way to or from the bathroom and wine table, stopping to look at my plate and saying lovely things to me. It felt comforting to be back among old friends.

Then from across the table, I heard Emma, one of Crystal's friends, say, "We'll have to plan some play dates when they get bigger."

"Ooh, he's really cute. I can't wait until mine is a little cutie like that." Crystal leaned over Emma's shoulder as she looked at pictures on her phone.

"You know, until yours shows up, you can borrow my young'un whenever you have a hankering to hold a baby. I know I'd kill for a night off." Emma rubbed her eyes.

Crystal laughed. "I'd kill for a glass of wine and a chance to see my feet again."

"I'd kill to be able to dump this craft shop and focus on being an art dealer," blurted Bianca, leaning against the wall near us with her eyes closed. In the sudden silence, her eyes flew open and she flinched as if punched. "Oh my, I think that was my inside voice coming out to play without permission again." She looked around the room, wide-eyed. "I'm sorry, too much wine and I'm just tired from all the remodeling."

"Well, it isn't right anyway to joke about killing," said Crystal's sister-in-law.

In the ensuing silence, everyone looked away. I finished my glass of wine and listened to the women's nervous tittering.

"My goodness, it's getting late," said Emma. "My baby will be up in a few hours for a feeding so I better get home and get some sleep."

That sparked everyone to say their goodbyes and bring their painted plates to a rolling cart that Bianca wheeled out.

"I had such a good time. This was such a fun idea for a baby shower," I said to Crystal.

"Yeah, it was great," she replied. "I wanted a baby shower that everyone could enjoy instead of one with all those silly games."

A woman putting on her jacket nearby suddenly looked hurt. Crystal noticed, reddened, and said, "Oh, I'm sorry. My hormones are just going crazy these days. *Your* baby shower was a ton of fun. I knew I couldn't come up with such creative games as yours so I thought it would be nice to do something different."

The other woman gave Crystal a thin, hard smile as she leaned in to hug her. "Oh bless your heart," she said, with a noticeable edge in her voice. "I'm sure everyone is thrilled to get a plate to commemorate your baby shower."

Crystal rolled her eyes at me over the woman's shoulder while she hugged her back.

A large grin broke out on my face, but I had it under control by the time the woman turned around. Kelsey and I said goodnight to everyone and left. We agreed to get together again this week for lunch or dinner.

I had indulged in a few extra glasses of wine knowing that I didn't have to drive. And although parts of the sidewalk felt wobbly, I managed to make it home without tripping over anything. The lock on the door must have stopped working properly since I left this evening—Mom needed to get it fixed.

The house was dark, but a small light still shone under the door to my old bedroom. I maneuvered carefully down the hall without knocking anything off the walls. This wasn't the first time I'd snuck back to my room without waking my mother.

"Hi," said Jonas when I opened the door. He was lying on the bed in his boxers, reading a book.

"Hi yourself." I leaned over and kissed him, tripping into his arms. I managed to extract myself and stepped into the bathroom to brush my teeth.

"Have fun?" he asked.

I thought I detected an ironic tone, but at that moment, I couldn't remember the difference between irony and sarcasm. And did it really matter?

Shaking my head but then regretting it as toothpaste flew everywhere, I said, "I had a really nice time." My words sounded a little slurred, but that must have been the toothpaste in my mouth.

"How much did you drink?" He laughed softly.

I spat and turned. "If the glass was never empty, that counts as one, right?" I giggled.

"Mmhmm," he said agreeably. He was a most agreeable man.

"I really liked spending time with Kelsey and Crystal and the others." I sighed happily as I took off my clothes and climbed into bed. "It felt like old times—even getting into an argument with Susie Q. It's been forever since I've felt at home."

He raised his eyebrows. He'd heard enough stories about Susie Q to last a lifetime. "Wasn't it just yesterday the sheriff arrested you for murder?"

"Don't ruin the mood. We can deal with my arrest tomorrow." I leaned over him and snapped off the light.

10

Wednesday Morning

Jonas

We got to Mimi's house around nine on Wednesday morning. Not early, but Elizabeth wasn't an early riser in general, and going out last night didn't help. A pickup was parked in front of the house next to Sebastian's plain white rental sedan. Pickups were more common here in Arkansas than Toyotas in California, and far more popular than the Subaru Outbacks we saw so often in Portland.

"Can you call Brent again?" Elizabeth asked as Mary drove us.

I had finally opened my eyes once I felt us turn onto the dirt driveway leading to Mimi's house. I resolved that we shouldn't drive with Mary again unless absolutely necessary. Elizabeth and I were going to meet the lawyer tomorrow, so it would be good to figure out if Brent would make a better fall guy for Duncan's murder than Tyler.

Mary stopped the car alongside a muscular, handsome blond man about my age who was perched atop a tractor by the side of the long driveway. "Good morning, Luke," she said out the window.

"G'morning, ma'am." Luke doffed his John Deere baseball cap, but only halfway in the style of a modern country gentleman.

"Everything okay?" she asked.

"Not yet." He swept his hand to indicate the tractor. "It just died."

Mary palmed her forehead as she shook her head slowly, muttering, "This week, of course." She fixed Luke with an eagle eye. "Do you think you can fix it? We need all this mowed down by Sunday so people will have a place to park for the estate sale." Mary waved her arms at the overgrown grass and weeds that threatened to take over the dirt road from both sides.

"Absolutely, ma'am," he said with a confident nod. "I can fix it." Then he leaned down further to get a better look in the car. "Is that Ella Mae?" He grinned. "How you doing?"

Elizabeth leaned over her mother. "Hey, Luke. I'm good. It's been a long time. What are you up to these days?"

Luke started to climb down but Mary flicked him back with an imperious wave. "Luke, you keep working on that tractor. We've got to get started at the house. You can stop by to visit with Ella Mae after you've finished mowing."

She started pulling the car away before his "Yes, ma'am," was finished.

"Mom," exclaimed Elizabeth as the car rolled closer to the house. "That was rude."

"Pfft," dismissed her mother. "He's fine."

"I knew Luke in high school," Elizabeth explained to me before turning to her mother. "What's he doing these days? I mean besides fixing Mimi's tractor."

"He does a lot of handyman jobs for folks. I called him yesterday and asked if he could mow before Sunday, with Duncan dead and all." She ignored her own awkward comment as we got out of the car. "He works for his father-in-law's contracting business."

"Father-in-law? Now, who'd Luke find to marry?" Elizabeth asked with a slight lilt to her voice and a tilt to her head, showing that cute, puzzled pose of hers that I found adorable.

"Suzanne Quentin," said Mary, and then she turned her attention to Sebastian, who sat in one of the rocking chairs on the porch. "Ready to work today, Sebastian?"

"Absitively!" Sebastian jumped to his feet, apparently eager to make some headway.

But Elizabeth had stopped midstride, her mouth agape.

I watched for the good ten seconds it took Elizabeth to gather herself while Mary unlocked the door for Sebastian, with Daisy crowding into the house after him, and then pulled out her phone and walked away from us.

After staring at Luke for a while as she rubbed the back of her head, Elizabeth said, "Well, I guess it makes sense."

I figured this had to be a good one. "Okay. Explain it to me."

"Susie Q always went for the blond, muscular, easy-going types. She probably dated a good chunk of the football team, but only the best players. She wanted their star power to make her shine standing next to them, and she wanted to make sure she could control them too." She wrinkled her nose.

"I take it that wasn't your type," I said dryly, thinking of my own dark hair and lean body.

But Elizabeth was caught in her musings. "No . . . Most of them were too dumb for me anyway. If I had to be explaining my jokes to someone, they didn't last long."

I nodded but then remembered something. "I don't think you ever mentioned Susie Q's last name was Quentin before. You know, I saw—"

She interrupted, "Wait, this is funny. Luke was the star football player and a year older than us at school. It was probably karma that he got a football scholarship to U of A." She snorted.

"Karma?" I asked, looking from Elizabeth to Luke.

"Because they're the Razorbacks," she said, giggling, as if that answered anything. At my puzzled look, she chuckled again. "Oh yeah, it's funnier if you knew his last name is Swine."

We both laughed at that.

I took her hand. "Growing up with a name like that in Arkansas, you better be easy-going. Either that or you get beat up a lot."

She walked with me, still watching Luke work on the tractor. "Nah, ain't nobody was going to tease the big, strong star football player." Then she smirked. "Oh, I almost want to see Susie Q again so I can use her full name properly. Susie Q Swine." She paused to savor the sound. "That just rolls off the tongue, doesn't it?" She leaned into me and fluttered her eyelashes.

"Be nice," I said, and pulled her up the porch stairs. I don't think I would have liked high school Elizabeth. I kissed the top of her head. Fortunately for me, I had only met the adult version. Now if we could just keep her there.

When we walked inside, Sebastian stood in the kitchen, organizing his materials for the day. Showing herself to be more like her mother than she would probably like to admit, Elizabeth picked up a dish rag to wipe down the already clean counters. I peeked into a box and rearranged the coffee mugs so the handles all pointed in the same direction.

Sebastian, by now accustomed to his time with Mary, took off his jacket and hung it over one of the kitchen chairs with the blue square facing outward. He stretched his back, pulled on his leather gloves, and said, "I'm in the mood to get cracking today." Then, with a wink and a smile, he clapped his hands twice. "Okay. Now I'm ready!"

We laughed at his imitation of Mary.

"What's so funny?" asked Mary, coming into the kitchen.

When we all shrugged innocently, she narrowed her eyes but let it drop. "By the way, he's home today," she announced.

"Who?" asked Elizabeth.

"Santa Claus," snapped her mother. "Honestly, Ella Mae, you just asked me to call him." Elizabeth's brows furrowed, but before an angry retort could leave her lips, Mary overrode her. "Brent Hollands." She pointed out the back window. "You know, down the hill on his cattle ranch. You need to go and see him. Maybe he knows something about Duncan."

"Fine," huffed Elizabeth as she tossed the dishtowel she was using on the counter. "I wanted to talk to him today. Let's go," she snapped in my direction. Then, looking my way with a sheepish expression, she calmed herself and asked, "Would you go for a hike with me, Jonas?"

"Of course," I agreed. I would gladly support Elizabeth, and getting away from the house would be nice. It would also keep me from being pulled toward repacking whatever Mary had tossed into boxes. "I'll put the leash on—"

Daisy knocked me in the legs before I even turned to whistle for her. Her preternatural awareness of an imminent walk was uncanny.

Concerned about ticks in the woods, we found some ballcaps that would help keep them from dropping into our hair and left the house. We already wore jeans and closed-toe shoes for protection because Elizabeth had warned me about the snakes they used to find in their woods. I'd made sure we included hiking boots on our packing list for this trip.

When she opened the back door, it squeaked from disuse and the bottom screeched against the porch. I'd have to look for some WD-40 and see if I could sand the bottom of the wooden screen door or move it higher. As we climbed through the picket fence separating the inner yard from the overgrown land near the stream, I asked, "Why don't you think Tyler is a good suspect?"

We'd had this discussion yesterday, but it didn't hurt to hash it out again before we spoke to another possible suspect. Neither of us really believed we'd find Duncan's killer, but we wanted to give some good options to the lawyer in case he needed to offer the jury an enticing alternative at Elizabeth's trial. At least that's how it seemed to work in legal thrillers.

I hoped it wouldn't come to that, though. An actual killer was still out there. Surely the sheriffs would solve this first.

"The kid?" she asked, and at my nod, added, "If I were a juror, I wouldn't buy it."

I followed Elizabeth along the stream before we reached a narrow point with flat stones protruding out of the water. She flowed across without stopping, but I paused first to check it out. "I get the feeling this isn't the first time you've done this," I commented as I followed her steps across.

"Nope," came her reply. "But it's been a long time. After my grandpa died when I was in middle school, no one was really interested in going exploring with me when Mom and I came up here. And then high school hit and I had other interests."

"But you still painted up here, right?" I asked.

"Oh yes. Sometimes there wasn't anything better to do so I'd go out on the back porch and paint something. Occasionally Mimi would teach me crocheting and needlework when her hands weren't hurting her."

Instead of risking the barbed wire fence dividing the Banks's property and the next, Elizabeth led us along the fence until we reached an opening protected only by a grid of metal tubes fixed to the ground and covering a depression of about six inches.

"The gaps are wide enough for cattle's feet to slip through, and their depth perception is pretty bad so they're scared of getting stuck or breaking a leg," explained Elizabeth as I paused to scrutinize the cattle guard up close. "But Brent can still drive a truck across from our land if he needs to bring something to this upper section."

"Hmm," I remarked. I'd seen these on TV and along our drive but never quite understood why they worked. With Daisy also having small feet, I picked her up and carried her as I stepped carefully across the slick metal tubes.

Once clear of the cattle guard, and as we continued through the unkempt land of the neighbor's property, I returned to our previous topic. "I think Tyler could be a viable suspect. He was on the river late on Sunday." I raised my eyebrows at her. "Plus, kids have feelings too. They can get mad and he's big enough to hurt an adult man." She hadn't spoken with Tyler and didn't know how upset he was over the thwarted college recommendation situation.

"Yeah, I know. Remember, I was one of those angry kids," Elizabeth said with a heavy sigh. "But I think it would look like we were just throwing him under the bus. All the women on the jury would think he was just a sweet kid and all the men would think there was no way a kid could get the jump on a grown man like them."

She seemed to be counting dead trees, and at the fifth one, she made a sharp left turn. I was impressed she had remembered how many dead trees to pass after all these years, but decided not to say anything that might make her feel like I was teasing her. She was always good about not bugging me about all my routines. Although, had she considered the possibility that another tree might have died in the ten years since she'd been here?

"I think Robert Jones is a better angle," she said. "Arrogant wealthy neighbor trying to buy the land and kills the property manager."

"Why?" I asked, ducking under a low-hanging branch she pointed out. The woods smelled different than the land down by the river. Up here, it was drier, with more shrubs and fallen branches.

"Who knows?" She shrugged. "But the local folks wouldn't like him. They never trust out-of-town rich people." Then she stopped short and looked back at me, her eyes wide. "I mean, except if they're friendly, nice, and cute like you." She went up on tiptoes and kissed my cheek. "Besides, you don't have anything to worry about. No one will bother you since they all think I'm the crazy murderer in the family."

Elizabeth smiled and shrugged, attempting to play off her last comment as a joke, but I could tell the idea was rattling her so I squeezed her arm for reassurance. The baby shower last night had been a nice break for her, but we'd both felt the stress of her impending court date.

We pushed our way through tall grass, past clusters of bushes, and skirted the trees that appeared unexpectedly in the path. This wasn't a groomed hiking trail like the ones we'd trekked around Portland or on our trip here in the different national and state parks. Not really a trail at all, the path was more a suggestion on how to head downhill toward the river. It didn't matter to me, as I've always enjoyed spending time outdoors. Daisy loved it too, but then she wasn't very discriminating.

The woods were noisy as a small breeze blew the tree limbs and bushes together. The cracking of small branches and occasional huff of some hidden animal made the whole place seem more alive than a typical hike back home. Daisy was sniffing and darting from side to side, but I hung onto her leash tightly. Who knew how she'd handle herself if she met another animal?

We broke into an open area where a large grassy meadow separated by clumps of brush and trees stretched down at a more gradual slope.

Suddenly I stepped into something squishy.

"Ugh." I wrinkled my nose as an unpleasant yet natural smell wafted up from my shoes. I looked down to see that I had stepped in a particularly large pile of dung hidden by some tall grass. "Hold on," I called out, and handed Daisy's leash to Elizabeth as I reached for a loose stick to clear off my shoes. Fortunately I had brought some extra poop bags in case Daisy needed them on our outing.

Seeing me pull out one of the small plastic bags, Elizabeth said, "There's no need to pick up the pile out here. It's a cattle ranch. He's got more cattle than Pawpaw ever had so you'd be busy for days picking up all the mess. Just watch where you're going." Then she laughed as she bounded after Daisy, who had just lunged away from her.

I wasn't positive if she was laughing at my city-boy naiveté or at Daisy's antics, but I decided it didn't matter since she had a pretty laugh.

Giving up on getting my shoe clean, I hurried after her and Daisy. We were approaching the trees again when loud grunting and shuffling noises made Daisy stop as her ears flattened.

"What. Was. That?" I asked. My city-boy radar was on high alert.

The aggressive grunting turned to a growl, but at a different pitch than a dog's. Daisy stood stock still and I actually saw the hair on her back rise before hearing a loud, long squeal.

I turned in time to see an enormous pig break through a bush and come charging out at us.

"Run!" yelled Elizabeth. She took off to the left with Daisy ahead of her. "To the trees, Jonas!"

I raced after her.

But the nightmare was running faster.

11

Wednesday Mid-Morning

Jonas

A loud shot rang out, startling us by its proximity. Instinctively we ducked, which of course was too late by the time we'd heard the shot.

I missed seeing the attacking pig drop to the ground. By the time I stopped to look back, the monster pig lay motionless on the ground while other unseen menaces squealed off into the brush.

I'd always thought pigs wallowed in mud and barely moved. This one was faster than Daisy. For the first time, I understood the term "greased lightning."

A man wearing a brown bandana over his face emerged from behind a nearby tree. "Ya'll all right?" He wore a long-sleeve camouflage shirt, long pants tucked into black boots, and a dark gray fishing hat. A belt with dangling pouches completed the picture. His whole getup seemed a bit extreme for the comfortable spring day, especially next to my jeans, lightweight fleece jacket, and hiking shoes.

"Yeah, at least we're standing. Jury's still out about my heart." Elizabeth was still panting as she leaned against a tree and covered her heart with both hands.

"Glad you didn't scare them off. I've been in that hide since before dawn waiting for that big momma to come out of the underbrush. She and her litter have been mucking up my land down by the river and scaring my cattle." The man wandered closer to the downed pig.

"Thanks for saving us. Can't believe I forgot to be alert for razorbacks." As Elizabeth was talking, the man rotated his rifle to his shoulder and shot the pig in the head.

I flinched. Even though I had seen him bring the rifle up to his shoulder and take aim, the sudden, loud report startled me. Shooting a dead hog when it was already down also seemed a bit unnecessary.

The man noticed my reaction. "Insurance," he explained. "Once knew a man who thought he'd killed a feral hog. But it was just playing possum, lying there waiting for him to come in range like a fool. The hunted became the hunter."

It sounded like the plot of a really bad thriller movie or the talk track from some Nature Channel documentary. When the man didn't continue his story, I had to ask, "What happened? Did the pig kill him?"

The man guffawed. "Naw. It was a wee little one. Still tore the crap out of his leg, though. Those tusks and teeth are brutal. The guy was hopping around on one leg with blood spurting out of the other and shot him again. That was the end of that." He nodded appreciatively at how his friend had persevered. "Ever since, I make sure any hogs I shoot are really dead before I get too close. That's also why I wear these thick snake boots. Any hog, or snake, tries to take a bite out of my shins, they have to go through them first."

I gulped. I hadn't expected today's hike to be dangerous—aside from confronting a possible murderer, of course.

Elizabeth said, "I'm Elizabeth, and this is Jonas." She pointed back up the hill. "That's my grandmother's place." Then she sighed. "Or I guess it was."

The man removed his hat and wiped sweat out of his eyes. "I'm

Brent Hollands. I'm sure sorry for your loss. She was a fine lady. I liked your grandmother."

"Me too," she replied. "Nice to meet you. I'm wondering if you know anything about all the damage done to her property?" She pointed back up the ridge. "Over in the woods in the corner of her property where it borders yours?"

Brent's lips pressed into a thin line. He looked like he wasn't going to answer, instead pulling some rubber gloves from one of the belt pouches and putting them on. Finally he said, "That Duncan made a big mess of it, didn't he?"

Elizabeth was taken aback. "You knew about it?"

Brent tugged on the hog's legs, rearranging the large animal so its legs pointed downhill. He pulled a knife out of a scabbard I hadn't noticed on his back. "Knew about it? Of course I did. I was paying for it." He turned his back to us, clearly uninterested in speaking further as he lifted a leg and sliced into the pig close to its hoof.

Elizabeth swallowed at the sight as I wondered if Brent's casual butchering was meant to throw us off-kilter so we wouldn't ask him more questions about Duncan. If so, it didn't work. I'd done my share of dissections in my biology days and Elizabeth kept her focus on his head, avoiding watching him slicing up the animal. "Why were you paying him to ruin Mimi's land?"

Brent grunted as he leaned over to grab another leg. "He wasn't supposed to wreck it like that. He was supposed to redirect the stream so it flowed down into my land. I'm fixin' to have a small pond up there so it's easier for my cattle to roam up the hill and still be close to water."

Elizabeth's eyes narrowed. Perhaps sensing her reaction, Brent looked up from the hog. "Your grandmother signed off on it. I got ANRC approval and everything."

Elizabeth's frown deepened. "Really?" Her voice dripped with skepticism. "What's-his-name agreed?" She waved uphill and looked at me.

I supplied the missing detail. "Robert Jones."

"Yeah." She nodded vigorously. "That's it. The rancher further along the ridge."

Brent pshawed. "He's no rancher. I reckon he just wants to have a little stream on his land to look purdy. To me that's a waste of valuable resources." He rolled his eyes before making another cut with his knife. "The guy who owned that land before him signed off and I got ANRC approval. Robert is out of luck on this. Or maybe I should say he's barkin' up a dry creek." He chuckled.

I furrowed my brow at his comment but merely asked, "We'd like to know why you argued with Duncan."

Brent looked up sharply at me. "How'd you hear that?"

I held his gaze, and after a moment, he continued, "Duncan was trying to cheat me. He wanted more money to finish the job. But no, sir, we had agreed on a fair price. Took me long enough to raise the money to pay for the work and the permits. Duncan knew what he was getting himself into long afore he started." With a sickening tear, he ripped off part of the hide. "I don't appreciate cheaters. Especially argumentative ones."

Brent looked up, his face stern and hard. He wasn't threatening us, but Elizabeth took a step backward anyway. Brent seemed to be a proud man, maybe unwilling to let an insult go unchecked. If his and Duncan's argument had gotten boisterous, would he have settled it via his own brand of justice? Brent clearly had the strength, skill, and stomach to kill. Plus, his land went all the way down to the river. The two men could have argued by the river, then Brent could have knocked Duncan over the head with something and pushed his body in.

Neither Elizabeth nor I said anything. Wrist-deep in pig innards already, Brent looked up again, his face softening as he remembered his manners. "Y'all want any of this meat once I get done dressing and butchering it?"

Swallowing carefully, I said, "No, thank you," before looking away. The sights and smells were starting to affect me too. "Rescuing us was more than enough."

Elizabeth raised an eyebrow as she flicked a glance over her shoulder at me. I nodded that I was happy to return to Mimi's house. Before we left, she said, "Thanks again."

His hands deep in the hog, Brent didn't look up and merely responded with a grunt.

After we left earshot, Elizabeth said, "Watching him butcher that pig might be enough to make me go vegan too."

*****

"What's ANRC?" I asked as we made our way back to the house.

"It's the Arkansas Natural Resource Commission," she answered. "You have to get approval if you want to make any landscape changes that affect water. Water rights are a big deal here in Arkansas."

"Really? A big enough deal to kill over?" I'd heard of arguments over water in dry areas like California, but it rained here a lot.

Recognizing my skeptical squint, she said, "It wouldn't be the first time. Farmers consume a lot of water for irrigation. Arguments between farmers, ranchers, and people who want to go fishing or boating can get pretty fierce. I remember Mom once had to treat someone who was hospitalized after a fight over water rights."

"Hmm," I responded as yet another disparity from life in a large urban city surprised me. "So I guess Brent is a viable suspect. He could have killed Duncan. He did still seem pretty upset about Duncan asking for more money to get the job done."

"Nor did he seem too torn up about Duncan's death," agreed Elizabeth.

"So Mimi had two neighbors who both seem like possible killers. And I thought you told me this was a great place to raise children," I teased her as I held Daisy back while Elizabeth crossed the stream back onto her grandmother's property. I corrected myself. We'd been on her property since we'd climbed back over the metal cattle guard.

We finished checking ourselves and Daisy for ticks and were drinking some cool water in the kitchen when Mary and Sebastian joined us on a break.

"Learn anything?" asked Mary. After Elizabeth filled her in on our excursion, she said, "I got a call from the temporary M.E. to let me know he was done with my lab now. He let slip that Duncan didn't drown."

"What?" Elizabeth blurted out.

Despite the serious topic, Mary smiled at Elizabeth's reaction as she rested her chin against a fist. "He was killed via a blow to the back of the head. Something thin and hard."

Like a paddle. Like a paddle swung by an angry high schooler who had a grudge against the victim and had been on the river Sunday evening. I turned to point this out to Elizabeth when I realized she was staring out the window down the dirt road as she cocked her head toward something outside and listened intently.

A moment later, two sheriff cars zoomed up, halting on the driveway with their lights still flashing. Instead of pulling all the way up to the house, they stopped by Luke, who was riding the now-working tractor. The sheriff and his deputy got out of the cars and approached Luke as he climbed off the tractor.

I followed Elizabeth out of the house, with Mary hot on our heels. When we neared the tractor, Deputy Walker noticed our approach and held up a warning hand. "Don't come any closer," he shouted.

The sheriff knelt on the ground where Luke was pointing as he checked the area while wearing latex gloves. He rose with an object in his hand and held it up so we could see it glinting in the sunlight.

"What is that, Owen?" Mary squinted to make it out.

"It's a Silver Dollar City memento," he said in a satisfied voice.

"How'd you know it was there? And why are two sheriff cars racing around doing lost and found?" she retorted.

"Luke called us," he answered. "And I bring backup when it's a clue to a murder." He put the shiny object in a plastic evidence bag, holding it up to the light as he inspected it.

"It was Duncan's," interjected Luke. "It was his good-luck charm. He would always take it out and rub it."

"I've never seen that before," said Elizabeth.

"You can tell that from twenty feet away?" scoffed Sheriff Tucker.

"How do we know you didn't just plant it here?" she asked.

Sheriff Tucker gave a quick, disgusted snort. "Sounds like some handy excuse you had all ready in case we found another clue."

Elizabeth threw up her hands. "I'd have to be an idiot to kill someone and then throw their lucky coin away in my grandmother's yard."

"It looks like it's got some fingerprints. I'll bet we'll find yours on it." The sheriff gave a self-satisfied nod and tucked the bag into his pocket. "Save it for your trial. I'll be telling the jury how we got a tip from this law-abiding citizen and came out to find proof that Duncan was here."

Mary shouted, "That's some very fancy detecting work there, Owen. Of course Duncan was here. He worked here, you fool!"

Trent said, "Dr. Banks. I understand why you're upset, but Duncan always kept that lucky charm in his pocket, pulling it out to show folks. He never let anyone touch it. No way he just left it by the side of the road."

"Someone's framing me. They must have planted it there. I've never seen or touched that before," Elizabeth exclaimed, but no one responded.

Mary directed a question to Luke. "What about when you were here helping Duncan last weekend? Are you sure it wasn't there then?"

With an earnest shake of his head, Luke replied, "No, ma'am, I'm sorry."

Mary jabbed a finger at the sheriff. "See. I told you—"

Luke interrupted, "'Twasn't there because he pulled it outta his pocket over yonder in the barn when we made a bet about a football game on Saturday." He quickly glanced at the sheriff as his face blanched. "That ain't illegal, is it, Sheriff?"

The sheriff just waved his concern away. If he started arresting everyone who bet on a football game, the jails would be overwhelmed.

Luke gulped. "I saw him put it back in his pocket too. Found it today way over here when I cut this tall grass near the house and saw something shining on the ground." He looked sheepishly at Mary. "I'm sorry." His voice trailed off as he saw the thunder in Mary's face and the dismay on Elizabeth's.

The sheriff gestured to Trent that they were finished here and watched him get back into his own vehicle. Then he fixed Elizabeth with a glare. "Make sure you don't leave the area," he warned her, and then added, "I've got you now," with a smug lift of his eyebrows.

"I've got you now," he repeated more quietly as he turned and got into his own car.

Their powerful engines roared on the dirt road and kicked up dust as they made U-turns and left us behind.

In the stunned silence, Elizabeth put her hands to her head and pulled her hair. Then she whipped around to stare daggers at

Luke. "What'cha go calling the sheriff on me? I thought we were friends?"

Luke stood there, eyes down, twisting his ballcap in his hands. "We was. I mean we are. I mean it's just I didn't have no choice. I touched that coin when I picked it up to see what it was. If them sheriffs found it, they'd think I done him in." His Adam's apple bobbed up and down as he gulped and looked up. "Besides, it's only doing right by Duncan. I don't lie. You know that, Ella Mae. I ain't no good at it."

Elizabeth's fear must have overflowed, as she started to cry. Twisting away from me, she ran inside.

Mary's frown hadn't left her face since she first saw the sheriff pull up the drive. Letting out a heavy sigh, she turned to Luke. "Did you at least see the dang cat?"

Startled at Mary's change of topic, it took Luke a moment to find his voice. He pulled his gaze up from the ground to meet hers and answered, "No, ma'am."

She sighed again and turned back to the house too.

Luke still stood there, staring awkwardly at me. "You think I should go finish up the mowing?"

I glanced at the house and then back to Luke. "I think it would be best if you took off for the day now. Finish the mowing tomorrow, maybe early before we get up here."

Luke tugged his cap back on his head. He nodded, looking relieved to have a set plan of action. "Sure 'nough. I've got plenty other projects to finish anyways. Okay then," he said, and waved as he trudged toward his truck. "Y'all have a good day now, ya hear?"

12

Thursday

Elizabeth

I woke up feeling invigorated. I had dreamt that today would be the day when we found the killer. Even though my dream didn't provide the answer, it felt good to hope. After being down in the dumps yesterday all afternoon and evening after the sheriff found yet another clue that he thought implicated me, I had my mojo back.

Yesterday afternoon, Mom remembered that the ANRC had an office in Ft. Smith. That was perfect, because Jonas and I were headed there this afternoon to meet with the lawyer Mom had recommended. We would stop by the ANRC offices and check Brent Hollands's story. He seemed credible enough, but something didn't ring true about his story. If Duncan was just going to redistribute Mimi's creek, why wasn't it finished yet? Was there something more that I wasn't seeing?

Mimi had been gone for months now, and Mom said that Robert Jones bought the neighboring land over a year ago. She didn't seem to know anything about redistributing the creek or an arrangement between Brent Hollands and Mimi. But Mimi and Mom not sharing everything didn't surprise me either.

During dinner last night, Jonas had wondered if Robert Jones wanted to build another house near his land and that's why he wanted to buy Mimi's land. Mom had the smart idea that we should check out the public records at City Hall to see if Robert had filed for any permits to build or change something on his property. He had seemed way too eager to "help" me by buying Mimi's land. And then he'd been upset—in fact a bit out of line—when I didn't agree right on the spot. The arrogance of some men was awe-inspiring.

So we would try to learn more about Robert first and then head out to Ft. Smith. Realizing that my uncharacteristic silence may worry Jonas, I parked the car and said with a tour guide's enthusiasm, "We're here." I added an arm flourish. Only a red umbrella to hold upright as I walked backward toward the building was missing to complete the effect.

"This is City Hall?" Jonas asked as he followed me into the lobby of a small, shared office building made of brick and fake siding. We stopped by the door reading "Jenkins City Clerk." Jonas's eyebrows furrowed when he noticed the nearby directory listed offices for an accountant, optician, and realtor.

I laughed at his expression. He never put on airs like a stuck-up, big-city boy, but he continued to be surprised when things here in Jenkins were different from his previous experiences. "The original building burned down a long time ago and they didn't have the money to build a new town hall. It's just a small town so they don't need a big, showy building anyway." I opened the glass door to the office.

We approached the empty counter, and before I could stop him, Jonas reached out and dinged the bell on the desk.

Seeing my look of disbelief, he asked, "What? The sign says, 'Ring for Service.'"

Before I could answer, a woman in the back hollered, "Hold your horses already. I'll be there when I get there." At least a minute passed before we heard slow, heavy footsteps approaching from the back room.

"Hey, Ethel," I said to the large woman who shambled over.

"Why Ella Mae." She took her time looking me over and then getting herself settled into a raised padded chair near the counter. "What a pleasant surprise."

"How ya doing?" I heard the Southern drawl return to my voice, as welcome as a sharp stick in the eye.

"I'm doing just fine, hon. What was all that ring-a-ding-dinging on the bell about? I heard you come in the door. I ain't deaf, just slow. You know it takes me a while to get out here." Ethel looked aggrieved.

I hastened to apologize. "I sure am sorry about that. I forgot to tell Jonas there was no need. He didn't know. He's not from around here and all."

Now Ethel gave Jonas a thorough assessment. "This is your husband?" she asked. When I nodded, she said, "Well, he may be cute but he sure is dumb." Making it into a big production, she slowly pulled the bell out of Jonas's reach as though to stop the simpleton from engaging in the horrid faux pas of more ring-a-ding-dinging. Ethel gave Jonas a mock stern look before bursting into a big, belly-jiggling laugh at her own actions.

Jonas made as if to speak, but Ethel, wiping her eyes, waved away his attempt to apologize. "Oh, don't you worry none, hon. I'm just teasing ya." She looked over at me. "Y'all have time to sit for a spell and catch up? I've heard so much about the both of you from your mama. She couldn't be more proud of you."

"My mother?" I asked, wondering if Ethel had gone senile since I'd left. Maybe she had me confused with someone else.

She laughed again. Her plump face could have been a ringer for Mrs. Claus. "Oh yes, dear."

I chewed my lip. That sure didn't sound like my mother.

Jonas jumped in. "We'd love to sit for a spell but I'm afraid we'll have to take a raincheck. We have to get to Ft. Smith so Elizabeth can see a lawyer."

Ethel's face grew dark and serious and her voice took on a sharper edge. "Oh, yes, I heard all about that. Terrible business." She cocked her head and fixed me with a hard look. "You didn't do it, now did you, Ella Mae?"

"No!" I was shocked she'd even ask.

"Oh, I knew it," Ethel said with a firm nod. "I just wanted to hear it from the horse's mouth. I figured those ladies were gossiping out of turn."

"What ladies?" I asked. Who thought I was a murderer?

"Oh, never you mind that evil gossip, dear." Ethel waved her hand as if to sprinkle fairy dust and erase the question from my mind. With her own magical change of mood, a sweet smile spread on her face as her voice turned breezy. "Now, tell me. What brings y'all to the Jenkins City Clerk today? How can I help you?"

My head was still spinning, but my knight, Jonas, stepped forward. "We want to see if any plans have been approved or submitted by Robert Jones."

"Oh, that newcomer who bought the land right next to your . . ." Her voice trailed off for a moment. In another shift of moods, Ethel reached out a pudgy hand and covered mine with it. "I'm so sorry for your loss, dear. We all miss her." Her eyes misted up.

I swallowed and nodded thanks. This maelstrom of emotions was exhausting.

Ethel patted my hand once more and then swiveled in her seat to the back room. She squeezed out of her chair and took a few steps away before stopping. "Oh, I plumb forgot to say excuse me while I go look in the records. Take a seat and I'll be back in a jiffy."

Ethel's jiffy translated into five minutes. When she turned the corner back into the front room, she said, "You were right, dear. Mr. Jones submitted a plan. It was recorded and approved."

Since Ethel's hands were empty, I asked, "What was it for? Can we see it?"

"No, hon. I'm sorry."

"But Mom said the town records are public."

She nodded sympathetically. "Yes, dear. She's right." She laughed. "She usually is, isn't she? But these plans were sealed."

"By whom?" Jonas asked.

"The mayor himself," said Ethel in a reverential tone.

Jonas and I exchanged a glance. He seemed as puzzled as I was. Then some of the lessons I'd learned from watching my grandmother and mother operate kicked in. Leaning over the counter, I put my hand over hers. "But you're such a dear, Ethel. You'll let us take just a teensy, weensy peek, won't you? You know we won't tell a soul. Then we'll all sit down and I'll catch you up on what we've been up to." I finished my coaxing by throwing in my sweetest smile.

Ethel put one hand on her cheek. "My goodness. You are quite the sweet-talker, aren't you?" She smiled sweetly back at us, blinked her eyes twice, and said, "But I'm sorry, dear. I can't break my word. I took a solemn oath to serve this city."

No matter what argument we tried, Ethel refused to let us see the sealed plans. So we left and drove up the ridge to Mimi's place since our appointment in Ft. Smith wasn't until early afternoon.

After I told Mom what Ethel had said, she huffed. "Well, if she's going to be all official like that, then I'll have to rev up Yahoo."

I forced myself not to laugh as we hadn't argued yet this morning and I didn't want to start something. "Mom, you can't just search the internet. If Ethel didn't scan and put the records online, then searching Yahoo won't find them." I was trying to be patient while yet again explaining how technology worked. As smart as my mother was on most things, technology still seemed beyond her grasp.

"Don't get all supercilious with me, young lady. I know what Yahoo is. I said W.A.H.O.O."

"What's a W.A.H.O.O.?" Jonas looked like he was trying to head off another fight before it started.

"It stands for Women of Arkansas Helping Out Others," answered Mom in a matter-of-fact tone as she dug her cellphone out of her pocket.

I laughed. "Since when does your gossip network have a name?"

"Since Lisa Hardy decided to name it."

"Who's she?" I asked.

"She's my friend, and conveniently also the judge who told the sheriff she can't make it to town until Monday and agreed to let you out on bail."

"Oh." My mouth opened and shut on its own a few times, but I couldn't formulate a coherent sentence.

"She called me Monday afternoon to check in on how I was doing," Mom explained.

"How you were doing?" I started to fume. "I was the one arrested."

"I thought I told you. Well, it's neither here nor there. It doesn't change matters at all." Mom waved a dismissive hand. "Now hush while I figure out what to trade to whom." Mom stood there staring out the window, mumbling to herself and counting on her fingers.

Trying to make up for being rude, I suggested, "What about one of Aunt Wendy's blueberry pies? Those are to die for."

"Honey, hush. It's not blueberry season yet. Besides, Wendy and her husband are out of town visiting kin." Mom started toward the front door so she could get a connection outside.

Jonas tugged on my arm, so I walked out of the room with him. He'd become a master at interventions between my mother and me. I decided to show him my second favorite spot in Mimi's house—after the kitchen, of course. I led the way up to the master bedroom but surprised Jonas by walking through the room and into the walk-in closet.

Yanking the hanging dresses to one side, I put my hand on the wall and turned to watch Jonas's face. His eyes widened and he laughed when my pushing caused a part of the wall to swing open, revealing a hidden, full-height attic. This section wasn't as large as the main one accessed from the other side of the hallway, but it was bigger than anyone would expect from the outside. The secret entrance was a favorite trick to show friends.

Ducking our heads, we walked into the dusty storage space piled high with boxes and old furniture, and lit by a few windows and a naked lightbulb with a hanging cord that I clicked on as I passed. Canvases were scattered throughout the room, on shelves, and stacked along the walls—most completed and framed but some still loose. I brought Jonas to my special spot in the back corner of the attic. A small threadbare carpet held a doll house and a low table with two chairs, some cards still spread on it.

We stood on the carpet, breathing in the old smells of oil-based paint, dust, and stale air. "I used to play up here for hours," I told him. "I remember Pawpaw would work up here rearranging the canvases while I played. When I got older, we'd sit and play cards until Mimi would holler to us to clean up for dinner."

"It's nice up here," said Jonas, and then he sneezed.

"It's probably dustier now since no one's been using it in a long time. And Pawpaw kept more lamps up here when we spent more time here."

Jonas started flicking through the boxes and canvases. "Will we need to go through these too?"

I sighed. "I suppose. I'd still like to find a few of my favorite paintings of Pawpaw's before the estate sale."

Jonas looked concerned. "We better get going, then. We only have a few more days."

We got to work. Jonas had just started on the second box of old junk and I was flipping through the canvases when Mom showed up just inside the door.

"Oh, here you are." She looked around and moaned. "I forgot about this attic."

A jacketless Sebastian stood by her shoulder, just inside the attic, looking around in amazement. Although the light wasn't bright, the floating dust did nothing to mute his bright red socks. Pulling out his notebook and price stickers, he leaned over and started flicking through the paintings, moving at a far faster rate than I had, but then again, he was only focused on ones that might sell on Sunday.

"I started the W.A.H.O.O network," said Mom. "This one's going to be tricky since Ethel's involved, but what I think is going to work is—"

I tuned out her detailed explanation of the horse trading that would be involved in the hopes of eventually uncovering the information we needed about Robert. I barely remembered most of the women Mom was rattling on about, and it wasn't like I needed to know how to W.A.H.O.O. from Portland.

*****

The less said about our afternoon visit with the lawyer in Ft. Smith, the better. A root canal would have been more enjoyable. I didn't want to think about the possibility of going to prison for something I hadn't done, let alone when the lawyer started outlining the length of prison term I faced for various charges. He was polite but didn't seem terribly interested in the suspects Jonas and I had uncovered so far.

He had dismissed our limited investigative efforts and said, "It's a little too early to worry about casting doubt on someone else. Let's see what happens during arraignment and the preliminary hearing. And then we've got the discovery process to see what kind of case they have against you. There's plenty of time for the sheriffs to find the actual killer and for us to discuss how we might approach a trial."

Jonas repeated his words to me in the car. All I really had retained from the conversation was the lawyer telling me how this nightmare would drag on forever. I knew he was trying to reassure me, but having this loom over my head induced a sense of dread and pessimism.

We made it to the ANRC offices before they closed. But that was also a bust as far as uncovering criminal suspects. Brent Hollands had been telling the truth, at least as far as getting pre-approval for the work on the creek. The only interesting piece of information we learned was that time was running out on the approval of his application.

I hadn't realized Arkansas had a use-it-or-lose-it philosophy in place for water projects. The ANRC approval gave Brent two years to finish the work before he had to go through another round of approvals. Based on what I'd heard, he wasn't likely to get Robert Jones to approve this plan if he had to resubmit it. Personally I was torn on how I'd respond if asked. I didn't mind him getting use from the water after it left our land, but only if the landscaping changes were done well. Anyway, he still had two months left to find someone else and finish the work before I had any say in the matter.

"Here we are, the Green Papaya." Jonas interrupted my thoughts as he pulled into the parking lot.

We'd decided to take advantage of the trip by eating dinner in one of the nicer vegetarian restaurants in Ft. Smith. Having several vegetarian restaurants to choose from was one advantage of traveling to the big city today. Jonas would be able to find something vegan that he'd enjoy. I still ate meat, but not as much as I did before meeting Jonas. And I couldn't give up dairy and eggs to go vegan. That was a step too far for a girl brought up by people who raised chickens and ranched cattle.

The outside of the building, with its red brick and large windows, resembled many other standalone restaurants. Inside was a bit nicer, with dark red walls offset nicely by black padded chairs and white tabletops. A bar with six stools ran along the side just past the entrance. The place wasn't crowded, but fuller than I'd expected for a Thursday night, and the food lived up to the delicious smells as we both got to satisfy our craving for some good Vietnamese food.

Our waitress stopped by to check on us while we ate. I gave her a thumbs-up, and then a man at the next table called to her, "Another Coke, please?"

"What kind?" asked the waitress.

"Dr. Pepper," he answered.

The waitress didn't skip a beat. "Sure thing." She smiled at us and left to go refill his glass.

When I glanced back, Jonas had stopped eating, his face wrinkled in confusion. "Didn't he ask for a Coke?"

I paused and then chuckled as I replayed the neighbor's conversation in my head. "Oh yeah, that's a thing."

"So I have to ask for a Coke?"

"No, it's okay if you ask for a soda. They'll just know you're a Yankee."

"But I'm from the Northwest."

"Most people around here would think the Northwest refers to Bentonville." When he still seemed confused, I added, "Arkansas." I smiled at Jonas. He was so cute when he was confused.

After we finished eating, the waitress cleared our plates. "Are y'all visiting or from around here?" she asked.

"We're visiting Jenkins," I answered, unwilling to get into my whole life story with a stranger.

"Jenkins?" asked the waitress. "Isn't that where they found that dead guy on Monday? What was his name now . . ."

"Duncan Fowler," supplied Jonas. "The check, please."

She snapped her fingers. "Yes, that's right. Good memory. I'll bet you're good with details, aren't you?" She gestured at him with our check but didn't hand it over.

He nodded and held out his hand.

I fidgeted in my chair, ready to leave. There had been far too much talk about murders and Duncan today.

"I was so sad to hear what happened to him," she said, and finally handed over the check.

"Yes," agreed Jonas, pulling out his wallet as he tried to get us out of here before this conversation became even more excruciating.

I looked away, hoping that would help me pretend not to hear her words.

"So sad." She sighed. "And he was just in here on Saturday night too."

"What?" I whipped my head back to look at her.

Jonas glanced at me and hurried to hand over his credit card.

She answered, "Poor guy breaks up with his girlfriend and then he dies the next day."

"He broke up with his girlfriend," I repeated dumbly.

"Oh, it was quite the scene. The manager almost called the cops." She lowered her voice. "Pie throwing was involved. Huge mess and they didn't even leave a big tip to make up for it." She shook her head. "They seemed friendly when they came in. I wonder what happened."

"Wait, wait." I waved frantically. "Who broke up with Duncan?"

"No." She leaned in conspiratorially. "It was the other way around. Duncan broke up with her. After she threw a pie at him, he stormed out and just left her here."

"Who?" I asked, exasperated. When she recoiled at my annoyed tone, I quickly apologized. "Sorry, it's been a really tough day." I forced myself to calm down. "Who did Duncan break up with?"

"Bianca. She runs that craft shop over yonder in Jenkins, I think."

"Delgado," I said, pressing my lips together. Bianca hadn't said a word about dating Duncan, or breaking up with him, during the baby shower.

The waitress snapped her fingers again. "Yes, that's it. You know her?"

My eyes went wide as I nodded at her before shooting Jonas a meaningful glance. But he didn't get it. Although he seemed surprised by the news, he didn't know Bianca and hadn't spent Tuesday evening in her shop gossiping about men. It seemed pretty odd that she hadn't said anything about Duncan all night when she had just been mad enough to throw a pie at him. What was Bianca hiding?

She'd made only that one comment agreeing that Duncan was a slob. Had she been embarrassed about getting dumped? My eyes narrowed. Or was she keeping quiet about killing him for dumping her? She was strong and outdoorsy. She could have surprised Duncan, whacked him in the head with something, and rolled his body into the river.

The waitress continued, "It was a good thing one of our regulars knew her. He took her home. He sits around here at the bar for hours in the evenings, just shooting the breeze with everyone. He's a funny guy. CB, I think they call him. Name is Cole, or something like that."

"Colton?" asked Jonas.

My husband was a surprising man. When had he met Colton? And knew him well enough to learn his nickname?

The waitress snapped her fingers yet again. "Boy, you two are on the ball tonight. You must know everyone down there." She took the credit card and walked off.

"How do you know Colton?" I asked Jonas.

"I told you. I talked to some guys outside the grocery store. Why were you going all bug-eyed over Bianca?"

I put both hands on the table. "Crystal's baby shower was at her store Tuesday. It was a gossip fest and she never said anything about Duncan. Weird, huh? And getting dumped in public sounds like a good reason to want to kill someone. Pretty suspicious when that someone winds up getting murdered the next night." I pursed my lips. "I wonder if Bianca has an alibi for Sunday night."

"I can ask Colton how she was acting when he took her home," said Jonas.

I smiled despite myself. "So now you're friends with Colton Buck? I'm not sure you should mention that to Mom. There's some history there."

"I'm beginning to think there are webs of history all over Jenkins."

At that I just plain laughed out loud. "That's for sure." I leaned back and scratched my cheek. "All bug-eyed? Since when is that something you say?"

He shrugged. "Been hanging around you a lot. Bound to pick up some of the vernacular."

13

Friday Morning

Jonas

Before Elizabeth woke up, I'd already gone for a run with Daisy, enjoyed my good coffee, and checked my email. The latter was part of my morning routine. Despite the comfort from the habitual process, it still felt different from the days when coworkers urgently requested my input on a project. These days, email consisted of newsletters, e-bills, and spam.

It was mid-morning by the time Elizabeth was ready to go and we'd told Mary what we learned last night about Bianca and Duncan. We were all getting worried about our lack of progress in solving the murder but had no better ideas, so we drove out to Mimi's house.

Before sorting through the final items, Mary spent a few minutes outside looking around and calling for Lucy to no avail.

Elizabeth flitted from one room to the next, haphazard with her sorting and selecting. I followed behind to pack all the items she wanted to save in a box. That was as efficient a system as I could manage given her lack of process today.

"Okay. Ready with another box yet?" I asked as I walked back into the attic after having loaded a full box into the car.

She turned, her phone to her ear. "Great, see you soon," she said, and hung up.

"That was Kelsey. She's got an open period at school today so we're going out to lunch," she said happily, and started dusting herself off.

"I could eat," I said.

"You can always eat," she said with a chuckle. "But this lunch date is just for me and Kelsey. She wants to distract me from worrying about my arrest."

"Oh," I said as I tried to remember if there was anything I could eat here.

She laughed. "Don't be so sad. You don't have to stay here. Do you want me to drop you off at Mom's house?"

"Sounds good." I grabbed her into a tight squeeze. "But I'll go with you to the restaurant and find something to eat somewhere else. I can walk around town and check out all the sights."

Elizabeth snorted. "All the sights? You've seen all the sights. It's Jenkins."

I shrugged. The lake was quite pretty with all the trees starting to fill in and I hadn't walked along the other side of Main Street. I'd be fine.

After winding our way down the mountain and across the river into town, Elizabeth parked outside the restaurant. She gave me a quick kiss, and as I strolled off, she called, "Enjoy the sights."

Now that she had mentioned lunch, I was hungry, so the sights would have to wait. I passed a fast-food place and a local joint whose only vegetable option appeared to be the sad tomatoes served on top of their burgers. I kept going.

When I reached the grocery store, Colton and Billy Ray were sitting out front again. I remembered they had a nice salad bar inside that far exceeded the other options I'd encountered so far.

From the bench, Colton asked, "You going to get something to eat in there?"

I nodded. "Do you mind if I sit with you to eat?" This would be a perfect opportunity to probe him about Bianca Delgado.

"No charge," said Billy Ray.

"Get some of their fried chicken," advised Colton.

"And potato salad. They make the best potato salad in the county," added Billy Ray. Then he glanced around nervously. "But don't tell my wife I said that."

"I'm vegan so that's not for me," I explained.

Billy Ray twisted his lips as he pondered my unusual word. "Don't worry. You can ask them to make you a special batch without the bacon. I'm sure it'll be dang tasty just the same." He licked his lips.

Colton shook his head. "Nah, it won't be. Them bacon drippings are what makes it so dang tasty. Otherwise it's just boiled potatoes, mayo, and some spices."

Billy Ray pushed down on the bench with both hands and strained. After a moment it finally became evident that he was getting to his feet. Colton got to his feet more easily.

I glanced from one to the other, unsure what I'd said to make them leave. But instead, they walked toward me.

Billy Ray clapped me on the shoulder. "We're going to get us some potato salad and fried chicken. You dun talked us into it."

We reconvened on the bench with our lunches. The greeting the men had received from the deli clerk made it evident this wasn't the first time they'd picnicked on fried chicken and potato salad.

The men's conversation rambled aimlessly for a while as I ate and listened.

"Sure you don't want a taste? I won't tell anyone you've fallen off the vegetarian wagon." Billy Ray held out a spoonful to me.

"No thanks. And it's vegan, not vegetarian," I said. Did he think there were vegan police roaming around looking for violators of the code?

I twisted to my right to look straight at the guys. How did one start an interrogation? I didn't want to be impolite, but would they respond well to the directness of a true detective? Should I have scripted this out or could I just wing it? I felt uncharacteristically tentative. "Colton," I started.

"That's my name. Don't wear it out," Colton said.

Deciding to go with the straightforward approach, I said, "Elizabeth and I went to dinner last night at the Green Papaya—"

"The one over in Ft. Smith? That's a great place. I go there all the time," interrupted Colton.

Before he could sidetrack me with a discussion about his favorite dishes, I continued, "The waitress said there was a blowup between Duncan Fowler and Bianca Delgado on Saturday night. She said you drove Bianca home after Duncan broke up with her."

"Yup." Colton lifted his plastic spork near his nose and took an appreciative sniff of his potato salad, as if he were savoring the aroma of fine wine. He then took a hearty bite. "Mmm, this sure is good stuff."

Before I could respond, we were interrupted.

"Good day, gentlemen." Sheriff Tucker appeared on my left, erect with his hands behind his back, as if standing at parade rest.

Billy Ray asked, "Going to pick up some of this delicious potato salad, Sheriff? I think we left enough for a tastin' behind."

"Not today." The sheriff pointed at me. "Is this a new member of your little club?"

"Nah, hasn't passed the initiation test yet," replied Colton.

"He's just having lunch and asking questions about Duncan," said Billy Ray.

The sheriff scowled at me. "Now son, you can't be going around asking questions about the case."

I was taken aback by his reaction but pushed back. "Last I checked, it's still a free country. Even here in Arkansas." I was clearly getting annoyed by the sheriff's attitude to resort to such a low retort.

The sheriff jabbed a finger at me. "Don't be poking your nose where it don't belong or I'll charge you with interfering in a criminal investigation." He jabbed again. "Back off." After one last stern stare, he strutted off.

Waiting until the sheriff was out of earshot, Colton whistled softly. "Boy howdy, something's stuck up his craw."

Billy Ray leaned back on the bench, patting his stomach in satisfaction. "He's still upset he didn't get that police chief position that was open over in Conway. He's been angling for a big-city job for years."

"Well, he certainly hasn't distinguished himself around here. All them thefts still ain't solved," said Colton.

"What was stolen?" I asked.

"Lots of people in the area have had something valuable stolen in the last two years," answered Colton.

I looked around. Only a handful of people were visible on the street. "How many people are we talking?"

"Mebbe ten or more. It's a regular crime wave. If it keeps up, I might have to lock my door when I leave," said Billy Ray.

"So the sheriff needs a big win," I said, and then added more quietly, "At Elizabeth's expense."

"Yep, Ella Mae's goose is as good as cooked," said Billy Ray. "Begging your pardon since you're vegetarian and all."

Colton grunted. "Best you don't get on his bad side. I don't know nothing about Bianca and Duncan anyhow. Just drove her home on Saturday. She was as quiet as a church mouse the whole way."

The two men returned to their earlier meandering conversation that sounded like it had gone on for years. I finished my salad, said goodbye, and headed off in the opposite direction of the sheriff.

I had looped down to the lakefront and back along the next street when I noticed a hairdresser ahead on the right. Elizabeth had been bugging me about my hair getting too long, and I realized this was a good time to get it done. Shear Heaven seemed a clever enough marketing name to attract walk-in clientele, so I ducked inside.

A woman sitting in the chair facing the door, her hair separated into foil-covered segments, asked, "What do you need, hon?"

"I need a haircut," I answered.

She burst into laughter. "He said it! Anita haircut." She slapped her thigh and laughed again, then twisted to the side. "I told you I could get the next person in the door to say it, Anita."

The woman beside her turned. She was the attractive older woman I'd seen jogging around town. "Oh, hush. Don't have a conniption over it." Anita swatted the woman by the door playfully on the shoulder. "You'll scare away my customer." Turning her attention to me, she smiled. "We don't get many handsome men in here. But I do men's haircuts too."

"How long a wait?" I asked, gesturing to all the women sitting in the other chairs.

"Oh, they're not waiting, just my friends here chatting. I'll get to you in a jiff." With another smile, she gestured me to an empty chair in the corner away from the group of women.

I thanked her, sat down, and looked around while the buzz of conversation resumed. Compared to most barbers I've gone to, this place had more comfortable chairs, more perfume, and more women. I was the only man there. But the scissors looked the same and Anita had said she cut men's hair, so all the essentials were in place.

One other stylist worked in the salon, sitting side-on to me and doing something with foil and chemicals to a woman's hair. She was much younger than most of the customers—about my age. Although she wore too much makeup for my taste, she was attractive.

After a few moments, the women were back to talking and laughing over each other. They ignored my presence. I returned the favor, barely aware of their gossiping about people, places, and incidents that were unknown to me as I absentmindedly did math games with the configuration of the ceiling tiles. I kept my ears open for any mention of Duncan or the various suspects we had uncovered but no one mentioned their names.

I looked up when the salon's front door opened. "Good afternoon, ladies," announced a woman carrying several shopping bags. After the others greeted her, she added, "I know it's hard to imagine, but I'm here for Anita to make me even more beautiful than I am right now." She held out her arms and modeled like a beauty queen, twirling her bags around, posing, and swiveling her hips. She put on quite the runway show until she caught sight of me. "Oh. Oh, my . . . I hadn't seen you sitting there." Her head darted around in confusion. "I didn't know there was a man in here."

"He's getting a *haircut*." The woman by the front door enunciated the word in an exaggerated fashion.

"Oh," was all the woman with the shopping bags could manage as her cheeks turned red with embarrassment. She scurried to a seat in one of the open chairs far from me.

"Mom." The young stylist looked to Anita. "Do you have any foil by you? I'm running out here."

Now that she had turned in my direction, the connection was obvious. She looked like a younger, softer version of Anita.

"No, hon. Sorry," answered Anita after taking a moment to glance down at a lower tray in her cart.

The younger stylist stood and stretched her arms out behind her, twisting her body just enough to make sure I had a good eyeful of her side profile before she sauntered to the back, swaying her hips. I wasn't interested in her, of course, but the sideshow was entertaining.

"How are we going to know what new hairstyles to choose now?" asked an older woman whose white hair Anita was finishing.

"Yes, Anita dear," said another woman in a red blouse. "Who's going to do your new photos now . . . now that he's gone?"

I looked over to see she was pointing at a set of photos hanging by Anita's station. Each was an artsy, close-up, angled shot of Anita with a different hairstyle and blouse and posing on a white couch. The soft lighting gave the photos a dreamy look. Although Anita wore stylish blouses and not lingerie, the scenes resembled boudoir photos—at least as close as one might get for something displayed in a public setting.

A tan woman about Anita's age idly flipping through magazines looked up over her reading glasses and asked in a teasing tone, "Yes, indeed, who's going to do you now?"

A few of the women tittered.

Through a clenched jaw, Anita answered, "I'm done with photography for now."

"Really? I thought you liked how Duncan worked with you," said the woman in red.

"Right, I thought you said he worked real hard to please you," added the tan woman.

Still facing the wall of photos, I froze as I finally connected the dots from her friends' snide remarks—Anita and Duncan must have been an item. Was Anita the reason Duncan had broken up with Bianca? How had he managed to get all these women to like him? And with all the other jobs that Duncan had taken on, when did he have time to spend with them, let alone be a photographer?

"Ow." The woman with the white hair flinched.

"Oh, I'm so sorry. A fly was bothering me." Anita waved in front of her, but I didn't see any insects nearby.

"No problem, dearie. Just be careful pulling my hair. I don't have a lot to spare."

Anita threw a quick glare at the tan woman, who blithely ignored her as she loudly flipped the pages in her magazine and recrossed her shapely legs. Getting no acknowledgment of her glare,

Anita then answered the woman with the red shirt. "Turns out he was moving on in directions I didn't like. We were no longer a fit. Photographically, I mean." She added the last bit quickly when it looked like her tan friend was about to say something else.

"Of course," she purred from behind her magazine.

Anita frowned and seemed about to speak when her daughter called from the back room, "Mom, do you know where the extra foil is?"

"Check the drawers on the left, Suzanne," Anita called back.

The woman in the red blouse moved closer to scrutinize the photos. "Anita, I love how simple and clean the shots are. It keeps the whole focus on how gorgeous you look."

"Thank you. The décor of his whole place—I mean his studio—was minimalist like that." Anita started noisily rummaging through the supplies at her station as if to distract everyone's attention from the photos.

But the woman in red was undeterred. "How long did it take for Suzanne to do your hair all those different ways?"

Anita's tone had turned brusque. "We took those over time. Suzanne did my hair before each shoot."

"Well, they look a lot like ones that I had taken for my anniversary years ago." The woman in red tilted her head. "Of course, I was wearing a little . . . less." She blushed and quickly flicked a glance in my direction, suddenly remembering my presence in the corner.

I felt confident that today was the first time a man had come into the salon in a long time.

Anita flushed. "It's time for some new art in here." She started pulling the photos off the wall and piling them on the counter. "I was going to take these down anyway."

"Oh, do leave up that one." The woman in red pointed. "That one is just perfect. You'll never need another beauty shot again."

"It's a good thing it's perfect. It's not as if Duncan Fowler can come back from his grave to take more beauty shots of Anita." The tan woman looked out from behind the magazine.

Anita waved at her friend to be quiet as she pointed insistently toward the back room where her daughter had gone. Then, noticing me still staring at the photos, she pulled the last one off the wall and turned it face-down.

"I'll be there in less than a minute, hon." Anita was looking straight at me. Suddenly realizing I had stood up from my chair to get a closer look at the photos, I blushed and sat down.

I needed to find Elizabeth to discuss what I'd learned about Anita. Would leaving now make Anita suspicious? I wasn't sure, and I did need my hair cut, so I sat back down.

When Suzanne walked out of the back room with a package of foil, the woman by the front door changed subjects. "Anita, did you try some of Meredith's apple pie on Sunday? Her top crust is so delish. I don't know how she gets it so flaky."

"Nope." Anita still sounded peeved.

"Oh, that's right, you missed church." The woman Suzanne was working on sniffed.

Suzanne jumped in to defend her mother. "She had another flare-up of her lupus and went to Hot Springs for treatment."

"Mm-hmm, another treatment," agreed a lean woman sitting next to the tan woman with a tad too much enthusiasm. She winked at Anita and then rolled her eyes from behind Suzanne's back at her neighbor.

Anita blushed, paused her cutting, and elaborately rubbed her hands. "I need those treatments to keep my joint pain down so I can work here and make you ladies look so beautiful."

Amidst a general chorus of ooh-ing and aww-ing, she added, "I was just so grateful the doctor could see me on Sunday, I had no choice but to miss church to see him. I'll just have to pray twice as hard next week—if I don't get another flare-up and have to miss again."

"I'll bet those treatments sure laid you out," agreed the tan woman as she covered her mouth with a hand, not quite hiding her muffled laughter.

The older woman Anita was working on placed her hand on Anita's. "You keep yourself healthy, Anita, and I'll keep you on my prayer list."

Anita patted her on the shoulder. "You're so sweet. And I'm finished with you now."

The woman said, "Oh, now go on and take care of that young man. I'm not in any hurry. I'll just sit here and visit some. I can pay you after you finish with him."

Anita switched to my chair. As she worked on my hair, the conversation grew louder around us.

The women had either accepted my presence, didn't care, or had simply forgotten I was still there with Anita's body hiding me from view. Some of the comments sounded downright nasty as the conversations swirled around me, but it was hard to tell because they were all said in such pleasant, friendly tones.

Anita finished my haircut quickly. I was at the register when a police car zoomed in front of the building and around the corner, going somewhere fast.

The ladies all quieted as they turned to watch it roar past the salon's windows.

"You don't think someone else died, do you?" asked the older woman.

"Oh Lord, I hope not," said another.

They paused in silence for a moment. Then, from a few chairs down, someone asked, "Do you think Meredith uses store-bought or homemade crusts?"

The upswell of indignant responses indicated that conversation had returned to normal as I hurried out of the salon and headed to Mary's house. I had to tell Elizabeth that Anita might have had a reason to kill Duncan too. Suspects were starting to propagate like cell cultures in a petri dish.

14

Friday Lunch

Elizabeth

"That was a lot of fun," I said as Kelsey and I walked out of the restaurant into the bright sun. "Thanks for distracting me."

"Do you remember how Aunt Eliza would distract us with cookies?" asked Kelsey wistfully.

Aunt Eliza was actually Kelsey's Great-Aunt Eliza. She had been close friends with Mimi and raised Kelsey's mother after her parents were killed in a car accident when she was a young child. During middle school, Kelsey and I spent a lot of time at both Aunt Eliza's house and Mimi's ranch. It had never felt like babysitting to us, but since our parents were at work, that's what it must have been.

"She did make the best cookies," I agreed. "Do you have time to swing by the bakery for a second-best option?"

She sighed. "No. I wish I didn't have to hurry back for class. Hey, do you want to come over later and look through Aunt Eliza's things? I'll bet there'll be something of yours in there."

"Oh, yes." I clapped my hands in excitement and then looked down at them. Funny how fast I had picked up my mother's habits. Well, at least this trip hadn't been as difficult as previous times she'd come to visit me. Maybe it was because I had come to Arkansas. Mom was more comfortable with a home field advantage.

"Oh, I forgot. I can't tonight. It's final costume fittings for the school play. Tomorrow?" At my nod, Kelsey hugged me. "Okay, I'll call you. Bye."

She dashed off, leaving me standing on the sidewalk and thinking about cookies. But I felt full and wasn't ready to end this little break from reality, so I strolled off down the street, trying to justify a stop at Crafts n' Creations to myself. Bianca did have all those new craft supplies that I didn't get a chance to dig through during the baby shower. I owed it to myself to take this opportunity. I was an artist, after all. It was important to support local craft stores. Otherwise, I'd have to drive all the way to Ft. Smith to visit one of those giant chain stores.

As I walked, I shook my head. Bianca killing Duncan just didn't make any sense to me. Duncan's murder was a terrible tragedy, but the perpetrator couldn't be someone I knew. I didn't associate with killers. Before I knew it, I found myself with my hand on the doorknob of Crafts n' Creations.

The door was locked. A sign in the window said, "Be Right Back."

Luke popped his head around the side of a compact SUV parked a few spots away from the store's entrance. "Ella Mae, what are you doing here?"

I frowned. He wasn't my favorite person at the moment. "I'm here to shop, Luke. What are you doing here?"

"Nothing." He wiped his forehead with an arm and looked down, twisting his ballcap in his hands. "Well, I mean, I was here because I was going to finish up some final bits of the remodel." He just stood there next to the SUV, stern as a sentinel. "Better not come over here," he warned.

My stomach sank and I froze. "It's not? Wait . . . Bianca's okay, isn't she?" At his gulp and nervous nod, I asked, "What is it, then?"

Before Luke could respond, we heard an engine roar before a sheriff's car screeched up a few spots away. My breath caught but then released when I saw Trent getting out of the driver's seat.

Intent on his goal, Trent hurried over to the SUV. "Where is it, Luke?" He paused to survey the area and noticed me standing on the sidewalk by the store's entrance. "Lizzy? What are you doing here?"

I wished he wouldn't keep calling me that. I was long over him and that felt too intimate, despite our connected past. "Why does everyone keep asking me that? It's a store. I'm shopping." My voice came out sharper than I'd intended. Perhaps Trent's presence still affected me after all.

"Uh, it's over there, Trent." Luke pointed inside the SUV's back passenger seat.

"Stay there," Trent commanded me in quite the officious tone, and then moved on to Luke.

I stood tapping my foot, wondering what Luke had found this time as I tried to avoid chewing on my fingernails.

"Welcome to today's special event, *Sheriff Search Live: Jenkins Edition.*"

I jumped and then breathed again as I saw Colton Buck. He had crept up alongside me and started narrating the action as if this were a sports event. Colton continued, "You've joined us just in time. Today, we're watching Deputy Walker looking all aflutter at the prospect of finding some important clue to some case he's working."

"Shh," I told him. Colton's nickname of CB wasn't just based on his initials. It also reflected his insistence on talking all the time. It was no wonder he volunteered to be the high school sports announcer.

"The crowd's restless as we haven't seen much action yet today. Oh." He raised his voice in excitement. "What's that? It looks like

Luke has served up a hat." His voice tipped back into calm. "That pass was a flop. Sorry, folks, but there's no blood in sight. It's just a John Deere ballcap."

"What is that, Trent?" I asked, rocking forward onto my tiptoes.

"It's Duncan's." Luke's Adam's apple bobbed up and down.

"How'd you know it was his hat?" I asked. "Lots of guys wear that hat." Case in point was Luke's own version, ratty as it was, that he was twisting in his hands.

"His name's written inside." Luke's excitement caused his voice to crack.

Trent flipped the cap around to show us the black sharpie letters on the inside bill. "Like on a kid's underwear before you send him to camp."

"An assist and spike for a point to the home team!" Colton's voice grew eager.

Trent smiled at Colton's idiocy and his own good fortune in finding a clue. To Trent, it must have felt like old times when Colton would announce his plays at the football games.

"What are you doing by my car?" Bianca's eyes narrowed as she strode up holding a container of soup.

Colton lowered his voice. "Now things are really heating up. A new team has entered the playing field."

"Excuse me, Ms. Delgado, but I'll need you to stand away from the vehicle," Trent instructed.

"It's my car. Who gave you permission to search my car?" she demanded, her voice rising.

"There's a challenge flag thrown, folks. Was this a rules violation? Let's bring in Bob, our retired referee, to give you his expert opinion."

Luke swallowed hard, his hat getting ruined as he continued twisting it. "Sorry, ma'am. It just that I called him. You told me to bring in the boxes from the back seat."

Colton's voice became more nasally as he invented another character. "Good afternoon, Colton. It's a beautiful day for our tournament. I see she's appealing the ruling on the field—"

"Colton!" I hissed, and he quieted. After Colton had retired and before his wife had died, she had kicked him out of the house whenever the weather permitted. Apparently she couldn't stand the constant chatter either.

Trent and Bianca approached the door to the store. Whatever he'd said had been drowned out by Colton's blabbering. We stepped back to give them space as Bianca silently unlocked the door. She stepped inside, kicking down the door stop, but stopped when Trent said, "Ms. Delgado, please stay here while I conduct the search."

Bianca stood fuming just inside her store while Colton and I watched from five feet away. Luke sidled up and stood next to Colton, but I didn't acknowledge his presence.

Colton couldn't contain himself for long. "How lucky we are today. New rules put into effect only this year give the visiting team extra time to score without the home team even being on the field. Can the deputy uncover the magic eight-ball for a score? Or will this play fail to pan out like so many others undertaken by the local sheriffs?"

I'd never admit it to him, but Colton's analysis was spot-on as Trent proceeded to quickly and efficiently check all the shelves and drawers. But for what I hadn't a clue.

Trent disappeared into the back room and Bianca stood impatiently by the door, crossing and uncrossing her arms as she almost followed him into the back a few times but stopped herself.

"It looks like another losing effort . . . No! No! I spoke too soon." Colton's voice grew louder and more excited as Trent burst out of the back room holding a plastic evidence bag and wearing a look of satisfaction. "I do believe the deputy has found something special here today, folks. We can't quite make it out, but it could be, yes, I think it does look like blood on some sort of rag—"

"Can it, CB," muttered Bianca in a threatening tone as her jaw clenched.

Colton shut up again. His commentator impression might have been ridiculous but there was nothing wrong with his instincts for self-preservation.

"Is this your bandana, Ms. Delgado?" asked Trent.

"No. And I have no idea how it showed up in my back room," she insisted.

I stared at Bianca. Her arms were wiry and strong from doing pottery and lifting things around her store. I wondered if she still did all that hiking and paddle boarding on the lake. She was strong enough to hit Duncan with something and kill him. She got dumped by him on Saturday night so she had to have been upset. Perhaps her anger had festered and grown until she was upset enough to kill him.

"Did you see Duncan on Sunday?" asked Trent.

"Sunday?" Bianca swallowed and then her voice strengthened. "No. I didn't see him on Sunday. I didn't kill him either. And I've also never seen that hat or bandana before."

I wanted to scream, "But you argued with him Saturday night," but Bianca wasn't done.

"It was you," she yelled, suddenly spinning to point at Luke. "You planted the evidence in my car and my store."

My eyes narrowed as I swiveled my head to stare at Luke too. How convenient that he discovered evidence in Mimi's driveway and then in Bianca's car. He could have killed Duncan and was desperately trying to pin the blame on someone else—anyone else.

If so, he wasn't doing a very good job of it. Discovering Duncan's Silver Dollar City medallion alongside Mimi's driveway had made me look more guilty. But why plant evidence implicating Bianca too? Was this some elaborate plot that Luke had devised?

That seemed unlikely. Luke just wasn't that smart. Maybe Susie Q had duped her own husband into doing something and then he'd gotten confused and messed things up. He had always been pliable and never the brightest bulb in the bunch.

Luke stood there looking miserable under the withering glares of two angry women.

"Was Luke in the back room today?" Trent asked Bianca, proving himself to be a decent investigator after all.

She whirled back around and started to speak, then swiveled to look at Luke. She sighed heavily. "No," she admitted. "He just got here as I was locking up to grab some soup for lunch." She lifted the soup container. "He offered to unload the boxes from my car, but I didn't want him crowding up the aisle so I left the store locked. I was only gone maybe five minutes."

"Hmm. The plot thickens—"

"Stop!" Bianca and I said in unison to Colton.

Bianca looked so dismayed that I decided to hold off on telling Trent about her breakup with Duncan. I'd call Trent later so he could use it to surprise her when he'd have her reaction recorded on camera for the jury to view.

Then, remembering that Colton also knew about Bianca's breakup, I looked at him and frowned. How had the town's biggest motormouth not already spread the word? Was he somehow involved in Duncan's murder? I edged away from him.

"Why don't we shut the door so I can take your statement?" Trent looked out the door at the small crowd gathering near me and Colton on the sidewalk. "Folks, you can move along now. Nothing to see here. Luke, please stick around and I'll be with you soon." He closed and locked the door, leaving us outside.

"Well, thanks for joining us today. It was another thrilling episode of *Sheriff Search Live*. Come back tomorrow for our regular episode of *Crosswalks of Jenkins*." Colton finished his little performance, gave a small bow to the mildly amused onlookers, and ambled off with a big grin. March was long after football season ended, so he must have been missing an audience something fierce.

I turned to head back to Mom's house, also happy, but for a different reason. With all this new evidence, the sheriff would be forced to get serious about looking for the actual killer. I should be off the hook in a jiffy.

*****

"Great news!" I yelled as I swung open Mom's front door. I knelt to greet Daisy with a big hug. She must have heard my happy steps approaching because she was already waiting to greet me with her doggy love right at the door. Having attended to the big bundle of furry affection, I stood and reached out to hug Jonas too. "You'll never believe—" I stopped in my tracks and blinked more than a few times.

"You got your hair cut," I said.

"Yes," he said, not seeming concerned by my reaction to his new 'do. "And I've got news too."

I cocked my head, thinking something was off about his haircut. He looked nice, but— "Wait! You didn't have the car. Where did you go?" I scowled, knowing what the answer had to be but hoping against hope that some other possibility had occurred.

"I ran into this place—Shear Heaven."

"Oh, no. You didn't? You wouldn't? You couldn't?" But the evidence was sitting neatly coiffed on his head, staring me in the face.

He touched his hair, trying to determine what was making my brain start to short-circuit. "What's the problem? You've been telling me I needed a haircut." He spoke softly, as if worried about spooking me further.

I sank into an armchair. "Of course, but not from there." My head flopped back and I rubbed my eyes. When I gathered my strength back, I told him, "That's Susie Q's place."

"Oh." He closed his mouth and leaned against the wall. "Yeah, I saw her and her mother there."

"You saw her mother too?" My pulse started to spike and I looked around, wondering if Mom was home yet and had overheard.

"Yes, but I'd seen her before, jogging. She's the one who actually cut my hair."

I frantically waved him quiet. "Do not, I repeat, *do not* say that to my mother. We'll tell her we took a drive and stopped out of town for your cut."

"Why? What's the problem with your mother knowing?"

"What can't your mother know?" Mom asked as she opened the door of her home office and stepped into the hallway.

I gulped and jumped out of the chair. "Mom! What are you doing home? Did you finish tagging everything in Mimi's house?"

"Close enough. I have patients to see this afternoon. Now don't try to distract me. It didn't work when you were in high school and it won't work now. What can't I know?"

I thought fast and came up with an even better distraction. Mom always thought she had the upper hand, but I had a lot of opportunities to develop excellent lying skills as a teenager. "That Trent found evidence linking Bianca Delgado to Duncan's murder."

"What evidence?" Jonas looked puzzled.

"Duncan's hat was hidden in the back seat of her car," I answered with a broad smile.

"Why can't I know this? It's good news. Really good news." Mom also broke into a big grin.

"It is awesome news and I wanted to be the one to tell you, not Jonas," I said. As Mom hugged me, I warned Jonas to keep quiet with my eyes, hoping that would be enough for him to realize not to contradict me.

"I heard some news relevant to the case too," said Jonas as Mom and I separated. "Anita Quentin had an affair with Duncan Fowler that ended not that long ago. It's possible she could have been angry enough to kill him."

Mom frowned at the mention of Anita's name. "Anita? And your hair is different. You didn't go there for a cut, did you?" I had to give it to her; Mom was fast.

I raised my eyebrows and shook my head emphatically, warning him again. He couldn't tell her he'd gotten his hair cut at Shear Heaven. Mom disliked Anita almost as much as I detested Susie Q. It wasn't exactly the Hatfields and McCoys, but we Bankses didn't mix with those Quentins.

Jonas's eyes flicked back and forth between us. "Mary, you know Elizabeth wouldn't have wanted me to go to that place. I overheard some people gossiping about Anita in town."

"Pah!" exclaimed Mom. "Some of these people have nothing better to do than gossip."

I breathed a quick sigh of relief. Jonas was not always the most adept with social skills, but he was smart and considerate. He'd avoided making Mom angry while also avoiding telling an actual lie. His unwillingness to lie was one of the things I loved about him, although this newfound ability to mislead was a touch troubling.

"Did they have anything else useful to say?" I asked, hoping to get us off the topic of Anita Quentin as quickly as possible.

Jonas grimaced. "Unfortunately I heard that she had an alibi for Sunday. Apparently she drove to a spa in Hot Springs to get treatment for her lupus."

"Lupus?" Mom scoffed.

"What?" I asked, turning to look at her.

She seemed about to say something—opening and closing her

mouth a few times—before she finally said, "I can't talk about medical conditions of patients, even former patients." She shook her head. "It makes some of the women think I'm all uppity that I won't add any gristle to chew on during gossip sessions when they know I have access to some juicy stuff. However, it's not only illegal and unethical, but it would also be bad for business. I'd lose all my patients if they heard me gossiping about someone else."

She still looked tempted to dish on Anita but then said, "I can't." That settled, she closed her office door behind her. "I'm off to see a few patients. I'll see you two for supper."

She departed with her customary dash, leaving Jonas and me standing in the hallway. I shook my head. "That was a close call. I still can't believe you went there." I squinted as I examined his head. It must have been a longer time than I'd thought since his last haircut because he looked like he did when I first met him.

Jonas touched his hair self-consciously. "If you're still upset with the haircut, I can try to return it."

I laughed and finally gave him the hug I had intended when I first arrived at the house. Despite his unintended disloyalty, it wasn't Jonas's fault. Then I had an idea. "Come on," I said, and opened the door into forbidden territory.

Jonas followed me into Mom's home office, a room I had never been allowed to enter while growing up. I had to keep myself from giggling with the glee of retroactive teen victory. "What are we doing?" he asked.

"Mom basically invited us to search her records."

"She did what?" he asked, astonished.

"She told us she couldn't gossip about her ex-patients. She emphasized the word 'she.' Did you notice?"

"No. There was no emphasis."

"Sure there was. Mom was just reminding me that she kept many of her older records here, especially for former patients. Her clinic is too small to store much." I was scanning through filing cabinets as I spoke.

"How will this help us titrate out all the suspects and pin down who we think is the best bet?" asked Jonas.

I laughed at him. "You know you use that word as if it were a normal word."

"Titrate is a normal English word," he objected. "We used it all the time at work."

I laughed again. "Well, sure. It's a biology word. Or chemistry, I guess. Normal people would say 'filter' or 'screen.'"

"Scientists are normal people," he insisted despite all evidence to the contrary.

"Yes, dear," I agreed blithely. Having met a number of his former colleagues, I knew better. "Here it is," I said, and pulled out a thick folder of papers.

Jonas followed me to the desk where I laid down the folder and opened it.

"It's Anita's," he said, looking over my shoulder.

"Of course. She's the one who claimed to have lupus. Let's see if that is true. I remember the blow-up right before she stopped being Mom's patient." I chuckled as I remembered that incident. "Most everyone is her patient around here. At least for a while. Then some of them get mad at her or don't like her answers, even though she's usually right, and find someone else in another town. Anita definitely fell into the 'get mad at her' bucket," I explained, still scanning the first page.

"Wow!" I pointed to the date on the page. "She's . . . she's . . ." I tried to do the math in my head.

"She's forty-seven," said Jonas.

"But Susie Q is my age. That means Anita was . . ." I counted on my fingers.

"Nineteen when she had her daughter," said Jonas.

"And that means she was eighteen when she . . . you know," I said.

"Probably still in high school," agreed Jonas.

"Wow! I never knew. I mean I knew she looked young, but she's more than ten years younger than Mom."

"Eleven," he clarified.

"Yes, yes. Hold on. This is a patient summary letter that Mom wrote. It must have been when Anita moved to a new doctor." My finger scanned down the page as I read through the jargon. "Look, right here. Mom wrote, 'No systemic or recurring medical conditions beyond those normally expected for a woman of her age and physical condition.'" I snorted. "Boy, Mom even made that sound like a slam."

"But no lupus," clarified Jonas as he finished reading the page.

"No lupus," I agreed. Cheerfully, I turned toward him and, since his face was right there, kissed his cheek. "She lied." I raised both hands and started doing my happy dance.

"It means she's a liar, but doesn't necessarily mean she's the killer," Jonas said, stopping my dance prematurely. "And what about your latest theory that Bianca is the killer?"

"Oh yeah." I turned back to the folder and flipped the page to read through the rest of Anita's medical records.

Jonas tugged at my arm. "Come on, we shouldn't be reading that."

"But if she doesn't have lupus, maybe the rest of her story is made up too. If only we knew which spa she claimed to go to on Sunday, we could check her story," I said.

"What if I knew the name?" Jonas asked, looking hesitant.

I frowned. "What? Did you, like, become her best friend while she cut your hair?"

Jonas shrugged noncommittally, but before I could snap at him, he added, "What if I thought a spa day was a good idea for a possible gift for a certain someone?"

"O-oh." My mood immediately brightened. "Well then," I said after planting another kiss on his lips, "I'll call them right now to double-check whether Anita really went there last Sunday, and afterwards, I'll conveniently forget I ever heard about the place in case *someone* wants to gift me a visit."

15

Friday Evening

Elizabeth

Over dinner, we discussed all the suspects. It might not have been the most appropriate conversation I've ever had with my mother, but then again, many of my interactions with her over the years couldn't exactly be classified that way. Anyway, it was a good distraction from worrying about what would happen in a trial. I don't know that any of us truly believed that one of our neighbors could kill someone, but we each had our favorites.

Mom kept pushing for one of Mimi's neighbors as the killer. Between Robert Jones and Brent Hollands, Robert seemed the more likely. We couldn't be sure if he had something devious underway as we still hadn't heard anything back from her W.A.H.O.O. network on the sealed property plans. Not that Brent couldn't kill someone, given his rifle skills and all, but at least his story had panned out so far.

Jonas and I were split on the two women. Even though Mom and I thought he was crazy because we'd known her forever, Jonas argued that Bianca Delgado had the strongest motive to kill Duncan and she was his top choice. He just didn't know her as well as we did. She was our friend, not a killer—although she did have a temper, was strong, and had just been dumped. On the other hand,

Jonas's scientific training and status as an outsider gave him a more rational perspective.

Jonas might have won us over but then lost his credibility by suggesting that the kid, Dale Cooper's son, was also a viable suspect because he was at the river late on Sunday and was mad at Duncan. But both of them couldn't have killed Duncan.

I was certain it was Anita Quentin. And Mom didn't disagree. To be fair, her agreement might have reflected more on their shared history than any points of logic I made. If the subject came up for a vote on who had to go to jail for killing Duncan, Mom would punch her ballot for Anita in a heartbeat—just to get her out of town.

I had to carefully tiptoe around revealing that Jonas and I had spied on Anita's medical status. We couldn't reveal we knew that, without a history of lupus, Anita's alibi for a visit to the spa proved her to be a liar. Despite that, Mom had no problem latching onto the idea that she was a liar.

"If her lips are movin', she's a-lyin'."

I laughed as I helped clean up after dinner. Jonas was drying and placing dishes into neat stacks while Mom held her traditional post as dish washer. "Bianca lied today too," I pointed out. "At least by omission. She fooled Trent by how she answered his question. Maybe I should call to tell him that Duncan broke up with her on Saturday night."

Mom looked at me. "Leave Deputy Walker alone. He has to put up with that sheriff all day, so he deserves his evenings off. Besides, you can do your own investigating on this."

I glared at her and huffed, "What have we been talking about all dinner?"

She nodded in acknowledgement. "Yeah, that wasn't bad. But you should talk to the Juniors too. You know they have their fingers in everything around town. If there's any gossip about Duncan to be found, they'd know it."

"Do I have to?" I winced at the thought.

Jonas looked puzzled, but before he could ask, Mom said, "It wouldn't kill you to ask them. And let's avoid dragging Bianca into this unless it becomes necessary. Too much gossip in this town as it is."

I chuckled. "Do you still go to her regular card games?"

Mom whipped her head to the kitchen clock. "Oh my stars, it's almost seven. I've got to go." She handed Jonas the soapy plate she had been washing without rinsing it.

"Go where?" Jonas asked as he rinsed it for her.

"Bianca's. With you visiting this week and my schedule all discombobulated, I completely forgot it was Friday night." She looked at the pile of unfinished dishes in the sink and then back at the clock.

"We'll finish," I told her, knowing how fastidious she always was about doing the dishes right after dinner. I didn't want her getting all twitchy during her card game.

"Oh, thank you, dear." Mom sighed in relief and dried her hands. She looked at Jonas with an earnest expression. "You just can't be late to Bianca's."

Jonas asked, "Why?" The question was perfectly reasonable if you didn't know Bianca.

Over her shoulder as she hurried to her bedroom, Mom answered, "Last time someone was late was five years ago."

"What happened?" asked Jonas. She had disappeared into her bedroom, so he looked at me and repeated his question.

I shrugged. Five years ago I wasn't living here.

Mom reappeared carrying her purse and paused with her hand on the doorknob. "We never saw her again." She opened the door and stepped through. "I'll be back late. See you in the morning." And she was gone.

Jonas turned to me, his eyes wide and mouth open. "She . . . It's too . . ."

I laughed and answered before he started hyperventilating. "Mom only meant the woman wasn't invited back. Bianca wouldn't kill someone just for showing up late for poker night."

"Ah." Jonas looked relieved.

Clearly he was more convinced Bianca was Duncan's killer than I had thought.

As I rinsed off a dish and handed it to him, he still seemed puzzled. "Who are the Juniors?"

"The Junior Auxiliary Club. It's a group of women who do charitable projects around town. They've been around forever. They basically run the city. Well, along with Anita's poker gang."

"What about the mayor?"

"Oh, he's just the figurehead. Someone has to run all the boring meetings and deal with the paperwork. His wife is one of the leaders of the Juniors. She's the real power behind the throne."

Jonas dried a coffee mug and lined up the handle on the shelf with the others. "And your mother gambles?"

I batted my eyelashes at him as I tackled the remaining pots. "Why, whatever do you mean by that, young man? You should know that gambling is illegal in the state of Arkansas outside of those new casinos."

Jonas shook his head. "That accent sounds more and more natural every day."

"Well, I reckon it does." Unable to maintain a straight face, I laughed.

After we finished cleaning up, I felt too antsy to sit home all evening. Mom's comment nagged at me. When I was younger, her constant pestering had pushed my buttons. Now, I had to agree she had a point. Going to see the Juniors might help narrow down our suspects, or uncover new ones.

"They meet on Friday night? Are we driving or walking?" Jonas asked after I broached the idea.

"Oh, they'll be in their meeting room. Though, I think I should go alone. They won't talk as openly with a man around."

He shrugged. "Okay. I'll take—"

Daisy ricocheted off my leg in her rush to get to Jonas before he even finished his sentence.

We laughed as once again Daisy knew what was happening before we called her or even jangled her leash.

"Are you going to tell your mother that you're going gossiping?"

I snorted as I locked up the house. "What do you think she's off doing tonight? Don't let her sanctimonious talk fool you. She's as big a gossip as the next one."

*****

I strolled around to the side of the old church, headed for the converted storage room that had served as the meeting/work room for the Junior Auxiliaries for as long as I could remember. This was the oldest Baptist church in the area, and its tall brick sanctuary near the street was surrounded by large trees that reached nearly as high.

I smiled to myself as I remembered how my mother had described the Juniors when I was growing up. She'd explained that they let men believe they ran the city only because it would devastate them to learn the truth. I wondered what new projects they were tackling these days. Growing up, I'd pitched in to help on a number of their larger fundraising or charitable events.

Mimi had been a member, which was probably why Mom had avoided joining them. Mom and Mimi had argued all the time, much like Mom and I did during high school, so they probably were both happy not to join the same group. Since Kelsey's mother had started participating in the Juniors when we were young, she and I went along with her mother and Mimi periodically.

As I'd expected, light spilled out onto the sidewalk through the open door. A core group of the older members could be found here most days—and evenings.

Knocking on the old wooden door, I poked my head inside. "Good evening, ladies," I said to the half dozen or so women who sat in a rough circle, knitting and quilting.

"Oh look, it's Ella Mae!" exclaimed Savannah Cooper, the mayor's wife, as the other women called out their own greetings.

It felt good. Even if one or two weren't as effusive in their greetings tonight, perhaps because of my arrest, no one ever welcomed me like this in our neighborhood Starbucks back in Portland.

"Come over here and give me a hug, Ella Mae." Ethel, the city clerk, shifted a pile of knitted blanket squares off her lap and struggled to her feet.

I complied and then went to grab a folding chair from the back for myself. "I knew I'd find some of you here tonight," I told them, plopping down.

"Well, sure. It's not like my husband was going to take me out dancing or nothing. Sitting here and chatting with the ladies beats sitting on the old couch and smelling his farts anytime," said Henrietta, one of the women with a less positive greeting, who led the group's holiday food drive.

The other women all nodded and burst into their own attempts to outdo each other with complaints about their husbands or children.

As that wound down, Savannah asked, "Honey, everything okay? I heard you got yourself into a spot of trouble on Monday."

"I'm okay." I looked down at my feet for a moment before smiling wanly at the thin, high-energy woman.

"I heard Trent Walker arrested you outside Harps." Henrietta shifted her purple reading glasses to the top of her head. She lifted her chin, so she seemed to be looking down her nose at me even though her tone remained polite. I seemed to remember she had been friendly with Anita. If so, that might explain why she wasn't smiling at Mary Banks's daughter, even if I'd never done anything to her and had helped out with the food giveaways every year during high school.

"The nerve of him. Savannah, you should talk to his mother," said Ethel.

"No, it's okay. He was just doing his job," I objected. Then, seeing them staring at me in surprise, my eyes widened and I shook my head. "I didn't do it, of course."

At that, their responses echoed through the small brick room. "Oh, of course." "Never entered my mind." "That sheriff!"

I blinked away a sudden tear because of their support. "We—Jonas and I—went to talk to a lawyer yesterday. I guess we'll see what happens." I slumped back in my chair, not in the mood to probe them about murder suspects. What was I expecting to get from them anyway?

Seeing me deflate, Savannah said, "Well, that's a fine how-do-you-do." She paused for a moment and added, "He's a fine catch from what I hear."

The other women were quick to voice their approval of Jonas as well. This reaction seemed more genuinely positive than before. Of course, who wouldn't agree that Jonas was fine? Even so, I was amazed at how fast news traveled in this town.

They must have tacitly agreed that they'd done enough prying for now, as they moved on to other topics. The conversation swirled around me while I fretted over the hearing on Monday. I'd been free on bail all week, but things were starting to feel serious. We had lots of suspects but were no closer to knowing who had killed Duncan than when I had been arrested.

Suddenly a word broke through my self-absorption. "Wait, did you say 'boudoir?'" I asked the woman who had spoken. I was embarrassed to realize I had forgotten her name.

"Yes, dear, but you're a newlywed, you don't need that. Henrietta was thinking of hiring Duncan to take some boudoir shots of her. Now, of course . . ." Her voice trailed off.

"I don't believe in that smut." I didn't see who had spoken, but it didn't matter as the room erupted again into another debate.

Jonas had mentioned some pictures at Shear Heaven that reminded him of boudoir photos. I wasn't thrilled that he'd been looking at sexy pictures of Anita Quentin. Hard as it was to get my mind off Anita, I couldn't figure out why Duncan Fowler had been taking boudoir photos of local women. Between teaching and the odd jobs managing properties, when did he have time to take boudoir photos? It all sounded sort of slimy, but most important of all, did it have anything to do with his murder?

The argument was still raging on. It wasn't clear who was on what side, or even how many sides were in play. In fact, it wasn't clear whether they were even debating the original topic. None of this appeared to bother the ladies, or seemed particularly relevant to the discussions entangling the room. I wasn't too concerned about this coming to blows, although I kept a close eye on the knitting needles in my vicinity.

As the noise level started to drop, I glanced at my watch. I'd sat with the Juniors for almost an hour and was ready to go home to Jonas. These ladies might not like their husbands, but I liked mine. Time to suck it up and find out what they knew about our two prime suspects' Sunday activities. "I was wondering if I could ask you all a favor," I started.

"Oh, honey, anything. What all do you need?" said the lady with the forgotten name.

"Well." I paused before deciding to tackle it straight on. "Did any of you see Bianca Delgado or Anita Quentin on Sunday?"

"Pfaw. Imagine seeing Anita Quentin at a church service on Sunday morning." Savannah snorted.

The others laughed.

"I saw Bianca, honey, later in the day. She called Sunday Night

Bingo in the gym." Ethel pointed over her shoulder at the main part of the church.

"No, Ethel. We didn't have bingo last Sunday," Savannah said with certainty.

"Well bless your heart for trying to help our Ella Mae. I'm sure you meant well but it must have just slipped your mind that I won one of the games on Sunday night," said Ethel.

"Well, my goodness, if I didn't know better, I'd have thought you were calling me senile." Savannah snipped her yarn with a particularly loud click of her scissors. "I'm telling you we didn't have bingo. We had that other doohickey instead." She waved her hand impatiently in the air. "You know, the whatsis."

"What in the Sam Hill are you talking about?" asked Ethel. "We had bingo. That doohickey was two weeks ago. Don't you remember, you complained about getting all gussied up and then getting rained on."

Deciding to leave before blood was shed, I blew them all a kiss and headed for the door. The argument paused as a chorus of "Bye-bye now" and "Stop by again" rang out. As I walked home, I felt as unsure as ever about what Anita and Bianca had done on Sunday.

Or even if Sunday came after Saturday.

16

Saturday Morning

Jonas

Early in the morning, I got out with Daisy for my run. Running along the lake trail was a delight, with the ever-changing shoreline and birds swooping and diving into the lake for their breakfasts. I was glad I'd asked Anita for running trail recommendations while I was getting my hair cut. I hadn't known talking to her was illicit at the time, but clearly she was off limits. So, even though she was the only other runner I knew in the area, I couldn't ask her for additional trail suggestions.

When I returned home, Elizabeth said, "I want to go paint at Mimi's place one last time."

Daisy was slurping up the water from her dish and looking ready for her nap, but I felt energized for the day. "You know, her house will still be there after tomorrow's estate sale."

"I know, but it won't feel the same with all her stuff gone."

I nodded and said, "Thanks," as she handed me a smoothie she'd made for breakfast. "Do you mind if I don't come with you?"

"Are you sure you want to sit around Mom's place all day? It's so nice out," she said.

"It is really nice out," I agreed. It was a perfect day to be outside—sunny and warmer than earlier in the week but no sign of all the bugs that everyone around here complained about. This area reminded me of Portland but with a lot less rain. An idea clicked. "I could go ask if the mayor will rent me a kayak to go down the river."

"That sounds like a great idea," she said.

"What's great? Finally finishing up the last of the rooms today?" Mary walked into the kitchen, showered and ready for a final day of sorting and tagging.

She was remarkably chill about us playing hooky today, so we moved on to discuss what had happened last night. Our collective results—a walk with Daisy, twelve dollars in poker winnings, and uncertainty over Anita's and Bianca's possible presence at last Sunday night's bingo game—didn't amount to anything useful. Although Daisy would probably disagree that any day that included a walk could be considered useless.

Daisy had already powered down for a morning snooze, but as Elizabeth prepared to leave the house, she shot right up as soon as she recognized her exit cue. Elizabeth and Mary took Daisy to Mimi's while I changed and packed some food, water, and other things for kayaking. If I couldn't rent a kayak, I would drive up to Mimi's place and join them. I finished my coffee before I left. After all, Dale hadn't yet made any changes to his store.

I walked past the aged, yellow-painted wood entrance of Dale's Bait, Boat, and Float storefront. Tyler knelt on the floor, stretching behind something on the lower shelf. A box full of electrical supplies sat next to him. A light on a higher shelf suddenly flicked on.

"Got it," he announced, sliding back out. "Oh, hey there," he said, noticing me standing just inside the open doorway.

"Who's there, Tyler?" Dale's voice was slightly muffled from the corner.

I took a step further into the store. "Good morning, Dale." He sat hunched over on a stool behind a glass display counter. Then, catching sight of another man seated across from him, I added, "Lester," with a smile and a wave to Principal Stapleton.

"Well, good morning to you, Jonas." Dale stood to greet me.

"Jonas." Lester smiled and waved back but didn't rise, turning his attention back to a magazine open in front of them.

"Tyler, carry this to the trash bin out back, would you?" Dale pointed at several empty boxes by the register.

Tyler sighed dramatically but did as he was asked.

"What can I do for you this fine morning? Would you like to join Lester and check out the new lures I've ordered? Some great new ones just came in too." Dale's voice was hopeful and excited, as if there was nothing better to do on a beautiful Saturday than sit around examining fishing supplies.

"I'd like to rent a kayak from you. I want to kayak down the river if you're able to drop me upstream?" I asked hopefully. Otherwise I'd kayak along the shore of Lake Capitola.

"Kayak, huh?" He examined me. "It's a bit early in the season, but the river's running fine and it's warm out today. Ever been before?"

"Certainly. I've gone many times back at home. Mostly river kayaking and sometimes in the ocean."

"Ocean, huh?" Dale looked impressed. He turned to Lester. "He's a regular professional."

"I'd say aficionado, not professional," I explained.

Dale laughed. "Better not let ole Colton hear you calling yourself a fish anything with you being named Trout and all." He slapped his leg as he laughed and looked around for his audience to join in.

Lester merely gave a polite "hmm" and returned his attention to the lures. I refrained from reinforcing any jokes making fun of my name. Although I would give him credit for an original one.

Tyler returned, leaning against the side door as he took a breather.

Dale noticed. "Let's go, young man. Get back to hooking up those new display lights. You've got the rest of the store to finish.

Or would you rather start on the restocking? I'm not paying you to stand around gawking." His matter-of-fact tone wasn't as forceful as Mary's could be, but he certainly wouldn't win any father-of-the-year awards. Tyler's shoulders slumped and he clomped back over to the box of display lights.

"Well, I'll be happy to rent you a kayak today, but I'm too busy to run you up to the drop-off point." He gestured to the near-empty store, but he didn't fool me—his eyes stopped when his scan grazed past the alluring supply of new lures.

"Would it be possible for Tyler to take me?" I asked.

Tyler's head darted out from behind the shelf as he looked optimistically at his father.

"Well, I don't know." Dale scratched his head. "He's got a lot to do."

Tyler's face dropped.

I pursed my lips thoughtfully. "What about if I pay for him to guide me. Besides, don't I remember hearing that you need him to finish taking a video of the river?"

"Dad?" asked Tyler, now standing and imploring his father.

Dale chewed his lip for a moment. "Well, I reckon customers come first. Especially a paying customer."

Tyler whooped and stepped toward the door, ready to hit the road.

"Hey." Dale pointed to the ground by Tyler's feet. "Put away those boxes first. You can't just leave them out for people to trip over."

Still smiling, Tyler snatched up the box of lights and headed for the storeroom.

"Don't be too easy on him now," Dale told me. "If I've got to restock the store, then the least he can do is practice his guide monologue. That boy ain't no natural-born talker. He needs the practice."

"Probably because it's too hard to get a word in edgewise at home, what with you there and all." Lester chuckled from his corner stool.

Whistling softly, Tyler worked quickly to collect the gear, as if trying to escape before his father changed his mind.

"Don't forget to sign out," instructed Dale. "You know the rules."

Tyler grunted but walked over to the counter and signed out our two kayaks on the rental log. I almost laughed when he had to pull out his phone to check the time after he glanced at the analog clock mounted on the wall. Telling time the old-fashioned way was a dying skill.

After loading two kayaks and assorted items onto a trailer and then hitching it to Tyler's truck, we grabbed some snacks and took off.

"Thanks," he said as we drove up a winding road that roughly tracked the river. "I'd have been stuck there all day."

"Sure. It didn't look like a whole lot of fun in there. Besides, it's nicer to have some company when out on a kayak. Safer too," I said.

Tyler scoffed. "This river is plenty safe. There's maybe one class III rapid on this stretch."

"I was thinking more about Duncan Fowler." I watched him carefully, but it took him a moment before he made the connection to Duncan's body showing up in the water.

"Oh," he said finally as he glanced around with the ubiquitous awkwardness of teenage boys.

I was already leaning toward Bianca Delgado, or one of the neighbors, as Duncan's killer, but Tyler's naive reactions were enough to tip the balance for me. If I had seriously thought he was a murderer, I would never have asked him to join me on an isolated kayaking trip.

After a short drive over the ridge, past where I'd normally turn into Mimi's place, Tyler pulled into a dirt parking area next to a flat, calm part of the river. "This is where we launch for a trip of about four hours. Sound good?"

While Tyler attached his waterproof sports camera and set up the kayaks, I put on my life jacket. I didn't need a wetsuit as this wasn't glacial runoff like some of the rivers I'd kayaked out West. We launched and started gliding down the river. The air was cool, crisp, and smelled like nature. Besides the occasional sound of a car in the distance, all we heard was water, wind, and leaves. This sure beat sitting around Mimi's house watching Elizabeth paint or Mary finish sorting all of the belongings.

"So your dad said I should remind you to practice your guide talk," I said.

Tyler rolled his eyes but began, "With the Ozarks and the Ouachita National Forests nearby, Jenkins and Lake Capitola are the heart of Arkansas tourist country."

I interrupted him. "Your dad write that?"

He rolled his eyes again. "Whatcha think? Guides have to memorize the whole thing before they can take people out, and I've got to test them on it."

"He's tough on you," I observed. When Tyler nodded, I added, "I'll bet that's why you like going out on the river by yourself."

Tyler leaned forward and double-checked the camera before explaining, "Just checking that I had the adapter in so the microphone is turned off. Yeah, I like being out on the river. It lets me be gone for hours, all day if I screw around."

"That's what you were doing on Sunday, just screwing around?"

He looked at the opposite bank. "Sorta." After a few moments of silence, he said, "Look, you seem cool. Do you promise not to tell my folks?"

"Well, it depends. Did you hurt someone?"

"No. Geez," he exclaimed. "It was just a party. On the banks." He pointed forward. "I can show you where when we get there."

Relieved by his confirmation that he had not done anything to

Duncan after all, I said, “So that’s why you got home late on Sunday?” When he nodded again, I said, “You know that wouldn’t have looked good if the cops had found out. You realize there’s a murder investigation going on and that would seem suspicious.”

He blanched as he turned to me. “But I didn’t do anything.” His kayak rocked in the water until he paid attention to his balance again.

“Anyone see when you got home?” I asked.

Frowning, he demanded, “What are you, the cops?”

I held up my hands briefly to calm him. “No, I’m just trying to understand what’s going on. Elizabeth, my wife—” He nodded that he remembered her so I continued, “She didn’t do anything either. I only want to figure out what really happened that day.”

The tension eased out of Tyler’s shoulders as he paddled a few times around an eddy. Then he volunteered, “The lady across the street.”

“What?” I’d been looking at the passing landscape to give him a chance to cool off and I hadn’t heard his soft-spoken words clearly.

“She got home right after I did. She saw me in the yard. I was . . . I was chewing gum to get the smell of alcohol off my breath.”

“Mouthwash,” I suggested. “It works better than gum. Or coffee.” Switching gears, I asked, “Who saw you?”

“I don’t know her name. She lives across the street. She’s old.”

“How old?” I asked, hoping this might eliminate some of our suspects.

“I don’t know. Your age. My mom’s age. Old,” he said.

I exhaled a steadying breath as I realized he had just described an age span from thirty to sixty. I didn’t believe I was quite this blind to human developmental stages when I was in high school, but then again plenty of people have pointed out I was not a typical high schooler as my interest in science and preference for following detailed routines made me stand out. And in high school, that was rarely a positive experience.

We fell into silence as we paddled down the mild river, avoiding the few rocks that protruded out of the water. As we curved around a bend, an open flat terrace full of flowers with a roof jutting up behind it came into view. The house must have belonged to Robert Jones, because the double-chimneyed outline of Mimi's house was clearly visible a little farther along the ridge above us. That meant we would soon pass Brent Hollands's land too. My geography was confirmed as the smell of pigs and cattle became noticeable.

"Pretty," I observed, pointing at the spread of trees running up the ridge to Mimi's place.

"Yeah." Tyler glanced up. "Dad's got big plans for that place."

Startled mid-stroke, my kayak swayed a bit as I stopped paddling. "He what?"

"Yeah, like he's always talking about turning it into some boutique hotel."

I pointed at Robert Jones's house. "That place? With the level ground and flowers?"

"Nah. The other one up there with the two chimneys. I think it's empty now."

I stared up at the ridge, silent.

"Hey, watch out for that rock," Tyler called.

Quickly, I looked down and did a hard pull on one side to sweep around the obstacle. "Are you sure he was talking about it becoming a hotel?" I asked.

"Yeah. Over the last few weeks, he's been yakking on the phone with some hotel people about building one next to the winery. He thinks he's good at secret plots, but he talks so loudly on the phone that everyone in the house can hear him."

Now the waters were getting truly muddied. Could the mayor have killed Duncan? How would that help Dale build a hotel on the land that had been left to Elizabeth? I had to tell her and Mary.

And what winery?

17

Saturday Afternoon

Jonas

Although I wanted to discuss what I'd learned with Elizabeth, Tyler and I still had another few hours on the river before we reached the end at the lake. Paddling faster wasn't going to make a big difference, but the time might give me a chance to puzzle out how the mayor might be connected to Duncan's death. In case Tyler spilled the beans to his father and lost us the advantage of surprise, I didn't want to ask him any more questions about his father or the winery.

As we wound around another bend in the river, the land became more wild and undeveloped, with no houses, chicken coops, or ranches in sight. After a few minutes, a deserted campsite appeared on the town side of the river. Clear signs of a recent party were evident—blackened logs from a fire, trampled grass, and bottles and empty bags of chips scattered everywhere.

I maneuvered my kayak close to the campsite at the water's edge. Tyler followed reluctantly, looking so embarrassed that I suspected this was the location of the river party he'd mentioned. Leaving all the litter behind annoyed me, but I tried to keep my tone nonjudgmental so he'd answer a very important question. "Is this where you were on Sunday instead of doing the videotaping for your father?"

"Yeah. I stopped the camera when I heard the people up ahead. I'll need to start the recording from here for my dad." He leaned forward to fiddle with the camera.

Relieved that he likely didn't kill Duncan if he had been at a party with a large group, I said, "Why don't you hold off on that for a bit." Then I paddled hard to beach myself before climbing out of my kayak.

"What are you doing?" Tyler sounded confused. When I jerked my thumb at the mess, he recoiled. "That's not mine." At my raised eyebrow, he whined, "There were a lot of others here."

"Come on. Cleaning up a little won't hurt us. We'll be back on the water in a jiffy." I bent over and pulled two garbage bags out of the pack behind my kayak's seat.

"What are you, a Boy Scout?" Tyler grumbled, but beached his kayak and stepped out too.

"It's just part of my hiking kit," I said, starting to pick up the glass bottles and aluminum cans. "I don't like messes, especially in nature."

There was some age-appropriate grousing and mumbling that I chose to ignore since Tyler started grabbing the plastic chip bags and candy wrappers and throwing them into a trash bag. He was a good kid, and it was unfair that he, of all the kids at the party, was the only one having to deal with the mess.

It took only five minutes of effort to collect most of the mess they'd left behind. I tied the sack of bottles to the back of my kayak so I could pull it down the river with me while Tyler rotated his kayak to face outward before turning on the camera to capture the rest of the trip.

The river and mountain scenery were equally beautiful now to the earlier portion of our trip. Recognizing the landscape as we got close to the end from my earlier run, I wondered what the full-day trip would be like. I was sure I could convince Elizabeth to try that before leaving town.

It was mid-afternoon when we stopped our kayaks alongside the small pier next to the Bait, Boat, and Float store. We were lifting everything out of the water as Dale and his friend Blake from the grocery store wandered outside. Dale might not make a lot of money during off-season, but at least his friends seemed to drop by to keep him company.

"Have fun?" Dale eyed my garbage bag full of clinking glass bottles suspiciously.

"It was an awesome trip," I answered.

Before I could figure out how to ask him about his hotel plans without implicating Tyler, he said, "Tyler, Hanson will close up shop today. He's almost finished with the restocking, so you lucked out." To me, he asked, "Do you mind driving Tyler up to the drop-off spot to get his truck? I've got something important to attend to."

He didn't even wait for my "Sure" before waving and heading to the parking lot.

Blake saw me holding the bag of bottles. "The recycling dumpster is on the other side. Best to walk around there."

I took the bag where he had pointed. When I returned, Blake had left also. Tyler signed the kayaks back in on the log and yelled, "Bye, Hanson," to some unseen person in the back room.

The voice responded, "See ya, Tyler."

We rode to the drop-off point in companionable silence. Before driving away, I handed Tyler a twenty-dollar bill.

"What's this for?" he asked, already half out of the car.

"I always tip the guide, especially the ones who don't spend the whole trip droning on from a canned script," I said with a wink. "I also show appreciation for those who respect the environment by packing out whatever they packed in."

He brightened. "Cool. Thanks." He took the bill and slid out. "See ya."

*****

Mimi's place was on the way back to town, so I stopped to see if the women were still there. Sebastian was just walking out to his car, his red bow tie undone and his face damp from the hard work in a warm, old house without air conditioning.

"All finished?" I asked.

"Finally. The crew will be here early to set up tables and chairs and take all the tagged items outside for the auction. Pray for no rain or it's going to be awfully crowded in there." He placed his jacket in the back seat and got into his car.

I watched him leave, then bounded up the porch steps. Daisy greeted me as I opened the door, looking rested from our morning run and ready for her next walk. I knelt to pet her, but she'd have to wait because I was tired now. I stepped back onto the porch as Elizabeth and Mary walked out the door as well, looking ready to depart.

"You'll never believe what I just learned," I told them, thumping Daisy on the side.

"What?" asked Elizabeth as she hooked Daisy up to her leash.

Mary's phone rang. "Hold on, I've got to get this." She walked around the corner of the porch as she answered it.

"Tell me already. You can't just stand there and wait," Elizabeth complained.

"But she said . . ." I glanced toward the side of the house where Mary had disappeared. Seeing Elizabeth about to burst from impatience, I changed course. I have very clear loyalties. "Tyler told me his father wants to turn this place into a hotel."

"What? A hotel? Here? But this land belongs to me now. He hasn't said anything to me about buying it." Elizabeth's forehead wrinkled in confusion.

"Unless that's why Robert Jones was so insistent on buying your place. He's setting up a large winery," I said, having had the advantage of more time to think everything over.

Mary stormed back around the corner. "Unbelievable!" she shouted, bouncing on her toes. Noticing our dumbfounded expressions, she added, "That no-account scoundrel!" She flung her keys onto the porch, and Daisy slunk behind my legs as she tried to make herself scarce.

"W.A.H.O.O. may be slower than your fancy internet, but it's reliable. Dale Cooper, our beloved mayor, the Honorable—my ass—"

Mary had to be furious. I'd never heard her swear. Elizabeth told me she reserved cussing for the devil and drunk drivers.

Mary continued, "—approved plans for a winery next door and, you won't believe this one, to re-zone this property for commercial use. This is our land." She slapped the front door, rattling it in its frame.

"Mom, Jonas just—" Elizabeth started to speak.

Mary interrupted her. "What business in their right mind would set up shop way up here anyway, where there's no traffic?" She started to pace. "Oh, this just makes me so mad, I could spit."

"A hotel," I said.

"What hotel?" she demanded, glaring at me as if it were my fault.

"Tyler, the mayor's son—"

She gruffly interrupted, "I know who he is. I live here, remember?"

I ignored her outburst. Elizabeth got emotional sometimes too, and I'd learned the best way to avoid escalation and stay on topic was to remain calm myself. I tended to be calm anyway, so this wasn't terribly difficult for me. "He told me his dad has been planning with some people to build a hotel on this land."

"Well, if thinks he can do that, he's got another thing coming. This is our land." Mary positively growled. This wasn't the best time to point out that it was actually Elizabeth's land per Mimi's will.

"They'd tear up all those beautiful old trees to build a parking lot?" Elizabeth pointed at the old oak and hickory trees shading the house, her voice heavy with sadness.

"I'm gonna give that sorry excuse for a man a piece of my mind." Mary bent over to pick up her keys.

"Wait, Mom. You can't go over there," said Elizabeth.

"Why not? It's time someone stands up to that low-down snake and tells him what's what."

"If he killed Duncan, he's dangerous. It's not safe for you to run over there," said Elizabeth.

Mary furrowed her brows. "Why would he kill Duncan? It's not his land."

Elizabeth paused. Her mother had a good point. "Maybe Robert Jones killed Duncan. Maybe he'll co-own the hotel. That would explain why he was so eager to buy the house."

"But what did Duncan have to do with it?" asked Mary.

Elizabeth snapped her fingers. "Maybe he stumbled across their plans and threatened to reveal them?"

Mary snorted. "If Duncan winds up the hero, that will really shake up some folks in this town."

I finally spoke. "When he came over, Robert said he was out on a boat until late on Sunday evening with the mayor, right?" At their scowling nods, I continued, "I know how to check out if that story is accurate."

I explained the log that they kept of all boats taken out from their shop. Tyler had explained to me that it was a safety regulation the state required. "Dale and Tyler aren't at their store now and the clerk who's closing up never saw me. I'll just peek at the trip log for last Sunday and see whether they had a boat out in the evening."

"I'm coming with you," said Elizabeth.

I shook my head. "Too many people in this town know who you are. Would someone named Hanson recognize you?"

"Yes." She blew out a frustrated breath. "But please be careful."

Understanding her anxiety, I gently rubbed her shoulders, "I'm not going to confront a killer, just look at a log."

She still made me promise to call her as soon as I left the shop.

"And keep your eyes open for Lucy while you're driving down the road," instructed Mary. "She's never missing this long. Mimi would strike me down from heaven if I let that cat starve to death."

I made it to Bait, Boat, and Float only fifteen minutes before closing.

"We're closing in just a couple minutes," said a rail-thin man with a large gap in his tobacco-stained front teeth. He sat behind the counter holding his phone as he jabbed at it with his thumbs, undoubtedly playing some game. His voice sounded like the clerk from earlier, so this must be Hanson.

"No problem. Can I reserve a boat for tomorrow afternoon?" I asked.

"We're not busy so there's no need to reserve it. Just come in when you want it," he said as he checked his watch.

"My wife gets anxious easily. Would you mind if we make the reservation anyway?"

He leaned over and pulled the boat log closer. Flipping it around, he pointed at the last box on the page. "Fill out the info and we'll have it ready for you. You should know since it's not yet summer that we need all the boats back by five."

I nodded, realizing that we'd have to cancel the trip tomorrow because we'd likely be too tired after the estate sale ended in the afternoon. I really did like the idea of getting back on the water, so perhaps Elizabeth and I could go next week before any legal proceedings started.

The log sheet started with Monday, so I had to find a way to flip back a page without Hanson noticing. I glanced around quickly, searching for inspiration. A small display refrigerator hummed a few steps away from where Hanson sat.

"I'd like to buy a bottle of water too," I told him.

Hanson grunted, looking up at the clock to see if it had struck five o'clock and he could refuse, then slowly slid off his stool and plodded over for the water. As soon as he turned his back, I quickly flipped the page back and looked at the box with last Sunday's date. A boat had been checked out to Dale at one o'clock, but he had returned it at four-thirty.

Surprised, I leaned back. Robert Jones had been lying. Why? He and Dale were back from the lake well before dark—and well before Duncan Fowler had been murdered. Had he killed Duncan or was he covering for the mayor?

Hanson set my bottle of water on the counter and glanced at the page where I hadn't written anything. "Oh, looky that, we almost had you down for last weekend. Can't hardly take a trip in the past without a time machine, now can we?" Chuckling at his own humor, he flipped the page back to the present.

Still in a fog, I wrote my name down to rent a small motorboat for tomorrow for three people at three o'clock and paid for my water.

I sat in the car and took a long swig of cool water, then called Elizabeth to update her. Neither of us had a good guess as to why Robert had lied to us. For such a small town, there sure were a lot of secrets hidden here.

It seemed as if everyone I'd met in Jenkins had one.

18

Saturday Early Evening

Elizabeth

Not long after Jonas left Mimi's house, Sebastian called Mom. He wanted to return to do one last pass through the house before his crew showed up tomorrow morning for the estate sale. We had only made it out to Mom's car, so we turned around, unlocked the front door, and walked back inside. Daisy was all too happy to lie down for another nap, clearly forgetting she hadn't had her walk. I texted Jonas to meet us back here when he accomplished his spy mission.

I was standing in Mimi's living room, looking around and reminiscing, when Jonas hurried inside. Without even greeting me, he said, "Robert was lying. They did have a boat out on the lake last Sunday, but they brought it back in before five."

"Ha! I told you it was one of the neighbors." Mom came down the steps from the second floor, stabbing her finger in our direction to emphasize her point. Sebastian had followed her, but was a few steps higher on the staircase. I could only see as high as the red pocket square in the ridiculous suit he insisted on wearing.

"Just because they got back before dark doesn't prove Robert or the mayor was the killer," I said.

Mom reached the ground floor. "Why else would Robert lie? I

knew I didn't like that man." When I didn't respond, she added, "Told you," with a jab of her finger. Then she swiveled and said, "Come on, Sebastian." Daisy must have thought her hurrying upstairs was part of a new game and raced up after her. I heard Mom trying to settle the dog down again so she wouldn't get in their way, reminding me of when Pawpaw and I would be banging around upstairs with some made-up game and Mimi would yell at us from the kitchen not to break anything.

The house felt stuffy as I began missing them again. I rushed past Jonas to the front porch, which was crowded with last-minute pictures that Mom wanted to pack into the car. I had no idea where she'd put all the stuff she'd grabbed from Mimi's house.

"We can keep more of your grandmother's furniture if you want," offered Jonas as he joined me outside. He must have seen me staring into the house through the large front windows and thought I was looking at the furniture.

"Nah. I don't really want it, it's just that I'm going to miss all the good memories here. In the house, in the yard. All over the whole property. Sometimes I think maybe I shouldn't sell it, but that doesn't make any sense." I blinked back tears. "Come on," I said, stepping inside.

He followed me through the house and out the squeaking back door, then sat down beside me on the swing on the back porch.

"We used to play cards out here and watch the sun go down," I said.

"It is pretty." He put his arm around me. "It was nice out on the river today. Maybe we can go out on a boat on the lake this week?"

I snuggled in. "That sounds nice." We swung slowly, watching the sun drop lower over the lake.

The mood was broken when my phone rang. It was Kelsey, so I answered.

"Can you still come over?" she asked.

"Now?" I asked. I'd forgotten we'd made plans for today during yesterday's lunch.

"Yes. Just for a little while. I found some stuff that I think you'd want to see."

"At your place? I don't even know where you live now."

"No, I'm at Aunt Eliza's. My mom and stepdad live here now. But you inspired me with your rapid-fire sorting of all your grandmother's stuff. Mom just put things in boxes and shoved them into the attic."

"I don't know, Kelsey." I hesitated. "Jonas and I are hanging out—"

"Please," she insisted. "You see him all the time and you're never in Jenkins."

I laughed, picturing her pouting.

Jonas nudged me. "It's fine. Go on over. I'm tired and sore from the river anyway."

I kissed him on the cheek and may have wiggled a little. Kelsey was right that I never saw her. "Okay, I'm in," I told her.

She squealed happily. "I'll have a pizza delivered."

"She's ordering a pizza for us. Do you want to stop and get something for yourself?" I asked Jonas.

"Nah, there's enough leftover fixings at your mother's place for a Buddha bowl."

We stayed a few more minutes enjoying our alone time on the porch and the romantic atmosphere of the sunset, then we walked hand-in-hand around the house to the front. Before we left, I poked my head inside the front door and hollered up to Mom, "We're leaving. See you back at your place later." I didn't wait for her permission, not that I often did when I was in high school either. Hurrying out to the car, I jumped in, eager to beat the pizza to Kelsey's place so it would still be hot.

Less than thirty minutes later, Kelsey and I were sitting on the floor of a spare bedroom in her Aunt Eliza's house, surrounded by ancient artifacts from our childhood while we inhaled the best pizza in the county. Drawings, photos, and random art projects were scattered on the floor.

"Oh my gosh, I can't believe she saved these," I said as I pulled out an assortment of friendship bracelets woven together with different patterns.

After admiring a few, Kelsey slipped one on her wrist while I found its match and did the same. She pulled out a sheaf of papers from another box and started going through them.

"Didn't Aunt Eliza die last year? How come you haven't gone through these before?" I took another slice of pizza.

"I did, sorta, right after my folks moved in here. But it made me sad and Mom wasn't in the mood to go through any of her things. You know how she was about her aunt." She held up a photo for inspection. "Remember this? Didn't your grandparents used to have that painting hanging on the wall too?"

I grabbed the photo. It was the same one I showed Jonas the other day of Pawpaw and Amos, his close friend and Aunt Eliza's husband. "Mimi still had this photo in her living room. I looked for the painting but couldn't find it." I studied the painting between the men with its thick bold strokes of vivid greens, blues, and browns. "Pawpaw was a good painter."

Kelsey was flipping through more of the old photos. "Do you remember when your Pawpaw showed us how to take pictures with that old camera of his? He used to brag that it took the best pictures ever."

"Oh yeah," I exclaimed. "I haven't thought about that in years. We didn't use that camera much, did we?"

"That's because we weren't very patient in the darkroom." She giggled. "I remember we were in there once and Mimi called us for lunch. You burst out of there and ruined a whole roll of film that your Pawpaw was developing."

"Oh yeah," I said again, covering my mouth as the memory

came flooding back. "I guess I always did like lunch. And Mimi had made her banana pudding for dessert that day." We both had a moment of reverential silence for Mimi's banana pudding. "I think that's the only reason Pawpaw didn't send me out to sleep with the chickens that night." I was just joking; Pawpaw was an old softie. I didn't know how my mother came from those two. Maybe I should check for adoption records.

We were laughing, but something about the discussion tickled my memory. I held onto the photo of the two men as I looked off into space.

"Look at these," Kelsey said, holding up some watercolor paintings we had completed long ago. She giggled and cocked her head to contemplate the two paintings like an art critic. "Uh, guess which one was yours and which was mine?" She showed me two paintings that resembled each other only because they both used paint.

I squirmed a little, not wanting to make her feel bad. "Okay, so maybe my grandfather's artist genes gave me a little edge." Then I laughed as she fluttered the two paintings next to each other—one looking like an actual painting of a backyard landscape and the other not like much of anything. "Yours were . . ." I fumbled for a polite description. ". . . more unconstrained."

Kelsey dropped them in my lap and shook her head. "Mine were crap and you know it. If it bothered me that you were a better artist, we would never have been friends." She flipped her hair and kept digging.

The missing connection finally clicked into place for me. "You'd call a digital camera electronics, wouldn't you?" I mused, scratching my chin.

"Huh?"

"If you were searching somewhere and found a digital camera, you wouldn't tell me you hadn't found any electronics, right?"

Kelsey looked up. "What are you talking about?"

"Trent told me they didn't find anything electronic at Duncan's house, not even a TV."

"Trent, huh?" Kelsey smirked. "I thought you were a happy newlywed."

"Stop. He told me on Monday when he arrested me," I protested.

"Uh-huh." She batted her eyelashes in an exaggerated fashion. Before I could object again, she added, "Yeah, that is weird, though. Who doesn't have a TV?"

"Right?"

"Why are you bringing this up now, though?" She set down the papers she'd been holding.

"Because it might be important. I've got to ask Trent something," I said, and put aside the remaining crust from my slice.

"You know, for a married woman, you seem to find a lot of excuses to keep contacting your ex-boyfriend," she chided me, one hand on her hip and the other waggling a finger in my face, a pose I imagined she used with her students regularly.

"Hush," I told her, and pulled out my phone to dial the cell number Trent had given me.

"You know his cell number?" For all her teasing, Kelsey seemed genuinely surprised.

"Shh," I hissed as Trent answered my call. "Hi, Trent." I hesitated briefly, wondering if Kelsey was right and I was doing this just to talk to him. Then I shook away my doubts. "It's Elizabeth. Did you find any camera or darkroom when you searched Duncan's place?"

Trent cleared his throat. "You know I can't talk about the case, Lizzy."

"Elizabeth," I insisted, glaring at Kelsey. Then I decided to lie to him—not for the first time in my life. "It's not for the case. I'm looking for my grandfather's old camera and some missing pictures. Duncan was in their house plenty of times. I'm wondering if he took it."

Trent pondered whether to answer me for a long moment. "No.

No camera or darkroom. But please don't tell Sheriff Tucker that I told you." His confident officer's tone turned hurried and heartfelt.

Realizing that he must have really felt anxious about his new boss, I kept my response serious and matched his earnestness. "Thanks, Trent. I won't, I promise." Then I hung up.

"You know his cell number?" Kelsey repeated.

"He gave me a business card when he arrested me, told me he didn't think I did it, and said to call him if I learned anything important," I explained.

"I don't understand. What did you learn?" asked Kelsey.

I stood up, energized now. "Didn't you tell me that Duncan stored art supplies in an unused classroom at school?"

"Occasionally, yes. So?" Her forehead wrinkled in confusion.

"Duncan took boudoir photos of women around town—"

"Shut the front door," Kelsey interrupted, her mouth falling open as she swatted at the air. "Are you serious?"

"As serious as a heart attack," I agreed, pacing now. "But Trent just told me they didn't find a camera or darkroom at his house. I wonder if it's at the school."

Kelsey chewed her lower lip. "So?"

"So," I echoed. "I think those photos might have had something to do with why he was killed." This felt like a significant clue, perhaps because we hadn't figured out how the hotel project might have led to Duncan's death.

At this point, I didn't want to share my theory that Anita Quentin had killed Duncan. Kelsey was better off not knowing in advance what I was considering doing next.

"School's closed now," said Kelsey, reading my mind.

"I know. Don't worry," I said, striding to the door. "I've got to run. Thanks for inviting me over. This was super fun. Let's do it again before I leave, and I promise to stay longer." I opened the door and ran down the stairs before she could wheedle my secret plans out of me. "See ya, Kelsey," I hollered over my shoulder.

*****

I burst into Mom's house. "Jonas! I think I know where Duncan's boudoir photos are. Come on."

It was just as well I hadn't figured out Duncan's hiding place until now. Stapleton had told us he would be busy with some activity at the school every other evening this week. Tonight was a perfect opportunity for what I had in mind. It was dark, but not so late that it would be hard to explain why Jonas and I were out walking.

"Where's Daisy?" I asked when Jonas appeared by the front door. Usually just thinking about a walk caused her to appear.

"She's still with your mother at Mimi's. Where are we going?" he asked as I handed him his jacket and ushered him out the door.

"To the high school. If I'm right, I know where Duncan kept a darkroom. I'll bet his camera is there and hopefully we'll find evidence for why Anita killed him." At Jonas's frown, I added, "Or Bianca, I suppose." If the killer was the mayor or Robert Jones or Brent Hollands or some other random person, this likely wouldn't help at all.

"But it's eight o'clock at night. Will the school still be open?"

"I have my ways." I grabbed his hand. "Come on."

We walked the few blocks from Mom's house to the high school. I understood why she preferred to live in town, with almost everything within walking distance, but to me, the beauty of Mimi's land and views far outweighed the inconvenience of driving a little bit.

When we reached the high school, the place looked deserted. A spotlight illuminated the front of the building, but that was easily avoided. Tugging on Jonas's arm, I led him to the dark parking lot in back.

"Elizabeth?" His voice sounded troubled.

"Don't worry. I'm not going to break anything. We'll be in and out in a jiffy, you'll see." I spoke in a lighthearted tone, as if I had no cares in the world, but in truth, it had been a long time since I'd done this and my nerves were jangling. We'd take just a quick look, and if we found anything, I'd call Trent so he could discover the evidence legally—and, of course, based purely on my brilliant deductions.

We approached the school building and a small loading dock hidden behind a brick wall that jutted out. If I hadn't known better, it would have looked like part of the school.

"Do you have a plan in mind?" Jonas asked.

"Yes. Wait and be amazed." At least I hoped so. Things might have changed in the last ten years.

The rollup garage door took up most of the loading dock's width. A heavy padlock secured the closed door to a metal rail drilled into the brick wall. I walked right past that and stopped by the small industrial green door to the side. I knelt and lifted the dusty rubber floor mat, relieved to see a key lying underneath it.

I managed to restrain my whoop of joy as I snatched it and popped up. After all, I didn't want Jonas to think my plan was based on the hope that the drama club presidents still left a spare key under the mat so they could sneak into the theater for late-night practice. And the occasional party.

The key worked. I walked into the high school, holding my breath until my quick scan failed to reveal the blinking light of an alarm. Relieved that things hadn't changed, I used my phone light to get us through the crowded backstage side hallway without tripping on the boxes of costumes and props. I turned it off when we reached the door leading to the school's main hallway. It was dark, but the glow from the emergency exit signs, computers, and fire alarms was enough for us to avoid hitting the walls.

"No lights?" asked Jonas. I was impressed by his cool demeanor.

I didn't know if he was anxious or not, but he had committed to be with me and would trust my plan. Or at least trust that he could get us out of whatever mess I got us into. I loved that man.

"No," I agreed, "we don't want to be seen from the street."

Jonas kept hold of my hand as he followed me around the winding corridors.

"For someone who hasn't been back here in years, you know your way around in the dark surprisingly well," he said as I pulled him around a darkened split in the hallway.

"Um, I may not have mentioned that I've been inside at night before."

"More than once, it appears," he said dryly as I stopped in front of the door to the unused room Kelsey had mentioned.

"More than once, yes," I confirmed, then grimaced as the door wouldn't open. The doors used to be left unlocked at night for the janitor. Maybe they didn't clean abandoned rooms so no one ever unlocked this one?

"By yourself?" he asked.

"Shh," I said, trying to think of an excuse to distract him from this train of thought. "We need to focus. Keep your ears open to make sure no one catches us."

I felt Jonas whip around. "I thought we were alone," he said. "How many other people would be here in the dark? Does the janitor work on Saturday night? Do you know any other nefarious nighttime alums?"

Now I looked around. He had made me nervous too. "I don't think so, but that's why we should be quiet and keep our ears open." I hadn't thought about a janitor. When we used to do this, I never worried much about getting caught. Mostly we stayed in the theater area, and that was only cleaned after performances.

But a locked door wasn't going to stop me. I reached up and removed one of my hairpins conveniently available for this purpose.

As I fiddled with the lock, Jonas asked, "You can pick a lock?" Glad that we were in the dark so he couldn't see my blush, I mumbled, "Yes. I've done it before."

"More than once, it appears," he said wryly when the door clicked open.

I pumped my arm exuberantly and hoped he wouldn't press the point. We had better find something incriminating inside, because it felt like my reputation with Jonas was dropping before my eyes.

Jonas merely said, "Hmm," as we entered the classroom.

In the moonlight coming through the windows, it certainly appeared abandoned, with bare walls, empty bookcases, and an unoccupied teacher's desk. Student desks and chairs were shoved together into random clumps around the room. I could faintly make out doors on the side walls. I walked over to one and tried it, but it merely opened into another occupied classroom.

Jonas, who had gone the other direction, hissed for my attention when a door he tried opened into pitch-black darkness.

After closing the connecting door, I crossed the room, carefully avoiding smacking into any of the desks, and stood by his side. Risking my phone's flashlight again, I angled it inside the pitch-black space. It looked like a large, windowless storage closet.

We stepped inside, and I pulled the door mostly closed behind us so we could use our flashlights. After a moment of scanning the walls, Jonas snapped a light switch, and a dull red glow brightened the room enough for us to see what was inside.

Forgetting my vow to avoid my mother's habits, I clapped twice in delight. "It's a darkroom." Echoing another of Mom's habits, I said, "I was right."

19

Saturday Evening

Elizabeth

On the right side of the small room, shelves held jugs of chemicals and tons of plastic containers full of various arts and crafts supplies. On the left, a long wood tabletop ran the length of the room. I gasped as I saw dozens of photos taped to the wall or hanging from clothespins attached to string lines running back and forth above us. A camera rested on the table with its back open, and rolls of film littered the table.

Jonas had already begun examining the hanging photos reflected in the red light of the darkroom as I picked up a small stack from the table. An older woman who looked vaguely familiar, wearing a lacy, low-cut chemise, gazed back at the lens with a sultry smile. I flipped through several pictures, but they all captured the same woman from different angles.

"See anyone you recognize?" I asked, grabbing another stack.

"No," he replied as he shifted to another line.

The woman in my next stack certainly seemed proud of her assets as she maneuvered around in the photos to make sure everything was captured on film. "I don't know if I could do this—posing in lingerie in front of a strange man." When he didn't respond, I looked at him. "You wouldn't like that, would you?"

Jonas didn't answer, keeping his head angled to look at the photos. Finally he responded, "I don't need photos, I've got you."

Good answer. But before I could respond, he added, "These are more risqué."

I stepped to him and gulped at what I saw. "Yeah, no. Definitely wouldn't do that." I pushed him away from the nudie pictures while I tried to pick my jaw up off the ground. Any thoughts of doing a boudoir photoshoot were immediately scrubbed from my mind.

"Wait!" He pulled one of the photos off its clothespin. "I think this is Anita Quentin." His eyes flicked up to the photos hanging nearby. "All of these." He started pulling down more photos.

I grabbed one and took a look. He was right. Anita was dressed—or undressed might have been more accurate—in an extremely revealing garment and leaning against a chair. I didn't recognize the empty, all-white background unless the Quentins had completely redone their house—and Anita had radically overhauled her decorating style—since the last time I saw it. Not that I'd been inside their place often, but her style had more resembled the living rooms overcrowded with quilts, needlework projects, and too-cutesy trinkets found on the covers of the cozy mystery novels most of the women around here enjoyed.

These photos had been taken in a much more sterile environment. I didn't know any photo studios in the area and couldn't imagine Duncan had rented one far away. Was this his home?

Finally noticing how quiet the darkroom had become, I glanced over. Jonas was intently examining one of Anita's mostly naked photos. "Don't be gross," I said, and snatched it away from him.

He started to say something but then his head spun to the door. "What was that?"

My breath caught as I held still, straining to listen for whatever he had heard. It was silent except for the sound of my heartbeat echoing in my ears.

Then I heard something too. A rattle, as if someone had let one of the heavy classroom doors close too hard, echoed in the empty hallway.

I moved to the darkroom door and looked out the open gap. Our abandoned classroom was still dark, but I saw a light flash across the hallway in another classroom.

"Someone's there," I whispered in an urgent tone.

Jonas flipped off the light in the darkroom, plunging us into complete darkness.

I squinted, trying to see better, and eased the darkroom door open wider so I could edge closer. "I don't think it's a janitor. I just saw a ski mask and dark clothes in the moonlight and a janitor would turn on the lights," I reported.

"That wouldn't be the police," he said.

"The killer." I could barely get the word out as a chill ran down my back.

The intruder appeared to be rummaging around by the teacher's desk in Duncan's classroom across the hall. That was where Jonas had found the note questioning whether I might be a problem. Did the note contain DNA that the intruder was trying to eliminate? But Jonas had stolen it and both of us had touched it, probably ruining any evidence for the police.

A very quiet click startled me before I realized Jonas had closed the darkroom door behind us. "Let's get out of here," he whispered in my ear.

I agreed. We couldn't hide in the darkroom. What if the killer was looking for it too? Then we'd be in trouble. We needed to call the sheriffs. Capturing violent killers was their job, not ours.

We tiptoed to the door of our abandoned classroom, trying not to be seen from across the hallway, and slid out as quietly as we could. The moon must have gone behind a cloud as it was even darker than before. Very slowly, Jonas let the classroom door close behind us.

The light from the other classroom flickered into the hallway. I froze, plastered against Jonas and the door.

Mercifully, the light shifted away from us, so I tugged on Jonas's arm and we crept back up the hallway to the theater, sneaking peeks over our shoulders as often as we could to make sure we hadn't been noticed.

I heard a long, loud scraping noise right next to me, followed by Jonas's soft "Ouch" as he ran into a chair lurking in the dark hallway.

I twirled to check if we'd been discovered.

The intruder in Duncan's classroom flashed the light in our direction through the glass door before opening it. Its squeak sounded extra loud in the empty school.

The intruder was onto us.

And heading our way!

Without thinking, I let out a mighty roar and pounded on the metal locker beside me.

The resulting boom both frightened and emboldened me. "Aargh!" I screamed, and started running toward the intruder.

The light flashed past me briefly before the intruder slammed the door shut again.

I reached the door and, in my adrenaline rush, foolishly yanked it open.

I stepped inside before realizing this put me in the same room as the killer. Slamming on the brakes, I tried to back up, but Jonas nearly knocked me over as he ran into me.

The intruder must have been freaked out too and burst through the connecting door from Duncan's classroom into the next classroom before slamming it behind them. I leapt forward, determined to stop them before they got away. If we caught the real killer, all my troubles would be over.

I ran the handful of steps to the connecting door, hearing Jonas's footsteps pounding right behind me.

Flinging open the connecting door, I took two strides before tripping over an overturned desk. "I'm fine. I'm fine. Go," I called to Jonas, who had slowed to check on me.

He skipped around me in pursuit as I scrambled back to my feet and followed a bit more gingerly.

Jonas opened the next connecting door that had just been banged shut.

"Ooh," came a loud, pained grunt from the intruder, who must have run into an obstacle at full speed.

Jonas stretched forward but the intruder bounced off a wall, barely eluding his grasp. Jonas stumbled to a halt to avoid smacking into an errant desk.

This time I sidestepped him, but a textbook slammed into my stomach. I gasped from the pain of the thrown book and fell to the ground. Why are textbooks always so heavy?

Three or four more textbooks came flying through the darkened room, fortunately missing me as they banged into cabinets behind me. One of the books must have hit a shelf, as more things splattered on the ground and something glass shattered on impact.

I heard one of the heavier classroom doors open and saw the reflection of the moonlight in its glass window before the intruder, obviously affected by smacking into the wall, stumbled out of it.

Jonas managed to extricate himself from the fallen objects first and then helped me up. "Hurry," I panted. He was the runner. If one of us was going to catch that intruder, it would be Jonas.

I exited the classroom in time to see Jonas hurry down the hall to the left in pursuit of the intruder.

At the Y junction, the intruder darted to the right, heading to the front door, clearly familiar with the school's bizarre layout.

Jonas's pursuit had slowed to a hobble as he lost ground. He must have slammed his knee into something earlier.

I caught up to him outside the school's main office as the intruder crashed the metal panic bar in the middle of the glass front door to make it open quickly.

A siren wailed as soon as the door opened, but it was too late—the intruder was gone, running down the driveway and soon out of sight around a corner.

We stood panting right outside the door.

Well, I was panting. Jonas was rubbing his shin.

"Ow, that really stings," he said.

I touched his arm sympathetically but then panicked again when I heard police sirens approaching. "We better get out of here."

"It's too late," Jonas said.

"No, it's okay, let's run. I'll help you." I pulled him up. "If we hurry, we can make it into the neighborhood before they arrive."

He pointed behind me and I spun. Had I missed another intruder?

But it was only the flashing red light of a camera above the doors. The camera must have captured my stunned expression clearly in the brightness from the spotlight. "When did they put in video surveillance?"

Jonas kept rubbing his shin. "Probably after certain students kept breaking in at night for reasons unknown." He stood up and winced a little as he put his full weight on the leg. "What are we going to tell the cops?"

My ever-practical husband had a point, but I was stumped. Then, the approaching sheriff's sirens motivated me to get inventive. "I have an idea," I said, relieved that returning to the scene of so many past crimes had sparked my creativity. "Let's tell them we were out for a walk when we saw someone dressed suspiciously sneaking around back and then breaking into the school. We followed the intruder inside to stop them but didn't catch them."

Jonas nodded and then looked straight at me. "When I ran into that chair, your scream half-scared me to death." His forehead creased in concern. "And then you just charged forward. Was that the best idea? I mean, that was probably the murderer."

I shrugged. "Maybe not. But I just knew you would come with me and the two of us could overpower one person."

"True, but what if they pulled a gun?" he asked.

I gulped. "I guess I didn't think about that." I shivered a bit, and he hobbled over and hugged me. Glancing back at the school's entrance, I asked, "And when did they wire up the panic bar to an actual alarm?"

"The what?" Jonas asked. "What's a panic bar?"

I pointed to the metal touch bar fastened across the middle of the glass door. "I learned what these parts were called when I had to pay to install new doors back in the day."

"Why would you have to pay?"

"Apparently something about breaking the school's glass doors makes Stapleton get all prissy about one needing to take responsibility for one's actions. Took me all freaking summer to pay for the doors. Did you know that panic bars cost like two hundred bucks each?" I still felt outraged at the scam of it all. "Mom wouldn't help me."

"Hmm," he said, wisely noncommittal in his response.

Two sheriffs' cars roared up, one blocking the driveway to prevent our escape.

"Don't move," yelled Sheriff Tucker as he slid out of his car and held his gun on us from behind the driver's door.

Trent jumped out of the other car, his gun also at the ready.

It seemed like an entirely unnecessary command since we had been standing in the same spot for several minutes waiting for their arrival, but I certainly had no reason to believe the sheriff was the smartest law enforcement official around.

"What are you doing here?" Trent asked as he recognized us, lowering his weapon.

"Stopping a crime," I snapped, about to yell at him for pointing a gun at us when Jonas squeezed my hand.

He was right. Since the sheriff was still pointing his gun at us, I probably needed to rethink my approach. "We were out for a walk and saw someone suspicious heading around the back of the parking lot," I said before giving the rest of our cover story to the men.

"I'll call dispatch and have them check the video feed from that camera," said Trent.

I suddenly got nervous. What if the camera had captured us going behind the school before the intruder? "Hey!" I shouted, startling both officers again. "What about the intruder? Are you going after them?"

Before they could respond, a sedan pulled up and stopped behind Trent's cruiser. "What happened?" yelled Stapleton out his window. The overweight oaf clambered out of his car much more awkwardly than either of the officers and seemed out of breath, either from panic or the effort of extricating himself from his car. "Is there a fire?" He looked wildly between the two officers. "You know there have been some cases of arson in schools nearby. We should check it out. Should I call the fire department too?"

I'd swear the sheriff rolled his eyes, but it was dark. He finally put his gun away and said, "Everything's under control, Lester. No fire as far as we know. These two miscreants claim they saw someone breaking into the school."

Lester finally focused on me and frowned. "Aren't you getting a little old to break into my school, Ella Mae?"

Jonas took a small step in front of me, redirecting Stapleton's attention to him, and held out his hand. "Hi, Lester." Jonas actually shook Stapleton's hand like he was having a normal meeting with a normal person.

Jonas continued, "We saw someone dressed all in black and followed them. We managed to scare them out of a classroom and chased them, but they escaped out of the school before we could catch them." He repeated the basic story to Lester, and conveniently, reinforced our tale for the two officers.

"Did you see the intruder set any fires inside?" Lester was still breathing hard.

"No. They looked to be searching Duncan's classroom but ran when I bumped into a chair and made some noise. We followed them through a few classrooms but fell over some of the furniture, so we couldn't catch up."

I was impressed with how Jonas had told the truth without mentioning anything about the darkroom or that we'd gone inside first. We'd have to discuss how to bring the darkroom's existence up to the sheriff without incriminating ourselves.

"Wow," said Stapleton. "Jonas, I guess we owe you a big thank-you for chasing off a burglar."

I stared at him. The nerve of that man! Whose idea did he think this was anyway? I took a deep breath to give him a piece of my mind when Jonas squeezed my hand again. This time shutting my mouth took more willpower, but I held off and let the air out with a heavy puff.

"Did you see who it was?" asked Lester.

Tired of him giving Jonas all the credit, I jumped in. "No. Whoever it was wore all black sweats and a black ski mask."

"Actually," Jonas broke in.

I whipped my head around to stare at him, along with everyone else.

"I think I know who it was," he finished.

"Well, pray tell, son," said Stapleton, unwilling to pause for the dramatic moment. He never had appreciated our drama club.

Jonas nodded. "I'm pretty sure it was Anita Quentin."

I gawked at Jonas in the sudden silence and then said, "Ahh," as I figured out his clever angle.

"What?" Trent was now looking at me intently.

"Nothing," I answered, concerned that I had been overheard. I wasn't about to explain that I'd figured out my husband was trying to use this opportunity to convince the sheriffs to go after Anita as the murderer. He was such a quick thinker to get her arrested for breaking into the school. We'd convince the police to search the abandoned classroom, revealing the proof of her affair. The key would be to carefully navigate explaining how we'd seen her naked pictures during the midst of a chase.

I nodded to myself. Duncan must have been blackmailing Anita over those nudie photos that he'd taken of her, prompting her to kill him. She couldn't let them get out; they would ruin her marriage and her business.

I smiled up at Jonas. What a clever man. And way better at this trickery business than I had expected him to be. I could have used him and his skills during high school.

"If the person was wearing all black and a ski mask, how could you be certain it was Anita?" The sheriff was clearly worried about accusing a longtime resident and local businesswoman of a crime on flimsy evidence. And probably not ready to just take the word of his prime suspect's husband.

Jonas snuck a sideways glance at me. "I recognized her 'run.'"

The sheriff cocked his head. "Her run?"

"From behind." Jonas at least had the decency to sound sheepish. "I've seen her running a few times this week. When she ran away down the street, it looked familiar."

My cheeks flushed in anger. "Why are you watching her run?" I demanded.

He looked at me. "I'm not. I wasn't. Not on purpose anyway. She was in front of me a few times. I'm just running and watching where I'm going." His voice faded as he recognized my glare.

What was with Jonas and Anita Quentin? It was like he was obsessed with her. First, he got all chatty with her at the salon, then he was staring at her photos, and now I learn he's literally been chasing her tail. Sure, some might say she was attractive, for an older woman, but that didn't excuse his recognizing her backside. I clenched my jaw and glared at him again.

I couldn't believe he was ogling Anita Quentin.

Wait until I told Mom.

20

Saturday Evening

Jonas

Elizabeth crossed her arms over her chest and glared at me.

I was confused. I expected her to be pleased with me for identifying the intruder. Elizabeth could appropriately point out that she had been right—Anita Quentin must have killed Duncan. Anita must have waited until tonight when the school wasn't busy to sneak in and steal back the photos linking her to him. She hadn't known he had a separate darkroom or that we were after the same evidence to clear Elizabeth of the murder.

"Well." Sheriff Tucker scratched the back of his head and looked off in the general direction where Anita had disappeared. For the first time since I'd met him, he seemed uncertain of himself.

Elizabeth's anger shifted into high gear as she directed her ire to the sheriff. "Well, get a move on, Sheriff," she commanded. "You can't arrest her if you stand around here star-gazing." Elizabeth liked to believe she was very different from her mother, but there were times when the relationship was unmistakable.

The sheriff's body stiffened and his eyes glinted in the reflected light as he looked squarely at Elizabeth. "You better watch your tongue, missy." He swung his gaze over to include me as well. "Any arrests here could include the two of you. I've got you both breaking and entering into the high school. That's a clear violation of bail if I've ever seen one."

Elizabeth's anger quickly sputtered out as she audibly gasped.

The sheriff appeared pleased by her reaction. "Deputy," he said with a glance at the other officer, "put them in the back of your unit."

"Wait," exclaimed Elizabeth. "Anita lied about where she was on Sunday. She's the killer."

The two officers and Lester all swung their heads to stare at her.

"Where was she?" asked Deputy Walker.

"She told everyone that she went to Hot Springs for treatment last Sunday, but the spa wasn't open then." Elizabeth pointed at the sheriff as if that was the final nail in Anita's coffin.

Sheriff Tucker tilted his head. He was unconvinced, but at least he didn't shut her down. Yet. "How do you know?"

"Jonas heard her tell the ladies in her salon. She flat-out lied."

Now everyone turned to look at me. The sheriff's face grew grim. "I thought I told you to stay away from any investigating?"

"I wasn't investigating. I was getting my hair cut," I explained.

Deputy Walker snorted. "At Shear Heaven?" He chuckled as the other two men joined in.

Elizabeth flung her arms up. "He's new to town. He didn't know any better." She stared them down until they stopped laughing.

I was still uncertain why it was so off-limits to men. Anita had done a good job on my cut. But after all the grief, I wouldn't challenge that local custom again.

She continued, "But he was there. And so were a bunch of the other women who heard her too."

The sheriffs had stopped laughing, but I could tell they were still undecided. During the silence, I decided to speak up rather than risk having Elizabeth locked up until a trial. "We have additional proof."

I reached in my jacket, then froze. The sheriff had moved his hand to grip his gun and shifted his stance. I swallowed and said slowly, enunciating clearly, "No gun. It's in my jacket pocket." I remained still, careful to not blink. Thankfully he nodded before I sneezed, and I slowly opened my jacket, showing them there was nothing dangerous strapped to my chest. Carefully and visibly using just my index and middle fingers, I reached into the jacket's inner pocket and pulled out a photograph.

Elizabeth spun around to stare first at the photo and then at my face. Her expression darkened and her glare returned.

Uncertain why she was angry that I had grabbed proof of Anita Quentin's relationship with Duncan Fowler from the darkroom, I ignored her for now and passed the photo to the sheriff.

He snatched it and brought up his flashlight to study it. With a sudden intake of breath, he rocked back on his heels. "Where'd you find this?" he asked me, shaking his head to stop Deputy Walker from coming closer to look at the evidence.

"Anita was rummaging around in the school when we frightened her off. I took this to show the authorities," I explained, feeling slightly uncomfortable at misleading him on the exact order of events.

"Duncan had a darkroom inside the high school across from his classroom," added Elizabeth.

"He had what?" asked Lester.

"We learned he took boudoir photos of women—" she continued.

"And some more risqué ones," I added.

Elizabeth glared at me again. "Downright porn if you ask me." She shook her head in disgust, but I wasn't clear on whether it was with the photos or with me.

Lester stepped toward Sheriff Tucker with his hand outstretched, but the sheriff waved him away too before fixing Elizabeth and me with a stern look. "You two ran around town poking your nose into places—"

"Well, you aren't looking for the real killer," Elizabeth interrupted.

The sheriff's voice took on a harsh edge. "You have no idea what we are or aren't doing." Then he slid the photo into a plastic evidence bag and put it in his jacket pocket before glancing at Deputy Walker. "Let's go over to the Quentins' house now and get to the bottom of this."

Elizabeth flashed a smile and turned away from the sheriff, as if to leave.

Noticing Elizabeth's attempt at escape, the sheriff said, "Oh, you're not out of the woods yet. Deputy." He glanced at the other officer. "Put them in the back and follow me."

Lester stepped toward the school.

"Lester," commanded the sheriff, pinning a suddenly guilty-looking Lester to the spot. "Don't go near that darkroom. There might be evidence."

Lester glanced at the school and then back at the sheriff. "I need to check if there's a fire," he said weakly.

"There's no fire," snapped Elizabeth. "You perv," she added, low enough not to be heard by Lester or the sheriff, but loud enough to get a chuckle from Deputy Walker as he was escorting us to his car.

For once agreeing with Elizabeth, the sheriff gave a crisp nod before instructing, "Just lock up the building. But don't go to sleep yet; I'll call you later to check on this darkroom."

Elizabeth didn't speak to me as Deputy Walker put us both into the backseat of his cruiser.

"Your grandfather's camera, huh?" he said to her, but she didn't respond.

When he started the car, Elizabeth asked, "Trent, please open the windows. I get car sick when I'm in the backseat."

His eyes, flickering to the rear mirror, held an unexpected smirk.

Elizabeth frowned at him and then looked away. "When the car is moving." She didn't say another word as he lowered our windows.

*****

When we pulled to a stop at what must have been the Quentins' house, the sheriff was already standing by the door. The evening was cool and quiet. I still hadn't gotten used to the complete absence of street noise in Jenkins—no cars and trucks honking, brakes squealing, people yelling to each other in the street, and no loud parties from the inconsiderate people in the neighboring apartment building.

The sheriff knocked on the door as Deputy Walker got out of his car and radioed dispatch with their status.

After another, louder knocking, the door finally flew open. "What!" yelled a tall and ruggedly handsome man before he realized the sheriff was standing there.

I recognized him as Blake, the man I'd met briefly outside the grocery store on Monday evening. If he lived here, he must be Blake Quentin, Anita's husband and Susie Q's father.

"Oh, Sheriff. Sorry." He shifted from foot to foot, understandably nervous about having two sheriffs suddenly appear outside his house. "Uh, what's going on?" He wore a white tank top and jeans and crossed his muscular arms over his chest, shivering a little in the night chill.

"Sorry to bother you at night, Blake," said the sheriff. "Can you ask Anita to come to the door?"

Blake turned back into the house, hollering, "Anita, Sheriff's at the door for you."

"Tell him I can't come to the door. I'll call him in the morning," Anita yelled back.

Sheriff Tucker leaned forward. "Please go tell her she needs to come to the door right away."

Blake jammed his hands in his pockets. "You got some warrant or something?"

"Go get her now or we're coming in for her," commanded the sheriff, his voice sounding more ominous.

"Okay, okay. Geez." Blake left the door open and disappeared into the house, yelling, "Anita!" as he searched for her.

Standing by his open car door, Deputy Walker was surprised by the squawk of his radio. "Walker," he announced.

The radio crackled as a man's voice said, "Dispatch here. The security firm sent video from that camera at the high school. It did show a figure all in black running out the front door followed a short while later by a man and woman." In a surprised tone, the man continued, "The woman looks like Ella Mae Banks."

Deputy Walker glanced over at us before clicking on his radio to respond. "Thanks, Dispatch. It's Trout now. Out."

Blake returned, dragging a complaining woman by the arm.

When Anita finally appeared in the doorway, Elizabeth laughed out loud. Anita's face was covered with one of those green overnight masks for improving the skin. But hers must have been slapped on too quickly over a flushed and sweating face because the goo was pooling and dripping down her cheeks. As if trying to distract anyone associating her with an all-black intruder, she wore tight, tiny yellow shorts that barely covered all the legally required parts and a hot-pink T-shirt. The distraction seemed to be working, as the sheriff and deputy were staring, speechless.

Giggling, Elizabeth whipped out her cellphone and snapped a few quick shots. "Looks like a swamp monster melting into a pile of ooze," she said.

Another car drove up and stopped behind Deputy Walker's. I twisted in my seat to see who it was.

Lester Stapleton had followed us, driving slower than the sheriffs but clearly wanting to catch the next episode in tonight's drama. His eyes widened as he saw the scene at the Quentin front door.

The sheriff frowned, but before he could say anything, Elizabeth called out, "She just put that on, Sheriff. It's still wet. It's dripping because she's still sweating from running away."

Anita glared across the lawn at us.

Without turning, the sheriff waved a dismissive arm in our direction. He didn't need Elizabeth's help. Ignoring his audience, he continued, "Anita, did you just break into the high school?"

"Why, Sheriff, what an odd accusation." She flung her arm to her head in an overly dramatic gesture, as if performing to the audience in the balcony seats.

I whispered to Elizabeth, "Should I suggest to the sheriff that he check her hip for a bruise? She hit something hard. It must be black-and-blue by now."

"What is it with you and that woman's hips?" Elizabeth hissed back.

I decided I could wait to mention it to the sheriff later, when Elizabeth wasn't nearby.

"We have video of you at the school," he said gruffly, failing to explain that the camera would only have captured her back.

Her face turned pale. Putting a hand to her cheek to hide her reaction from her husband, who was standing at her side, she asked, "Blake, dear, could you please go get me a towel? And a glass of water."

Throwing up both hands as if in surrender, Blake said, "Sure," and plodded off.

Once he'd left the vicinity, Anita leaned forward and spoke softer, just barely loud enough for us to hear. "Okay, yes. I did go inside. But only to get something that's mine." She crossed her arms to cover up her lack of a bra. Now that she'd decided to confess, she must have felt there was no longer a need for her attempt at distraction.

The sheriff reached into his jacket pocket and pulled out the plastic baggie. "Is this what you were looking for?"

"Give me that!" She lunged for the photo, but the sheriff pulled it out of reach.

"It's evidence," he said.

"Okay, put it away already." She looked over her shoulder to make sure the coast was clear and lowered her voice again. "I hired Duncan to take some photos of me as an anniversary gift for Blake. I don't want him to know so it will be a surprise."

Next to me, Elizabeth muttered, "Oh he'll be getting a surprise, all right."

The sheriff put the plastic baggie back in his jacket. "Where were you on Sunday night?"

"Sunday night?" she repeated, and then, "Thanks, hon," to a returning Blake. Buying herself some time, she wiped the green goop off her face and took a long drink of water. She handed both to Blake and he faded back.

Anita answered the sheriff, "I was out like a light early on Sunday. I was exhausted from a busy day."

Elizabeth poked me in the shoulder. "I'll bet," she said, raising her eyebrows.

"Is this about Duncan Fowler's murder?" Anita asked.

The sheriff nodded and then lifted his head, staring over Anita's shoulder. "Blake?" he questioned, freezing Blake before he could completely disappear into the house. "Can you confirm Anita's whereabouts on Sunday night?"

Blake's eyes shifted between Anita and the sheriff. "I spent the evening in the TV room watching an MMA match and then an action flick. I didn't see Anita until quite late when I went to bed."

Anita nodded along, as if encouraging him. "That's right. I didn't see you until morning when I woke up." Then she snapped her fingers. "Wait. I use a CPAP machine to help me sleep. It keeps track of when I'm using it and if I have any sleep apnea episodes.

Hold on." She rotated and grabbed a phone from somewhere out of sight. After tapping on it briefly, she turned it so the sheriff could see the screen.

"See," she said, excitedly jabbing at it. "It shows I was asleep at eight o'clock and slept all the way until seven on Monday morning."

I wondered why she had gone to sleep so early. Was she lying and had figured out some way to trick a CPAP machine? It seemed unlikely that Anita had the technical skills and foresight to plan such a convincing alibi only to get caught slapping a sleeping mask on her sweaty face.

The sheriff grunted as he stared at the proof. He must have been starting to believe Elizabeth's theory of Anita as the killer was accurate, as he seemed disappointed to have merely caught Anita breaking into the school.

Anita put a hand on her waist and struck a jaunty pose, relying again on her revealing attire. "Do you need anything else, Sheriff?" she asked with a lilt to her voice. Without waiting for a response, she turned to the side and bent over to pick up something small—something so small I couldn't see it. After pausing to make sure the sheriff had a good look at her assets, she gracefully eased her way back to standing. "At least for now?"

The sheriff cleared his throat. "Um, no, thank you."

"What about breaking into the school?" shouted Lester from his car.

"Yes, we'll deal with that in the morning," said the sheriff, causing Anita's pose to become a bit less carefree and a frown to form on her face.

Switching her tone from sultry to catty, Anita asked, "Before disturbing us, did you at least interview Bianca Delgado about Duncan's murder?"

The sheriff's body stiffened again. "Why?"

"That woman," she said with distaste, "was sleeping with Duncan Fowler."

I heard Deputy Tucker's surprised inhale.

Anita must have taken his reaction as her cue to make an exit, undoubtedly figuring that was the best audience response she was likely to get from tonight's performance.

Blake was left standing by the door, unsure what to do now that his wife had exited stage left. "So that's all, Sheriff?" he asked.

The sheriff nodded.

Blake said, "Okay, good night. I guess I'll see you all tomorrow at the estate sale. I'm hoping to pick up some tools cheap." He started to close his front door.

"Actually, about that." The sheriff hesitated as he turned to look at us. "I'm afraid it's going to have to be postponed."

"What!" exclaimed Elizabeth as Blake paused in surprise as well. "Why? Does my mother know?"

The sheriff answered, "I called and left her a message on her cellphone."

I could tell Elizabeth was frustrated by the news. As she started to call her mother, she repeated, "Why?"

Deputy Walker jumped in. "We're bringing in a crack forensics team to do a full DNA search of your grandmother's place and a few other locations." Then, in an awestruck voice, he added, "All the way from Little Rock."

"Stupid cell signals. They're so unreliable in those hills," complained Elizabeth as she hung up.

Blake frowned. He must have been really eager to get some bargains to add to his tool collection. Elizabeth's grandfather must have kept an extensive assortment in his workshop that would be attractive to a contractor like Blake. Mary and Sebastian had certainly spent a good hour out there one day while Elizabeth and I boxed up photos and knickknacks.

From his car, Lester said, "It'll be like *CSI: Jenkins.*" Then he paused for a moment. "Don't tell the mayor I said that. He'll want to approach the TV networks to see if they'd be interested in making that into a show."

Elizabeth pointed out an important detail. "But we've been in and out of that place all week. What are you looking for? Won't it be completely contaminated?"

She glanced at me for confirmation, and I nodded. "Anywhere we've touched or been would have our DNA."

"They'll be investigating a few specific locations, and their experts think it could be helpful," said the sheriff cryptically.

I started to explain basic biology to him, then remembered how he had reacted when he'd caught me asking questions outside the grocery store and shut my mouth.

Deputy Walker's voice grew excited. "They're bringing in some cool specialty tools."

"Wow! This really will be like *CSI.*" Lester sounded enthusiastic too.

Blake awkwardly said, "Okay, see ya later," and quickly shut the door.

The sheriff walked down to our car and leaned over. "Do you have anything you've neglected to tell me about Bianca?" Although his voice was gruff, he waited for a response. He was paying close attention to us for the first time since I'd met him.

"We also heard that Bianca was dating Duncan. They had a messy breakup last Saturday night at the Green Papaya in Ft. Smith," I told him.

The sheriff frowned but didn't comment. He might have been concentrating rather than disapproving. It was difficult to discern, as a frown was Sheriff Tucker's predominant expression.

Elizabeth added, "Duncan broke up with her and apparently pie was thrown." It wasn't obvious which of these infractions Elizabeth felt was more serious. She was clearly following the reveal-everything strategy to distract or dissuade prosecution from the school break-in. Had that ever worked for her with Mary?

I completed the story. "Bianca likely still would have been pretty mad at him the next day. The waitress told us Bianca even had to get a ride home with Colton Buck."

The sheriff dropped his head, shaking it slightly. All I could hear of his muttering was "that CB."

Elizabeth spoke up again. "The only other thing I ever heard Bianca say is that Duncan was a slob."

Puzzled, I turned to look at her. "That's weird."

Everyone looked at me, so I explained, "When I was getting my hair cut—"

Snickering from Deputy Trent and Lester, who had wandered out of his car, interrupted me. This town was going to have to get past their hang-up about a man visiting Shear Heaven.

Ignoring them, I continued, "Anita told everyone in the place that Duncan was neat with a minimalist style."

Deputy Trent said, "Well, clearly one of them was lying."

The sheriff leaned on the cruiser with his chin on his fist for a few moments, thinking. In a decisive move, he stood erect. "Time to go pay a visit to Bianca and see what we learn."

Lester hurried back to his car too, eager to start Act Three.

As Deputy Walker drove away, Elizabeth leaned over to show me the close-up photos she'd captured on her phone of Anita with her dripping green face mask.

With a Cheshire cat grin, she said, "Mama will want copies of these."

21

Saturday Later Evening

Elizabeth

Trent seemed to be showing off as he let the sheriff's car get a bit ahead of us before squealing around a corner and zooming down the street before screeching to a halt outside Bianca's house. But it didn't have any impact on me. A guy driving fast hasn't impressed me since high school. While stopped at Anita's, I had moved into the center seat to see the show better, so now I just squeezed in close to Jonas and held on.

I wondered if Trent would break down Bianca's door, but in the end, it didn't matter, because she was sitting on her front porch talking to the mayor and his son. They all looked up, eyes wide, at the arrival of the two sheriffs.

Even that busybody Stapleton pulled up. He must have still been trying to get me thrown in jail for wandering around his precious high school after dark. I mean, please, we didn't even break in—we used a key. I wondered if my lawyer could use that to get me off. At least that would make him good for something. He certainly hadn't done anything to get me off this murder charge yet.

Besides, we didn't hurt anything, except maybe a few desks. And the desks hurt Jonas.

Again the sheriff channeled his inner John Wayne, striding up to the porch with his chest puffed out while Trent acted as his sidekick, standing alongside his car door. "Bianca, I need to ask you some questions," announced the sheriff. Geez, why couldn't his dialogue have matched his entrance?

I felt like calling out his stage directions: "Now he will pause and take a breath." But I restrained the urge, knowing that otherwise his next step would be to return me to jail.

As predicted, Sheriff Tucker paused and took a deep breath. "Where were you on Sunday?"

"I didn't do anything wrong," replied Bianca.

Curious. Would an innocent person respond by announcing they weren't guilty?

At first the sheriff didn't react, facing her down with his arms crossed. Finally he said, "We know you and Duncan broke up on Saturday night, and rather flamboyantly, as I understand."

He resumed staring at her, but this time she broke down into tears almost immediately. "Yes, okay. It was just terrible. We were dating. We didn't tell anyone because we didn't want the whole town talking about us. Then that scumbag broke up with me at the end of dinner. He let me babble on about vacations we could take together and when we might move in together. Then he just up and announces he's interested in someone else, someone younger."

The mayor and his son moved in closely, drawn to the spectacle and almost grotesquely eager not to miss a word.

No one spoke as she sobbed again and caught her breath. "Like that's something I can do anything about—some flaw that I let myself fall into. I can't make myself be younger, but I keep fit. I eat right. I'm attractive, aren't I?" She held out her arms as if asking for an inspection.

Sheriff Tucker stayed silent, just watching her. He didn't say anything to make her feel better about herself.

My heart went out to her. It was hard to stay quiet and watch the sheriff speak like that to someone I liked. For Bianca to feel like such a helpless failure about someone she'd given her heart to was, well, heartbreaking. I wondered if her answers would wind up keeping me out of jail. I had almost broken down and told her she was beautiful when the sheriff barked, "Where were you on Sunday night, after dark?"

Bianca looked startled, her eyes darting from side to side. Then she sighed. "I admit it—"

Next to me, I heard a sharp intake of breath. I whacked Jonas in the side to stay quiet.

Bianca continued, "I went into Duncan's house to retrieve some clothes I had left there." She stopped talking and dropped her head, looking down at her hands in her lap. Even in the glow from the porch light, we could see a blush creep up her neck. "And some photos he'd taken of me," she added in a quiet voice.

"Show me the photos," commanded the sheriff.

Still looking down, she shook her head. "No. Those aren't pictures to show around. They're sort of . . ." She looked around at her audience of the mayor, his teenage son, Stapleton, Trent, and the two of us. "Sort of revealing."

Finally dredging up some civility from somewhere deep in his soul, Sheriff Tucker managed to say in a partially humane voice, "I'm sorry, but I still need to see them."

"But I didn't break into his house. I had a key. That's not breaking and entering, right?"

I leaned forward, eager to hear the answer. This was a truly important question. But the sheriff didn't address my legal dilemma. "I won't keep the photos unless they're critical evidence. But it's important that I see them."

She went inside her house, returning shortly with a few photos. I couldn't see them from the curb, but they were the same 5×7 size as the others in Duncan's darkroom.

The sheriff pulled out the plastic baggie from his jacket, careful not to show the contents to Bianca, and compared the photos side by side. He reviewed them quickly and methodically, his head swiveling back and forth.

As he handed Bianca her photos, I realized he hadn't been acting like a pervert. He must have been looking at the backgrounds in each of the photographs. If they both had the same setup—doorway, white walls, and furniture—then it was a pretty good bet they had been taken by the same photographer in the same place.

Grudgingly I admitted to myself that maybe Sheriff Tucker wasn't completely incompetent. But I held out my final judgment on his professionalism until I saw whether he put me in jail for the little incident at the high school. I had used a key, after all.

"Why'd you go so late?" he asked Bianca, studying her face carefully.

She squirmed a bit under his intense stare. "I waited until most people finished taking after-dinner walks. We had kept the relationship a secret. Now that it was over, I didn't want anyone to see me. And you know how hard it is to do that in this town." She shook her head in exasperation. "I didn't want rumors to start, especially now that he'd dumped me." She sniffled again.

Of course, throwing pies on a Saturday night in a nearby restaurant wasn't the best idea if she wanted to keep the relationship hush-hush.

"Are you sure you didn't track him down in person and then kill him?" he asked in a low tone, still watching her intently.

"No!" She jerked her head back in surprise. "I didn't go anywhere near the river on Sunday."

The sheriff kept his eyes locked on her. "Can anyone prove when you got back from Duncan's house on Sunday night?"

Bianca squeezed her eyes shut and pressed her hands against her head, trying to force the memory loose. Her eyes suddenly popped open as she looked around wildly before jabbing her finger at the mayor's son.

I had been following her dramatics so intently, I had forgotten the mayor and his son were still standing nearby.

We all turned to stare at the kid, whose name I could never remember.

"Tyler, that true?" asked the sheriff.

He started shaking. "Yeah, I saw her. I got home around nine—"

"Nine!" interrupted a clearly surprised Dale.

"—and was just walking around in the yard to cool off," he finished.

Next to me, Jonas whispered, "Translated to mean he was trying to get the smell of alcohol off his breath and clothes."

"Where were you that you were just getting back?" asked the sheriff.

"I, uh, was slow going down the river and getting my kayak—"

"Tyler." Jonas leaned forward so the kid could see him in the back seat. "Tell the truth."

The kid's eyes darted wildly for a moment before he sighed. "Okay, jeez." Then he looked at his father. "Don't have a cow. It was no big deal, but I was at a party down at the river with some friends. At Roundtop Bend."

He looked back at the sheriff, but his courage must have started to wane as he dropped his eyes and his voice softened. "I didn't see Duncan or his truck. Everyone else was fixin' to leave the river to go to"—he glanced sideways at Stapleton and his father—"someone else's place."

The mayor started sputtering at his son, as if he himself hadn't gone to Roundtop Bend for parties back when he was in high school like the rest of us, but the sheriff cut him off. "Dale. Not now."

Worried that the abrupt quiet meant the investigation was coming to an end and my next stop would be the county jail, I blurted out, "But if Bianca didn't kill Duncan—"

Quickly Jonas inserted, "And if Anita didn't kill Duncan—"

I added, "And if the kid didn't kill him—"

"Tyler!" the crowd shouted at me.

"Then who did?" the sheriff finished, asking the critical question that had us stumped.

Everyone went silent once again until Bianca asked, "Have you talked to him about where he was on Sunday night?" She was pointing straight at Dale. "Our esteemed mayor wasn't home when Tyler and I saw each other. His truck wasn't in the driveway."

"Me!?" The mayor turned red. "Me?" he kept repeating.

Sheriff Tucker broke in. "Why not? It was obvious by your reaction to Tyler that you weren't home at nine on Sunday when he got home. Where were you?"

The mayor looked like his head was going to explode.

Bianca spat out, "Don't be lying now. Tell them about paying Duncan to delay and mess up his work for Brent Hollands. Come on, spill it. What crazy scheme have you cooked up this time?"

The mayor glared at Bianca and the sheriff but didn't respond.

"Robert Jones said the two of you were out on the lake together, but you brought your boat back at four-thirty on Sunday," said Jonas.

"And why were you secretly having Mimi's land rezoned to be a hotel?" I demanded. "A hotel!" I repeated for emphasis, glaring at him.

His mouth dropped open, shocked that his secret was out.

Sheriff Tucker's face turned sour. He jabbed a finger toward Trent. "You and me are going to have a chat when this is all over."

It wasn't fair for him to blame Trent for not digging as hard as we had. He couldn't tap into the W.A.H.O.O. network, after all. Plus, Trent wasn't worried about going to prison for something he hadn't done. Although, he *had* said he didn't think I killed Duncan but still let me stress out about the murder charge all week without finding the actual killer. I glared at Trent too, for good measure.

The sheriff glowered at the silent mayor. "Dale?"

"Okay, okay." The mayor buckled under the pressure of everyone glaring at him. "Well, fine. You all spoiled the surprise. Yes, we have a plan to build a winery and a boutique hotel up on the ridge."

"We?" asked Trent.

"Robert is building a winery and I'd build the hotel." He noticed Bianca's and Stapleton's outraged expressions. "What? It's a good plan. We'll need the rooms and the supporting attraction if Jenkins does wind up winning that final Arkansas casino slot. All that extra sales tax revenue will be great for the city, for the sheriff's department, for the schools, for the voters—"

"And for you." Stapleton interrupted the mayor's stump speech before he got going. His face was screwed up in scorn—a familiar expression to me.

"Well, of course. I'm not a charity." Looking back at the sheriff, he quickly added, "But I had no need to murder anyone. The plans were all legal. We planned to buy the land when Elizabeth put it up for sale, fair and square. Robert and I had a lovely dinner at his house and I left well after nine."

Instead of drilling in further on the mayor's story, the sheriff surprised me by swinging his head back to Bianca. "Did you go up to the Banks' ranch on the ridge on Sunday?"

Bianca's face filled with confusion. "No. Why would I go up there to her old ranch? She died a few months ago. No one's living there, right?"

She turned to me for confirmation, but I didn't respond, suddenly realizing what the sheriff had revealed. "Mimi's?" I asked.

The sheriff heard me and nodded slowly as he turned his attention away from Bianca.

"I thought Duncan was killed at the river," I said, still shocked. How had this been hidden from us? How had the sheriff learned?

Trent bent over to look in the window. "We think so. We know he wasn't killed at the river. That's why we have the special forensics team coming in. We couldn't exactly tell you everything we knew, seeing as you were the main suspect and all."

Sheriff Tucker frowned. "Deputy Walker, we don't share *any* information about cases with civilians, especially not suspects. Am I understood?"

"Yes, sir," replied Trent, snapping to attention.

I looked at Jonas with my mouth agape.

Dale gestured excitedly with his hand as if asking to be called upon. "Wait. There's someone else who could vouch for me. When I drove back along that dirt road from Robert's house, I passed that appraiser guy who's always doing the estate sales in the area. He was on your grandmother's porch. I'd swear Duncan's truck was parked next to some white sedan, but I didn't see Duncan."

"You didn't stop?" Trent asked the mayor.

"Why would I stop? There was nothing going on but a guy on a porch. Duncan was up there working after school lots of days. I didn't want him finding out my plans prematurely."

After the sheriff and Trent exchanged meaningful glances, Dale gasped. "Are you thinking . . . Do you think . . ."

"Mama!" I shouted, suddenly remembering.

Everyone looked startled, but I didn't apologize. "She's working late to finish up at Mimi's house tonight with Sebastian." Noticing their blank expressions, I added, "Sebastian Edwards. The appraiser guy." Then I fumbled for my phone, trying to get my shaking fingers to press the buttons to call her.

Her phone rang and rang, eventually clicking over to her voicemail. I tried twice more before leaving a short, breathless message for her to call me immediately. Shaking my head, I announced, "No answer."

Trent looked up from his own phone. "The clerk at the Best

Western hasn't seen him since this morning and no one answers in his room." Calling the only hotel in town sure was fast thinking.

"We've got to get up there. If Sebastian was the last one to see Duncan, then Mama's in danger. She's all alone with him!" I cried to the sheriff.

22

Saturday Late Evening

Jonas

Over the river and through the woods to grandmother's house we raced. We had to get there in time to save Mary.

Deputy Walker drove faster than even Mary had along those winding mountain roads as he followed the sheriff's cruiser. Elizabeth and I swayed heavily into each other as the centrifugal forces pushed and pulled us around each curve.

I knew that Elizabeth's white-knuckled grip on my arm had less to do with the deputy's driving and more out of fear for Mary's safety. I hadn't heard her refer to Mary as "Mama" during the whole time I'd known her. Through the back window, we got the occasional flash of light, presumably from the headlights of Lester's car bringing up a slower driving caboose in our caravan.

Without bothering to park by the workshop under the sheltering overhang, the sheriff stopped his car on the side of the dirt road across from it to save time. Deputy Walker slammed on his brakes and stopped his car behind the sheriff. Most of the house appeared dark, and there was no sign of movement. As Deputy Walker jumped out, Elizabeth yelled, "Trent! Open our door too."

He yanked open the rear door and shouted, "Stay here," but didn't pause as he hurried to join the sheriff on the porch. They drew their guns and flashlights, then stood to both sides of the front door, gesturing at each other. At some unseen signal, they burst into the house, shouting. It was just like on television.

We got out of the car, watching as their lights flickered through the downstairs windows.

"Hold!" yelled one of them.

In the sudden silence, we were surprised when a large furry animal burst through the open front door, aiming at us.

It was Daisy. She raced over, agitated to the point of nearly frantic as she reached us.

I knelt to give her a quick pet as she danced around, clearly out of sorts. "Your mom would have taken Daisy if she left. She must still be here," I said as Elizabeth nodded tightly, still staring at the open door and dark house.

Distractedly, Elizabeth leaned over to pet her too, but Daisy barked and danced backward, still watching us intently as she tried to catch our attention. When we didn't respond, she barked and then dashed off in a beeline for the workshop.

Realizing Daisy must have smelled someone hiding in the large shrubs nestled against the side of the workshop, I shouted, "Sheriff." Elizabeth yelled, "Trent," at the same moment.

Daisy stopped near the shrubs and started barking loudly.

"Someone must be hiding over there," called Elizabeth as the deputy ran out of the house.

Deputy Walker took in Daisy's tense posture and continuous barking and then called for the sheriff to join him.

Sheriff Tucker glanced back and forth between the house and the dog. "Go ahead. I'll cover you," he instructed the deputy. "Get back in the car," he yelled at us, and then took up a position where he could watch both the front door and the dog.

We were too tense to follow his directions completely, but moved behind the car where we could still keep an eye on Daisy and the shrubs.

"Sheriff!" warned Deputy Walker as he approached the bush with his gun. "Come out with your hands up."

"Daisy, come here," Elizabeth called, clapping her hands twice. Daisy actually raced back over to us. Evidently a week of obeying Mary had trained her to respond to this command. Elizabeth grabbed Daisy by the collar to keep her from returning to the bushes and interfering.

Lester's car pulled up along the dirt road, but I waved to stop him. Despite that, he drove closer and got out, perhaps not understanding my directions. And then the passenger door opened and the mayor got out too. Perhaps he thought he needed to be here in an official capacity, but most likely he couldn't resist the excitement.

When I turned back, Deputy Walker was down in a crouch, moving into an opening in the bush. He was holding his flashlight out in front of him but pointing it at a forty-five-degree angle from his body. That was a smart move, as anyone shooting would aim at the light, figuring the person holding it would be right behind it.

"Oww," yelled the deputy suddenly, and then, "I'm okay, it's okay," as he probably realized his boss was pointing a gun in his direction. He squirmed awkwardly back out of the shrub, with the flashlight left behind.

"False alarm," Deputy Walker said as he freed himself and held up a bedraggled creature.

"Lucy," cried Elizabeth as she released Daisy to take the cat from the deputy.

Daisy decided that was her cue to explore and leapt forward, practically diving through the gap in the shrubs.

I ran after her, flopping down to reach into the shrubs to get her out.

"No Mom? Sebastian?" asked Elizabeth from behind me, her voice growing frantic.

"No," answered Deputy Walker. He raised his voice to update the sheriff. "They must be gone."

"Deputy," I called.

I heard Elizabeth's sharp intake as she echoed him. "Gone?"

I repeated myself.

"What?" the deputy asked impatiently.

"There's evidence here," I said.

A few seconds later he was on his belly next to me, half surrounded by the bush.

I pointed at the bright yellow pocket square shining in the flashlight's glow. It was stuck in the old bird's nest where Lucy must have been hiding. "That belongs to Sebastian. He hasn't worn it since Sunday."

"Sheriff!" called the deputy as he backed out of the shrub, leaving the evidence untouched.

I backed out as well and was just standing up when the screech and groan of the back door rang out in the momentary silence.

Daisy started barking again and raced off, the two officers following after her.

Elizabeth and I did the same at a more cautious pace. We were trailed by the even slower Lester and Dale.

When we reached the side of the house, we stopped short, shocked by what we saw in the backyard.

Blake Quentin stood there facing the sheriff and deputy, still wearing his John Deere hat and white tank top but now with a jacket thrown on top. Daisy barked at him.

What was he doing here? He must have driven straight here when we left his house to question Bianca.

"It's, uh, not what it seems," Blake babbled as he wrung his hands together. "You all scared me to death. I, um, I—"

"Where's my mom?" demanded Elizabeth.

Blake swallowed. "I was trying to call 911. That appraiser guy. He—"

"Where is he?" demanded the sheriff. "Where are both of them, for that matter?"

Blake looked panicked, his eyes flickering back to the house before refocusing on the sheriff. "All that yelling in the house scared me. I thought people were coming in to kill me. I snuck out back so I could call 911. I swear," he whined. "Can't get no signal inside that house. That's why I came out here."

Something around us was different. I turned, sniffing.

Suddenly I realized smoke was drifting down from above.

"Fire!" I shouted. Without stopping to explain, I raced back around to the front.

I burst through the open front door and ran up the stairs, yelling "Mary" over and over. The sheriffs had been interrupted in their search of the house when we yelled for them to come to the bushes where Daisy had cornered Lucy. That meant Mary must be upstairs if she was still here.

The thought flicked through my brain that she hadn't answered because she was already dead, but I didn't stop my search.

I paused just briefly at the top of the stairs, frantically looking at all the doors. "Mary!" I screamed again, but no reply.

Loud steps on the ground floor made me look down, but it was just Deputy Walker making his way into the house.

Only the master bedroom door was closed, raising my suspicions. It banged open against the wall as I flew inside.

I heard the deputy pounding up the stairs behind me.

No one was in sight.

The bathroom was empty. As I turned, a draft of smoke hit me in the face.

I realized where she had to be and yanked open the door to the hidden attic.

Smoke poured out. A fire crackled and snapped as it burned up the stacks of papers and oil paintings in the far corner.

The smoke eased for a moment as the open door let out all the trapped smoke, but then the fire made a whooshing noise as the increase of oxygen fed it.

On the floor only a few steps inside were two bodies. Staying low, I scrambled over to the smaller one. It was Mary.

She wasn't breathing.

23

Saturday Night

Jonas

This couldn't be happening.

I held my breath while I put my fingers on the side of Mary's neck to check her pulse. Thankfully, I was wrong, and never happier about that. Mary was merely unconscious and breathing shallowly. I glanced over at the other body, but in the dark and smoke, I could only tell it was someone bigger wearing pants and shoes.

I coughed as the air grew worse. The fire roared louder than an airplane taking off as it engulfed another stack of oil paintings.

Deputy Walker tapped me on the shoulder. He had followed me inside. He gestured at Mary and me, then at the other figure and himself.

I understood. I would get Mary out of here. I pulled her along the attic floor and into the bedroom, where the air was marginally better.

With the flames getting closer, we were running out of time. "Sorry," I muttered at Mary's unconscious figure as I braced myself and then lifted her over my shoulder like a sack of very heavy potatoes.

I staggered into the hallway and managed to make it down the stairs without dropping her or falling.

When I reached the ground floor, the others were standing just inside the door. In tears, Elizabeth rushed forward and helped me carry Mary while the sheriff hurried up a few stairs to meet the deputy and share his heavier load.

We stumbled outside and away from the house until we reached the sheriff's car, where we set Mary on the ground as gently as possible.

Blake stood with his hands cuffed to a metal bracket in the back of the car with Lester and Dale standing guard, though mostly staring at the house with their mouths open. "I told you I was trying to call for help, Sheriff," Blake hollered as soon as the sheriff and deputy exited the house. "That assessor fellow was threatening Mary. I got the drop on him and tied him up and went for help."

His explanation made only partial sense. How had the fire started? Who had tied up Mary? Before I could ask him, the sheriff and deputy reached us and set down the other body. It was Sebastian Edwards, minus his jacket and with his hair in disarray and his white dress shirt filthy.

While Blake continued to protest his innocence, the sheriff ignored everyone and radioed for the fire department to respond and send the paramedics.

While he was talking, Deputy Walker pulled out a small knife and sliced through the ropes tying Sebastian's arms and legs.

Sebastian reached up and pulled the duct tape off his mouth. He coughed and wheezed before gratefully accepting a bottle of water that the deputy had retrieved from his trunk.

Elizabeth knelt over her mother, listening to her breathing. Then, undoing the top button of her mother's shirt, Elizabeth gently felt around her neck and head. Growing up as the child of a rural doctor had imparted at least some basic first aid knowledge, and she didn't attempt to roll Mary over in case of more serious injury.

A loud crash startled us. Everyone whirled around only to see smoke and flames pouring out of the attic window. Something must have fallen and broken it.

"He did it." Blake started thrusting with his free hand toward Sebastian. "I don't know how that fire started. He must have set some delayed fuse to kill Mary but messed up and got caught in the fire himself."

In a hoarse voice, Sebastian said, "He's lying," and then coughed again and flinched from the pain.

"Shut up! Both of you!" shouted the sheriff over their racket and the growing noise from the fire.

"I saw the whole thing, Sheriff," said Sebastian.

"I said shut your trap!" The veins on the sheriff's neck were taut.

Everyone froze, except Elizabeth, who quietly raised one of her hands to show me without attracting the others' attention. A small amount of blood smudged her palm. Mary must have been knocked out by a blow to the back of her head. Elizabeth bit her lip and looked to the county road, urging the ambulance to hurry.

Sebastian gulped but added, "On Sunday, I mean."

The sheriff looked ready to slug him, or shoot him—whatever action would get him to be quiet—when he suddenly froze. "What do you mean, Sunday?" As if anticipating an interruption, he whirled to point at Mr. Quentin. "Not a peep, Blake. You'll get your chance."

Sebastian took a small sip of water, coughed, and then explained, "I was here on Sunday night. I saw him"—he pointed a shaky finger at Blake—"fight with that other man, Duncan, the property manager. They were tussling on the porch. Then he hit Duncan with something and Duncan dropped to the ground. He never moved again."

If he was telling the truth, why hadn't he told the sheriffs about the murder? Why was the body discovered down at the river? And why had he not said anything all week as we were worried about Elizabeth's arrest?

"That's a lie. I was never here on Sunday. I told you I was home watching TV," yelled Blake. Then he stopped short when the sheriff spun around with a fierce look on his face.

The sheriff's hand on his holster seemed to add the emphasis needed to get the quiet he was demanding.

Elizabeth had been holding Mary's wrist and counting. I was amazed she could focus during all the commotion. She looked up at me, her eyes wet from tears, and nodded with a small smile. "Her pulse is better."

The sound of approaching sirens made us all look toward the main road. It seemed unlikely the fire department could make it here in time to save the house as flames erupted through the roof.

Deputy Walker asked Sebastian in a scolding tone, "If you saw a murder, why didn't you call 911?"

"I was scared," said Sebastian. "I wasn't even positive about what I saw. If he was dead, it would be my word against his. I'm the stranger in a small town. I'd get blamed for it and wind up in prison. I've seen it happen before."

"I'm not sure who's telling the truth here. Maybe you're both in this together," said the sheriff, waving his arms even as his face tightened with skepticism.

Trying to piece together all the scraps of this puzzle made me think of something important. There was no time to lose, so I dashed off across the dirt road toward the house.

Elizabeth screamed, "Jonas!" and although the others yelled for me to stop too, I kept going. The house couldn't have been more than fifty yards away, and the fire didn't look to have spread downstairs yet. Besides, the kitchen was right by the front door.

The house was hot and smoke was spreading on the first floor. I skidded along the kitchen linoleum, banged open the door under the sink, and grabbed the small trash bin.

I was back outside in seconds, before the sheriff or deputy could have even started to consider going in after me. I jumped off the porch and ran back to the others, still clutching the container in my arms.

"Jonas!" Elizabeth looked relieved as she hung onto a barking Daisy. She seemed torn as to whether she wanted to hug me or shake some sense into me. "Why did you do that?"

Dale stepped forward to look into the bin, perhaps trying to see if there were jewels tucked away inside. Finding no discernable treasure, he looked up at me with a puzzled expression. "Son, that seems like a pretty stupid thing to save from a burning house."

The sheriff just gave me the stink eye. He may have been closer to going in after me than I'd thought.

I didn't explain. "Deputy, could you shine your light in here."

He did, and I started pulling out the papers and cans. Dumping them on the ground felt wrong, but it was the most efficient way to sort through them. The others crowded in, trying to see what I was doing. Elizabeth stayed close. She may have been truly concerned about my mental well-being. I had, after all, just run into a burning building and was now throwing trash all over the ground.

Finally I found it. "Aha!"

I held up a business card, a little worse for wear but looking just like I'd seen it twice before. "Look. One of Blake's brand-new business cards."

Sheriff Tucker scowled. "So?"

"On Monday morning, I found it on the ground here by the porch," I said. "On Monday evening I saw Blake handing out his new business cards and bragging to the guys outside the grocery about the design. It's the same card. This proves he was here on Sunday."

Lester's expression tightened in concentration. "That's right. Blake told us he'd just gotten them back from the printer."

"I told you!" exclaimed Sebastian. "I told you. I saw them fighting on the porch. That other guy practically tackled him." He gestured at Blake. "His head got smacked into the column. He was stunned for a moment and I thought that was it. Then he reached down and grabbed something wooden, swung it, and knocked the first guy to the ground." He coughed again and gulped down more water.

"He's lying," said Blake. "He must be working with Bianca. They must have cooked up this whole thing for some reason. Didn't I hear that you found Duncan's bloody bandana stashed away in Bianca's store?"

The sheriff started to answer, but Elizabeth dashed to Blake's side and yanked his cap off his head. Blake winced and Sheriff Tucker grabbed her arm, seemingly worried she had removed the cap in order to get the best angle to smack Blake.

"I'm not going to hit him," Elizabeth snarled, yanking her arm from his grip. "Take a look at the back of his head."

When Blake backed away, she demanded more insistently, "Sheriff, do it. Now."

The sheriff's posture went rigid and his jaw tight. Although he complied, he clearly was not accustomed to taking orders from suspects. He shifted to grab Blake's arm, then twisted him around and shined his flashlight on the back of his head.

Clearly visible beneath his thinning hair, Blake's scalp was discolored red and purple and had a good-sized bump. Exactly as you'd expect if his head had been banged against the porch's wood columns.

Blake visibly wilted as he realized his story had fallen apart. "Well, shucks. I almost got away with it. That Duncan deserved to die. He dishonored me and my family. He seduced my wife against her wishes—"

Elizabeth glanced at me, raising her eyebrows.

"—and then, if that weren't bad enough, he disrespected Anita by dumping her for that younger hussy."

Tilting my head, I pursed my lips. Was Blake really so filled with a sense of family honor that he had committed murder? Was it because he was mad at Duncan for having an affair with his wife? Or had he killed Duncan for having the nerve to dump his wife and make her look like a fool? Finally I shrugged, unable to decide; either way, Blake had killed Duncan.

Finally convinced he had the right killer, Sheriff Tucker unlocked the cuff attaching Blake to the metal bar inside the cruiser's door and re-cuffed both hands behind his back while formally accusing him of killing Duncan Fowler and reading him his rights.

Suddenly Elizabeth stepped forward and slapped Blake hard. "You tried to kill my mama. You set the fire, didn't you?"

The sheriff pulled her back but didn't reprimand her. He kept his gaze on Blake, awaiting the answer.

Blake answered, "Even though I wiped it up on Sunday, some of my blood might still be on the porch. If it all burned down, then that forensics team wouldn't find any of my DNA." He ducked his head to avoid meeting anyone's eyes. "I didn't want to hurt Dr. Banks, or even this guy, but they saw me tonight. Why were they still in the house?" he asked, as if it were their fault that he tried to kill two more people.

The sheriff just nodded, then pushed Blake into the back seat of his cruiser and closed the door.

Through the open window, I saw Blake rest his forehead against the metal barrier restraining him from the front seat.

Sebastian clambered to his feet, futilely trying to wipe the dust and grime off his pants. He had started to steal away to his car when Deputy Walker cleared his throat.

"Care to explain what you were doing here late Sunday night?"

Sebastian hunched over a little, looking startled that anyone still remembered he was here.

The sheriff turned back, neatly trapping Sebastian between himself and the deputy. "While you're at it, you can explain why you moved the body."

Dale's and Lester's eyes had ping-ponged from the deputy to the sheriff. They gasped and stared at Sebastian.

"Not me. He must have done it after I left." Sebastian tried to redirect their attention to Blake, still sitting limply with his eyes closed.

"What about your pocket square?" I asked, pointing at the deputy's jacket until he pulled out the evidence bag and held it up. The yellow cloth shone brightly under the glare of his flashlight and the flicker of the flames behind us. "Despite your rotating color plan, you haven't worn this since we met you on Sunday afternoon. You must have taken off your jacket outside or done something so the square came out without you noticing it."

"That's ludicrous. There must be ancient scraps of all kinds of stuff around this old house," Sebastian blustered in protest.

"Open your car. I need to search it," said the sheriff.

"You have no right." Sebastian stamped his foot. "You don't have a warrant."

"A lawyer, huh?" scoffed the sheriff. "We don't need a warrant when we have probable cause to believe you have evidence of a crime in your car. Do you have any leather gloves?"

"Yes! He does. He wears them to protect valuables," Elizabeth blurted out.

"Give me your keys," demanded the sheriff. "Leather gloves leave palm marks that are unique too. Not as perfect as fingerprints but still good enough to convict you."

"You're making that up," complained Sebastian, but he looked uncertain.

"Not like you're attempting to make up your legal defense from television scripts," replied the sheriff. "Point of fact, each cow has a unique hide." He pulled Sebastian's keys out of his pocket and headed to Sebastian's car with the rest of us trailing behind him.

The inside was empty but then the sheriff popped the trunk. On top of several cardboard boxes rested Sebastian's leather gloves. Sheriff Tucker carefully placed them in an evidence bag and then started looking at the other items. He pulled out a thick cardboard tube lying alongside the boxes. Removing the cap, he slid out a rolled-up painting and gingerly unrolled it.

"That's Pawpaw's painting," yelled Elizabeth with aggrieved indignation. She had remained with Mary, who still lay unmoving.

"You fool." Sebastian's friendly salesman voice changed into a snobbish sneer. "Your Pawpaw, my patootie," he spat. "He couldn't paint that any more than I could ride a bucking bull for eight seconds. That's a Thomas Hart Benton work. It's worth over a million dollars." He shook his head and muttered, "Backwoods idiots."

"Is that why you were here on Sunday night? Stealing this family's valuable artwork?" asked the sheriff.

"Welcome to the game, Sherlock. When I saw the masterpiece in the photo, I figured it had to be here in this dump somewhere. The place was too crowded and messy to find it during the day on Sunday. I came back later to look for it on my own but couldn't get inside the house. I was about to leave when that property manager came wandering by, so I had to hide on the side of the house."

"It's not a dump," whispered Elizabeth. She stared at the house as sobs began to shake her body. I went to hold her while we watched the flames consume her grandparents' home.

The firefighters had finally arrived while Blake and Sebastian were confessing, but the house was beyond help. They let it continue to burn and cleared a safety circle around its perimeter to make certain the fire didn't spread to the workshop, barn, or surrounding woods. As they did this, the sheriff directed the deputy to move all of us out of the way.

Deputy Walker handcuffed Sebastian and put him in the back of his own car. Elizabeth talked to the paramedics while they assessed her mother, who had revived but lay there quietly, sipping water and taking in the destruction.

After a few minutes, the sheriff returned. "I still don't get why you moved the body?" he asked Sebastian.

Sebastian shook his head as if the answer were so obvious the sheriff should have figured it out already. "If the house became a crime scene, then it would be tied up for days with forensics and cops all over the place. There wasn't much blood. That man quickly wiped away what little there was and hurried away." He cast a quick glance down at Mary lying on the stretcher. "I wanted to finish and get out of here. I'd only spent one day with her by then, but I mean, have you ever worked with Dr. Banks? Let me tell you, I couldn't get this job done soon enough. Besides, the guy was already dead. He wouldn't mind; certainly couldn't argue."

The mayor and Lester frowned and tsked. Despite my lack of Southern upbringing, I had to agree with them—Sebastian had poor manners.

Sebastian, now on a roll, continued, "During the week, I tried to get some time alone inside to search for the painting, but that woman"—he tossed a hand in Mary's direction—"she's like a force of nature. Never left me alone. Not once. And always, always with new things to do. Things that were certainly outside the bounds of my contract. All I wanted was to find that painting and get out of here."

Lester and Dale both coughed and then pretended that the smoke had bothered them rather than their reaction to the description of Mary.

Elizabeth walked up and squeezed my hand. "Mama'll be okay, but they'll check her out at the hospital."

I smiled back, grateful to hear the good news.

Elizabeth had missed Sebastian's description of her mother, but that was probably for the best. I didn't know if she would have agreed or been upset with him.

Deputy Walker asked, "And you planted evidence all around town? In Bianca Delgado's car and her store? Were you trying to make us think she killed Duncan?"

"No," said Sebastian, surprising us all. He'd acknowledged all his other misdeeds. Why not this too?

Sebastian continued, "I only took the piece of wood that he used to whack Duncan in the head and left it down by the river with the body. Figured the cops would think he was killed there when the murder weapon was discovered by the body."

Sheriff replied, "That did confound us for a while. The medical examiner told us Duncan had been killed elsewhere and then moved to the river. And the murder weapon was part of a picture frame, so we knew it wasn't something normally found in the woods, but we couldn't figure out why someone would move the body and bring along the murder weapon, especially since we had the prints from the leather glove."

The mayor asked, "If not Sebastian, then who planted the bandana and hat?"

The sheriff turned to glower at Blake, who was now watching us and the firefighters.

"I don't know nothing about a hat," said Blake. "But yeah, I used Duncan's bandana to sop up some of his blood and then hid it in the back of Bianca's shop on my way home. She was one picky broad. Refused to pay me the rest of the money she owed me for redoing her store." He shook his head. "Fix this. Fix that. Clean up that." He mimicked a woman's voice. "I figured I'd fix her."

Elizabeth poked me in the ribs, then leaned in to whisper, "I'll bet Anita had one of Duncan's hats from their affair and stashed it in Bianca's car out of jealousy." She nodded to herself as she became more confident in her theory. "She could have done it on Monday morning after she heard about Duncan's body turning up. I'll bet she couldn't stand losing Duncan to Bianca."

I started to tell her that she was just trying to prove she was partly right about Anita being guilty of something when the sheriff cleared his throat and glared at us.

"Do you have something to contribute, Mrs. Trout?" he demanded. "I don't think it's wise for you to be keeping secrets about this murder investigation."

Elizabeth took a deep breath, but before she could respond, I squeezed her hand and quickly said, "Mary's doing better." I turned to Elizabeth. "Let's go over to be with her."

Elizabeth exhaled and nodded. I pulled her to the ambulance, with Daisy banging back and forth against Elizabeth's legs, excited and anxious about all the noise and strange activities as the firefighters hosed down the house and workshop. The flashing red lights everywhere threw strange shadows into the night.

We stood by Mary's side as she rested on the gurney next to the ambulance, watching Mimi's house burn. The firefighters used a lot of water to protect the surrounding structures and woods.

Elizabeth still had tears in her eyes, but said softly, "At least we got all the important things out of there first."

"You did say you didn't like the furniture," I added.

She snorted.

Then Mary coughed. With a half-hearted flick of her wrist, she waved the paramedics off. "It's just a cough. I'm okay." She coughed again and then managed to sit up, slowly, as if to prove to the paramedics that she was truly okay. "And hurting a little," she added with a wince.

Elizabeth bent over and hugged her mother.

"Did you find the cat?" asked Mary.

Elizabeth laughed and cried at the same time. "Yes. Lucy's alive, but now I don't know where she went in all this craziness."

Mary simply nodded and took another sip of water.

"Glad she's doing better," said a voice by my ear. Lester had wandered over. "That rescue of yours was pretty impressive," he added.

"Ahh," I mumbled, embarrassed.

He clutched my shoulder and looked me straight in the eyes. "No, seriously. You're quite an impressive young man. I've seen how well you've handled yourself this week. You've been calm under stress, even handling high schoolers well." He glanced in Elizabeth's direction before returning his gaze to me. "And let me tell you, that's no easy task."

I swallowed and looked down only to notice Mary and Elizabeth staring at Lester.

"Would you consider taking a position as our high school biology teacher?" His expression turned somber. "Sadly, we've had a sudden opening."

Stunned, I didn't respond at first. Then I said, "Thanks, but I don't have a teaching degree or anything." I frowned, surprised at my own words. Why hadn't I told him no? I paused as I realized teaching wasn't the strangest idea I'd heard. I continued, "I'll have to give it some thought and talk it over with—"

"Why not?" Elizabeth jumped into the discussion. "I think you'll be great as a teacher. And it's not like we have to hurry back to Portland for any reason."

Lester responded to my earlier objection. "Having a teaching degree is not required in Arkansas to work on a temporary basis. You can be a substitute and then take classes at night to finish the certificate part time while you do the job if you decide you want to stay on longer." He chuckled. "I don't think the test would be too challenging for someone with a degree in biology."

I considered his words as the flames crackled around us and the firefighters worked to keep the fire from spreading. Teaching was a big responsibility. "I wouldn't have to start teaching art classes, would I?"

He laughed. "Nope." Then he moved in for the close. "Congrats! Come see me Monday morning and we'll get all the paperwork signed." He actually smiled briefly at Elizabeth before turning and leaving—although I noticed he never asked if she would be interested in teaching art.

Elizabeth stood and hugged me. "That's awesome. You'll be great." She looked down at her mother, still lying on the gurney. "I like the idea of staying around here for a little while to help Mama recover."

Mary smiled gingerly and reached up to squeeze Elizabeth's hand.

Elizabeth looked around us, as if capturing the image in her head of the surrounding woods, the hillside, and the river in the distance, and the beauty of the land she knew so well. Then, as something large in the house fell with a boom, she winced and chuckled softly. "I, uh, guess we'll also have some insurance money coming, and maybe we could rebuild the place."

She turned to deliver a brief glare in the mayor's direction. "Besides, I don't want to see any hotel built on this land." Then, gaining confidence, she pointed a finger down at her mother. "But a place with better Wi-Fi and cellular coverage." Elizabeth smiled for the first time since we arrived at the property tonight. "We'll see how we like it. I can work from anywhere and now you've got a job here."

I nodded slowly. Teaching sounded far more appealing than sitting in a lab all day, and with my unexpected windfall, we didn't have to worry about money. I smiled back at them. "Yes, let's do it."

It felt good to have a plan in place. A school schedule would give me a routine I could live with. "Besides," I added. "With everything that's been revealed tonight, at least there won't be anything else to cause us problems. All of Jenkins's secrets are out in the open now."

"Oh honey." Mary laughed. "Bless your heart."

*****

Thanks for reading this first book in the *Ozarks Lake Mystery* series. I'd greatly appreciate if you could leave a review for other readers at Amazon and/or Goodreads. Even a sentence or two helps.

If you haven't read my other books, **turn the page** for a sneak preview of the first book—*Uncle and Ants*—in the *Silicon Valley Mystery* series.

Check out the books in the *Silicon Valley Mystery* series on Amazon:

Uncle and Ants
Chutes and Ladder
Serf and Turf
Hit and Mist

Sign up for Marc's mailing list to receive free content, learn of new releases, and receive special offers:

http://www.marcjedel.com

Preview: Uncle and Ants—Silicon Valley Mystery #1

Chapter 1. Monday Afternoon

Be careful what you wish for when you're ten years old because it just might come true. I've had a complicated relationship with my younger sister Laney since we were kids, but I never wished for her to wind up hospitalized from a falling drone.

Until the ICU nurse called about Laney, my Monday had rocked. Hard to beat clear blue skies and seventy-five degrees on a beautiful late August day in Silicon Valley, and even though my work kept me stuck inside, at least my latest software build appeared to be bug-free and working well.

I hung up to rush to the hospital, only then realizing I'd forgotten to ask the nurse about Laney's condition. Screwing up phone calls was one of my special skills that only came in handy with telemarketers.

When I reached the hospital, I hurried inside, more concerned than I'd want to admit to Laney. Over the years, our relationship had survived on a steady diet of teasing, and it had only begun to deepen since her husband's death.

She moved to town a few months ago, so she and her two daughters were around more often. I hadn't interacted this much with my sister, or young children, in what seemed like ages. I don't see my own two kids often since they started college across the country, close to where my ex-wife moved. I haven't fully accepted that they're old enough for college anyway. I also haven't fully accepted that I've crossed forty.

An unoccupied information kiosk responded to my query for Laney with a map to room 512. Darting through the crowded lobby, I hopped into an elevator right before the doors closed.

As I got off the elevator and walked to Laney's room, the quiet struck me—no loud beeping monitors or garbled announcements over the loudspeaker. An electronic sign reading "L. Tran" glowed next to room 512. Taking a deep breath to slow my rapid heartbeat, I knocked softly and said, "Hello?"

No answer. I stepped through the door, peeking around a movable privacy partition, and, to my surprise, found an elderly Vietnamese woman sleeping in the only bed.

While I like to tease Laney about her advancing years, she doesn't turn thirty-eight until next month. She's also white. About thirteen years ago, Laney married a nice Vietnamese-American man and took his name. A good guy, he always shared a laugh with Laney over people's reactions when a white woman with long, dark, curly hair and hazel eyes showed up for a dinner reservation under the name Tran.

I did a double-take as it struck me. Why was this old lady in Laney's bed? Had Laney already died and been replaced?

I calmed my overactive imagination, took another deep breath, and stepped back outside the room to double-check the sign. It definitely listed her name. Was it a mistake or software bug? Annoyed, I rubbed the back of my neck and considered my next move. Down the hall past the elevators, a police officer stood talking to a nurse. Perhaps they'd know how to find Laney.

They paused their conversation as I stepped in front of them. The cop was a few inches taller than me, and although I don't usually notice men, I paused at his Hollywood-style good looks. He held himself erect in his uniform, crisp, neat, and fitted to his muscular body like it had come straight from the tailor.

I'd like to think my clothes also fit that well. Other people might comment on some gray in my slowly receding hairline and a tendency toward a dad bod, but I saw none of that when I stepped out of my shower each morning. Self-delusion was another of my skills.

The cop's striking green eyes stood out from his dark brown skin and closely cropped black hair, penetrating me as I started to fidget from one foot to the other.

I didn't think I'd done anything wrong, at least not that the cop should know about. But he looked like he'd set me straight anyway. A badge above the pocket on the left side of his chiseled chest read "Sergeant Mace Jackson."

His name sounded more like an action movie character than a real person. That, combined with his looks, meant that if things ever went south in a conflict, I'd want Mace Jackson on my side. After all, action movie heroes always win.

Under the scrutiny of the sergeant's gaze, I directed my attention to the nurse, whose badge read "Ruth."

"Excuse me. I think there's something wrong with your directory or door signs. I'm looking for my sister's room. Laney Tran? The sign outside room 512 says it's hers, but some old lady is in there."

Nurse Ruth said, "Oh, you must be Marty. I called you earlier." She pointed behind her to room 518. "This is Laney's room."

"Her name is on the sign by the wrong room," I repeated, again highlighting the error needing correction.

The cop scowled and looked hard at me. "Your sister is in the hospital and you're worried about a sign?"

When I'm nervous or worried, or even when everything is fine, I've got a bad habit of obsessing over things that don't work right. Trying to ignore the distraction of the glitch, I said, "Sorry. Is she okay? Can I see her?"

"She's stable and should recover just fine in a few days," Nurse Ruth said. "You can call the doctor for more details or wait for her to come back. I have to check on the other patients. And yes, you can go see her, but she's not awake." The warm smile she was directing toward the cop became forced when she aimed it at me before walking away.

I had more questions and wished she hadn't left me alone with the cop. They've made me nervous ever since a difficult experience during my freshman year of high school. Let's just say that I hadn't yet mastered the U.S. postal system.

Squaring my shoulders, I looked up at Sergeant Mace Jackson, who was standing in the doorway to Laney's room. "Do you know what happened to Laney?"

Instead of answering, he asked, "Can I see your ID please?"

"I'm Marty Golden. I'm a software engineer," I said, as if that explained everything. Well, it did pretty much cover my life. I've got a cool job at a startup. It's not the most successful startup in the world, and I haven't received a big payday yet, but hope can sustain a person for quite a while. Even if that meant work consumed all my time. That's life in Silicon Valley.

"Some ID please," he repeated with an edge to his voice.

I fumbled in my front pocket for my wallet as a light sweat prickled on my forehead. When I pulled out the wallet, my badge fell on the floor. As I bent down to pick it up, Sergeant Jackson reached for my license, almost smacking me in the head. I stood up, holding my license, but dropped it when my wrist bumped into his retracting hand. When I bent over to pick it up again, I heard his exasperated sigh. After standing up a second time, I managed to execute a successful handoff. In one fluid motion, he flipped my license over, reviewed the information, and returned it to me as smoothly as James Bond handles a martini.

Then he pointed at my shirt. "Did you get called back from vacation?"

"What?" I glanced down. I was wearing my normal work attire: Hawaiian shirt and a pair of shorts. Different colors and designs every day, but all Hawaiian-style. Today's was one of my favorite patterns with the leaves on the palm trees in the shapes of different tropical fruit. "No. I came straight from work when the nurse called. How'd Laney's accident happen?"

Noting my defensive tone, the sergeant raised his eyebrow but answered, "She was in a pretty unusual accident. Witnesses reported that she was driving through the intersection of Saratoga and Doyle when she tried to avoid an ice cream truck running the red light. The truck was hit by a falling delivery drone and then your sister's car T-boned the truck. She barely missed getting hit by the drone herself. It would likely have killed her in her little car. It totaled the truck."

I couldn't believe my ears. "A drone?"

"Like I said, it was a pretty unusual accident."

I shook my head in disbelief. Granted, a modern delivery drone was heavy, not one of those lightweight, older-generation drones that were only good for taking videos and annoying your neighbors. But still, this shouldn't have been possible. "That's near her daughters' school. How could a drone hit there? The areas around schools are no-fly zones."

"We're investigating. So, do you—"

My phone buzzed, and I held up a finger to excuse myself. Sergeant Jackson pressed his lips together but said nothing as I stepped away.

"Hello? Marty here."

"Is this Marty Golden?" a woman said in a clipped tone.

"Yes, that's what I said. I'm pretty busy right now. What's this about?"

"Well, now, you don't have to be rude. That's just unnecessary. We teach our children to be polite. It's the right thing to do. Manners start in the home, you know."

I rubbed my nose in confusion. A rogue drone had nearly killed my sister and I hadn't even seen her yet. "I'm sorry. Who is this?"

"I'm Mrs. Quarles, school secretary. Skye and Megan are with me in the office. Their mother hasn't picked them up. We're not a babysitting service here at the Discovery School, you know. You're their emergency contact, so please come get them now."

Trying to take care of Laney and her girls was more than I'd signed up for. Wait, had I signed something? I couldn't be considered a responsible adult. If someone didn't believe me, they just needed to ask my ex-wife. I wanted to tell Mrs. Quarles to call another parent while I stuck around to talk to Laney's doctor and make sure she was okay. "I'll be there soon" was what I mumbled into the phone instead. Probably not the best way to get across my point.

I turned to see Jackson staring at a fixed point on the wall with narrowed eyes and hands on hips.

"I'm sorry. That was my nieces' school. I need to pick them up since Laney is here."

He took another slow, deep breath. "Before we're interrupted again, here's my card." He handed me the first paper business card I've seen in years. "I'd like to talk to her to find out if she saw anything unusual. Tell her to call me when she wakes. But I won't be back until Thursday because I'm on furlough for the next two days."

"Furlough?" I didn't know that word.

"Unpaid, mandatory time off. All thanks to the city of San Jose not having enough money to pay us." He grumbled at this before striding off to the elevators, chest held high like a champion headed off into the sunset.

I looked around but didn't see the cameras or director following our star, then stepped into Laney's room to see her before I left to pick up the girls. She looked to be asleep, with a bunch of tubes and wires running from her to surrounding machines. Bandages covered part of her head, and the rest of her face was bruised. I moved to her side and squeezed her hand, but she didn't respond.

The nylon satchel that she used as a catchall briefcase and purse rested on the chair next to her bed. Her computer, phone, wallet, and some papers were nearly spilling out. Grimacing as I noticed a splotch of blood on the side, I grabbed it all to take home with me for safekeeping. Maybe I would even wash her satchel so the blood wouldn't remind her of the accident. Well, I'd think about washing it.

I used the twenty-minute drive from the hospital to my nieces' school to check in with her doctor and update my own kids, who were away at college. To avoid enticing some elementary school hoodlum to break into the car, I grabbed Laney's bag as I got out.

The desert landscaping that most in the Valley have adopted to deal with the long-term drought prevailed along the path to the office. Assorted cacti, succulents, and rocks decorated the red dirt, creating an eye-catching display, but I still pined for green grass.

My nieces sat talking just inside the glass walls of the school office, their backs to me. Skye, reed-thin and pretty with dark hair and glasses, was a girl with plans. Twelve going on thirty, she liked school and was constantly reading fantasy books. Megan, her younger sister, wore her long hair up with various colored hairpins sticking out every which way. Megan was nine, or eight, or possibly a mature seven. I never could remember. The free spirit of the family, she bounced off the walls with energy.

When I opened the door, Skye noticed me first. Interrupting Megan mid-sentence, she said, "Hi, Uncle Marty. Did you come with Rover?"

From a side room behind the counter, a woman's disembodied voice called out, "No dogs in here! That's simply not allowed."

Before I could speak, Megan chimed in, "You got a dog?" Without pausing to hear the response, she continued, "Hey, where's Mom?"

"Yes," I answered Skye, glancing around and rubbing my chin. What was that voice talking about? There were no dogs in sight.

Megan jumped up and started a little celebration dance at the idea of having an uncle with a dog.

Oops. "No, sorry. I was answering Skye. I didn't get a dog. It's my car, remember?"

Megan's dance ended with a lurch. "Just the dumb car?" She slumped back onto her chair.

"Well, it's not dumb."

A woman walked toward the counter. This had to be Mrs. Quarles, the school secretary. "You gave your car a dog's name?" she asked in a scornful tone.

I'd never met this woman and didn't understand why she felt it was acceptable to judge me, but my parents had taught me to always be polite, so I answered, "I work for a car service called Rover that drives the cars for you. It's like a taxi, but with no driver. We call all the cars Rover. You know, like, 'Hey, Rover, come'—"

"Why not Buddy?" Megan interrupted. "That's a better dog name. Buddy would always be your best friend ..." Her voice trailed off as she hugged herself, thinking of her imaginary best dog friend.

She had me there. "Well, our marketing team decided on the name. Maybe they're not as smart as you and didn't think of Buddy."

Megan looked up at Mrs. Quarles. "Uncle Marty makes the cars go wherever you want."

Skye clarified, "He's an engineer."

I smiled. So the girls had paid attention when I'd told them what I did. Turning to Skye, I said, "I think you'll be interested in a new feature we just added."

Looking excited, she started to ask me about it, but Megan jumped in again. "But wait. If they all have the same name, how do they know which one should come?"

Can't argue with a child's logic. So I did the adult thing and ignored her. "Come on, girls, get your backpacks and let's go." I turned to shepherd them out the door.

Mrs. Quarles called out, "Excuse me. You need to sign the girls out first."

"I'm Marty Golden, the girls' uncle. You called me."

"Yes, Mr. Golden, I am aware of who you are. You still need to sign the form. It's in THE RULES."

I heard the capitalization.

Mrs. Quarles continued, "We all have to follow THE RULES. Please show me your ID so I can verify that you are who you say you are, and then sign this form before the girls can go."

I thought about bolting for the door, but the girls probably wouldn't follow fast enough to make a clean break. Besides, we had to follow THE RULES. I didn't notice any stone tablets with THE RULES etched in them, but the school might have sent them to the mason for cleaning.

After I signed, the girls followed me out the door. I didn't know how to tell them about their mother lying unconscious in the hospital, nor did I understand how this could have happened in the first place. Drones didn't just fall out of the sky nowadays. It's impossible, or at least it should be. Package delivery services worked out all their bugs years ago and were now safer than driverless cars. Fewer random pedestrians or unexpected street construction projects at a thousand feet in the air.

So how did a drone almost hit Laney? I wanted Sergeant Jackson to figure that out now, not waste two days on a silly mandatory furlough.

*****

Other Books by Marc Jedel

SILICON VALLEY MYSTERY SERIES

Book 1. Uncle and Ants
Book 2. Chutes and Ladder
Book 3. Serf and Turf
Book 4. Hit and Mist

Sign up for Marc's mailing list to receive free content, learn of new releases, and receive special offers:

http://www.marcjedel.com

Acknowledgements

An extra hug, kiss and lots of love to my wife. Not only does she put up with me bringing all these fictional people home all the time, but she's also embraced the role of emotional choreographer—helping me imbue my characters with their social skills and emotional expressions. Because apparently people have feelings and act upon them. Who knew?

Special thanks to all the family, friends, and others who I met in and around Arkansas when I was young. No character in this story directly resembles any real person but I may have borrowed some names and attributes more than others.

Thanks to my awesome beta readers, especially Lynne, Donna S., Donna N., Bill, and Julie for their early feedback and improvements. Bless their hearts—and I don't mean that sarcastically.

Thanks for my developmental editor, Kristen Weber, for her many recommendations and especially for her ideas to improve the novel's beginning section. Extra thanks, as always, to my awesome editor, Cara Quinlan, for her word choices, copy edits, and overall improvement suggestions.

About the Author

Marc Jedel writes humorous murder mysteries. He credits his years of marketing leadership positions in Silicon Valley for honing his writing skills and sense of humor. While his high-tech marketing roles involved crafting plenty of fiction, these were just called emails, ads, and marketing collateral.

For most of Marc's life, he's been inventing stories. Encountering more funny and odd people and situations as he's gotten older has made it even easier to write what he knows and make up the rest. It's a skill that has served him well as an author and marketer.

The publication of Marc's first novel, UNCLE AND ANTS, gave him permission to claim "author" as his job. This leads to much more interesting conversations with people than answering, "marketing." Becoming an Amazon best-selling author has only made him more insufferable.

Like his character, Marty from the *Silicon Valley Mystery* series, Marc lives in Silicon Valley, works in high-tech, and enjoys bad puns. Like his characters Jonas and Elizabeth from the *Ozarks Lake Mystery* series, he grew up in the South and spent plenty of time in and around Arkansas. Marc too has a dog, although his is neurotic, sweet, and small with little appreciation for Marc's humor.

Visit marcjedel.com, for free content, special offers, and more.

Made in the USA
Las Vegas, NV
29 March 2021

20339047R00163